"The Winds of Fate blow favorably upon those who have the courage to chart their own course." — Blackbeard

ROSE GREY
AND
PIRATES, NYMPHS, AND A SMOKING MONKEY

WRITTEN AND ILLUSTRATED

BY

J.D. MILLIGAN

THE FAIRY TALE TIMES

PUBLICATIONS

All inquiries should be directed to:
www.jdmilligan.com
ISBN 979-8-9917948-0-0
Library of Congress Control Number: 2024923835

THE FAIRY TALE TIMES
PUBLICATIONS

For Henry with love

THE BERMUDA

The Dazzling Pearl

CASTLE OF WINKFIELD

THE NYMPH BEAST

CASTLE OF BELLEFONT

EVERWOOD

Port of Bellefont

The Dark Market

The Salty Parrot Tavern

Spring Fair

BLACKW

The Revenge

Angel of Doom

BRANDYWINE RIVER

Devil's Dagger

ATLANTIC O

0
2.5 MILES
5 MILES
DEVONSHIRE
HILLSIDE ACADEMY
CASTLE OF ARCHMERE
BELLADONNA'S COTTAGE
SHALLOWS
Buttercup Lane
River Road
The Golden Jewel
N
E
S
ISLE OF LUMIERE

CONTENT

ILLUSTRATIONS

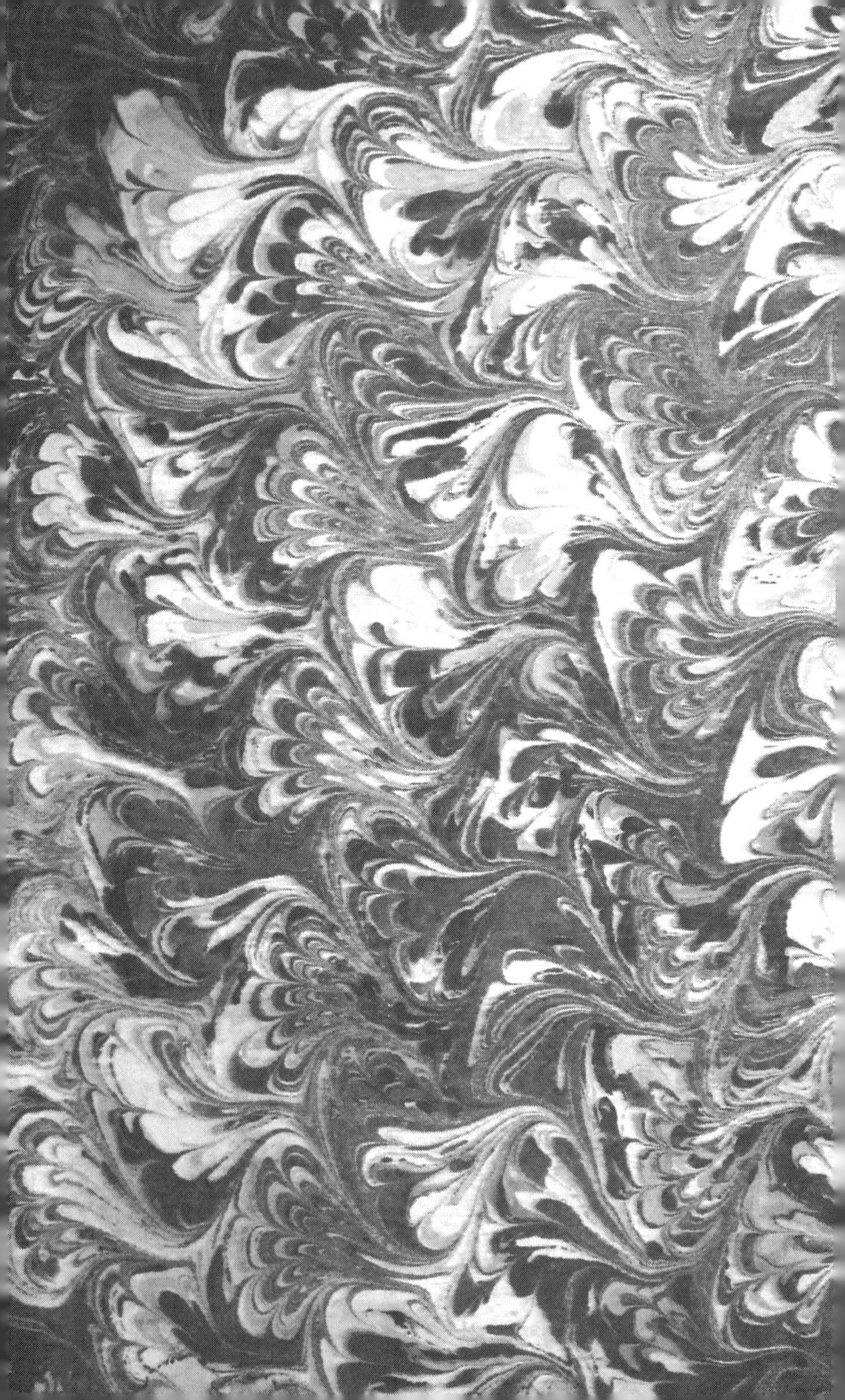

Prologue

Dear Theodora,

I'm alive and well and hope to be back home soon. Unfortunately, my latest journey on the Lioness to deliver goods to America ended in disaster. As we passed through the notorious voodoo'd waters of the Bermuda Triangle, a storm came out of nowhere, and wham...it tore our ship to smithereens. After a few minutes of thinking I was a goner, I luckily found a piece of wreckage to float on. As the storm cleared, I thought maybe I had died because I saw a glowing light on the horizon that looked like heaven. But then a wave hit me in the face. I gulped a big mouthful of salty sea water and started choking. That's when I knew. I wasn't dead, and I needed to get to that brightly lit island — before I was shark bait.

Luckily, I made it there without becoming some hungry fish's dinner, where a nice couple found me washed up on shore. I am now staying with them until I can find a ride back home. In the meantime, the nice couple has been telling me about this place. Oddly enough, most islanders are travelers who stumbled upon Lumiere, just like me. As I explore the villages, I have been looking for survivors from our ship, but I haven't seen anyone yet. The people I have met so far warn me to avoid exploring the woods unless I have a weapon to protect myself with. Believe it or not, they tell me this place is filled with enchanted creatures. I was shocked at first, but I actually believe them. Because when I first reached the shore, I saw some little lights spiraling around me. I sensed they were smarter than the average mosquito, so I pretended I was dead until they flew away. In town, some chaps, or should I say hoodlums, were bragging to me about capturing these magical beings. I think they thought I was a pirate just like them. I wanted to fit in, so I played along. They told me that if I caught one of these magical creatures, I could get a pretty penny for it. There's a dark market here where pirates barter for them. There's also a rumor of a ghost girl that roams the forest. The islanders call her the phantom nymph. Supposedly, she transforms into a terrifying beast then eats people alive. Horrible thought. They say, she ate part of a pirate captain. Poor chap! This place is unbelievable, to say the least. Anyway, I've decided to stay a bit and try my luck at catching one of these magical creatures. I would like to bring home a fortune for you and me. And this is my chance. I'm giving this letter to a crewman on a ship who is traveling back home. I trust this chap will deliver this message to you, my love. Wish me luck and I hope I will see you soon.

Kisses, Pitney

Chapter One

Two Scallywags Capture A Golden Birdie

Trees seemed to touch the sky in the mystical forest called Everwood. As a bird call pierced the silence in the early dawn, a soft breeze stirred the underbrush, only to scatter dried leaves haphazardly across the earth. But as the first light filtered through the branches, a man with a faded headscarf and a frayed eyepatch appeared from out of the brush. With a quiver of arrows slung across his back and a longbow dangling from his hand, Black-eyed Baxter wasn't just a hunter—he was a scallywag, a shyster, a desperado, and a good-for-nothin' pirate. And as everyone knew on Lumiere, pirates weren't hunting deer in Everwood. Oh no. They wanted something much more valuable, much more powerful, and much more precious, something that could only be found on the Isle of Lumiere. The scallywag pushed through the brush, chopping at tree branches like they annoyed him, when suddenly, he stopped. With his one good eye narrowing, he spotted something glinting in the grass ahead. He caught his breath, and in an instant, he was on his knees, pawing at some leaves. "Ha!" He barked. "Ain't this my lucky day!" As he scratched his eyepatch with his filthy nails leaving streaks of dirt on his weathered skin, there, sprawled on the ground, was a creature more beautiful than *anything* he'd ever seen.

It was a golden starling. Lying there motionless, it shimmered with an otherworldly glow. Breathtaking to look at—every feather looked like spun gold, as they caught the sun's rays.

"They'll all talk about this…about me." Baxter chuckled, his laughter low and deep.

With blood like the Gods, the golden starling was said to bring unimaginable fortune to whoever possessed it. To pirates like Baxter, it was the ultimate prize. But as he wrapped up his treasure, he noticed something. The bird was still alive! Its wound, which initially looked fatal, had mysteriously disappeared. Baxter froze, as the bird's eyes flickered open.

"What in blazes—?" he muttered, leaning back as the starling flapped its wings like two small propellers, desperately trying to escape. With no time to spare, the pirate shrugged off his jacket and flung it like a net, catching the bird mid-flight under the weight of his coat. "Ha! Well, aren't you somethin' special," Baxter murmured. He wrapped up the bird excitedly and held it bundled against his chest, cackling triumphantly. When he was done rejoicing over his new prize, the black-eyed scallywag tipped his

head back and whistled a sharp melody that sliced through the forest air.

"Baxter? Is that you?" Said a timid voice from out of the shadows.

"Hurry up already! I'm over here."

From out of the dense woods emerged Two-fingered Tex. His right hand had reminders of his past betrayals. Tex was Baxter's cohort in crime and bad-deed-doing buddy, and there was no one Tex was more loyal to than Baxter. Tex swung a cage of twigs and twine off his back and dropped it on the ground with a thud. "I finally found ya!"

Looking bothered by Tex's lack of speed, Baxter growled, "Hurry up and open the cage already!" His buddy unlatched the shabby door as Baxter unfolded his coat and shoved the frightened creature inside. They both stood over their new prize gloating. "We'z gonna be rich from this golden beauty! You wait and see Tex—she'll go for lots of gold, buddy!

"Yesiree, she's a dandy, Baxter! Yessiree…yesiree—"

"Tell me you set the other trap!" Baxter demanded, like a warning. His gaze darted around the clearing, every shadow seeming to shift in the growing light.

With a toothless and oh-so-greasy grin, Tex whispered back, "I did. The birdies will eat the sweet poison—um…I mean nectar." Tex snort-laughed, which sounded frightening. "They're as good as dead!"

Baxter joined his buddy snort-laughing, which sounded just as frightening."Excellent! Excellent! Now let's go see what we got!" And they disappeared into the dark forest.

Reappearing out of some brush, the two pirate buddies were now over the top of their trap. Dew-dropped webs sparkled in the morning light as spiders awaited their prey. Like Baxter and Tex, they anticipated their prizes, too — more magic birdies falling prey to their poisonous nectar trap. Feeling anxious, Baxter pulled out his telescope.

"Watch-a look'n at?" The two-fingered pirate asked stupidly.

Baxter started hitting Tex with his scarf repeatedly.

"Okay, okay," Tex grumbled.

"What do you think I'm lookin at? You imbecile!" Baxter barked, "We need to hurry up and trap'em before the Cap finds out we're missen," The black-eye pirate griped, "Imagine what he'd do if he knew we had these treasures."

Tex snickered, "McSly would probably shishkebob'z us —for sure."

The two snort-laughed out loud in unison again, proud of their criminal accomplishments.

Born to be bad, Tex and Baxter were part of Captain Corbin 'Peg-leg' McSly's crew. McSly was known as one of the most ruthless pirates who hunted down magical creatures on the isle. But recently, Baxter and Tex had read a story in the newspaper about a pirate, Pitney "Evil Grin" Torp, who captured a golden starling on his own and became instantly wealthy after selling it at the dark market. So the minute McSly's ship docked to fill up on supplies at the port of Bellefont that morning, the two secretly set their sights on capturing some treasures for themselves.

As the two pirates waited, they noticed a twinkling light fluttering about. "A fairy bug," Baxter whispered. "They're so annoying!"

The fairy, who had watched Tex set the trap earlier, fluttered near the birds and whispered in birdie language, *Eating that nectar will send you to your doom!*

When they heard the fairy's news, the birds screeched in a panic, immediately scattering into the sky.

"Only a cursed fairy bug could do this!" Baxter roared, with rage. His good eye darted between the fleeing birds and the glimmering fairy as the clearing erupted into chaos. "We've been tricked!" he snarled, shaking his fist at the shimmering pest."Quick, Tex—your bow! Shoot the bug!" he barked, his voice escalating to a shriek. "No, wait —get the golden starlings! No, no—blast it all, shoot everything!" Tex flailed wildly. Baxter's rage turned Tex into a frenzy of useless motion as he fumbled to get his weapon.

Chapter Two

The White-Haired Beast Excused Herself

Rose suddenly shot upright in bed. Her electric-blue eyes were wide with alarm, as the cries of birds echoed in the distance, desperate and haunting.

She pushed a strand of platinum hair from her face, her heart pounding. "What now?" she whispered, glancing nervously out the window of her bedroom. The dense forest was still. But the cries lingered, filling her chest with a strange dread.

Feeling nervous that she might be screaming for her life next, like the birds, was Rose Grey. She looked no more than 12, but she was really —205. Yes—205 years old. Rose was a nymph, and as everyone should know, nymphs were immortal, which should explain her extraordinary age.

As Rose lay there tossing and turning all morning, she couldn't stop thinking about the screeching birds. One would think that the daughter of a powerful deity—yes, super powerful—could fly through the air and save the

precious creatures. But unfortunately for the birds and Rose, she could not. Suddenly a tiny door popped open from a box hanging on the wall. A small bird sprang out, coo-cooing several times in a row like an alarm. She slipped out of bed and started pacing the bedroom. Her bare feet brushed the wooden floor.

"It's the pirates again," she grumbled bitterly. A squirrel gathering nuts outside the window looked like it was listening to her. "The scallywags have been terrorizing Everwood for weeks now!" She whined towards the squirrel, who looked like it was actually listening to her, but it was not. Contemplating what to wear now, Rose finally decided on her navy blue dress. Although it was her only outfit, she liked the idea of having options. That morning, like every morning, the magnificent nymph sat before her mirror, combing her long platinum hair while overanalyzing her face in the mirror.

"I swear I have a monstrous nose, strange marks on my forehead, and my eyes are like a fish—no wonder fairies think I'm a beast!" She mumbled to herself. Distracted by the sounds outside, she stopped combing her hair momentarily and looked out the window of her treehouse at several grey geese in a pond below. They were honking at nothing and swimming in circles.

"That's so like me, acting busy and important—but going nowhere," the nymph whispered to a squirrel, who was observing her from a branch.

The squirrel tilted its head, as if pondering her words, while the nymph let out a sigh.

Just below Rose's treehouse were her three nymph sisters. They were already up and sitting at a lavishly decorated table near an oak tree. Trays of pastries, a warm pot of tea, and a vase of flowers were in the center. As the rays of the morning sun illuminated the table, the sisters drank their tea and read about the latest gossip in their papers.

Rose and her sisters were daughters of Poseidon and Amphitrite, the God and Goddess of the Sea. For hundreds of years, the sister nymphs lived secretly in a meadow called the Shallows. It was breathtakingly beautiful there. Flowering bushes and trees surrounded its edges. But what was most important was that it was unknown to anyone. The sisters could live there unbothered by humans as they traveled the world performing their nymph duties of protecting ponds worldwide until otherwise notified.

Zoe, the eldest of Rose's three sisters, was the leader of the sister family since she had the most experience with failing. With long raven hair and chilling lavender eyes, everything about this extraordinary nymph seemed perfect, because Zoe was a master at— what not to do. The sisters found this large amount of experience in failure valuable, so naturally, she always had the last word about anything they did.

Rose's second eldest sister was Reeva. The long, chestnut-haired beauty had a passion for reading. Books, newspapers, signs, or labels, it didn't matter what it was. Reeva wanted to absorb the knowledge. However, as far as actually experiencing life, she would rather read about it, of course.

Chloe was Rose's third eldest sister. An amber-haired beauty with a cheeky smile loved to joke about everything. She especially enjoyed poking fun at all the sisters but particularly Rose until she cried. Although she was annoying, Rose would still say, Chloe was her best friend— in a weird way.

The three sisters were radiantly powerful beauties, as nymphs were known to be. But unfortunately for Rose, she was born without such powers.

Unsure how their sister Rose could have caught such an evil curse, the sisters decided to create something to protect her—an invisibility cloak. They feared that any pirate who saw Rose's unusual snow-white hair and metallic gold symbols, the marks of a God, would assume she was a magical creature, which she was. But without magical powers, poor Rose could be captured quite easily.

However, as careful as Rose was, during her various expeditions on the isle, there were moments when the magical cloak would slip off, revealing her identity. Because of this, the local paper, *The Fairy Tale Time*, started rumors about her. The fairies, the only reporters for the paper, seemed overly anxious for attention so they fabricated a little in their stories.

Pepper Thistleton of Thorn wrote, "I saw a figure with long platinum hair near the water's edge. Suddenly, it disappeared, and then an enormous serpent with green scales leaped out of the water."

Luna Berry of Lark reported a different experience, "I saw it. One minute, it's a nymph with long platinum hair, beady snake eyes, and a long fork tongue. She stuck it out at me. I swear. The nymph may look like a harmless young girl, but she's really— a scary monster!"

Shea Snapdragon wrote, "There is a nymph in Everwood— a ten-foot-tall beast with strange hairy nostrils and rotten breath."

Since poor Rose could not help her sisters monitor ponds worldwide, she kept herself busy making art or artistically inclined messes, as Chloe would describe them. Her art and found treasures filled her treehouse. A black boot, colorful feathers, and a broken twig wrapped in a pink scarf hung on a wall in her bedroom. Lemon-yellow paint was drizzled on top of it like a fancy cake. A label was next to it that read: Boot-iful. Next to it was another unusual piece. Two broken window shutters, a wooden bowl, and furniture molding were hammered together carefully and covered with scarlet red paint. The word 'hello' was painted on it near a tiny hole that looked like a peephole on one of the shutters. The label next to it read: Hello from outer space.

Chapter Two

One can only guess what was going through Rose's mind when she was creating these works of art.

As Rose combed her hair that morning, she fixated on one piece in particular. Crushed yellow flower petals, charcoal, and green grass stains were combined on paper to resemble someone, possibly resembling a girl. A label next to it read "Creepy Sibling in Banana." It was a recent attempt by Rose to draw her sister's portrait. "Half monster and half innocent princess," She whispered like she was happy about the insulting image, adding, "—so Chloe! Ha!"

A voice from below Rose's treehouse window called out,"Wake up, Oh-Great-and-Powerful One!"

Rose got up and leaned out the window, acknowledging her taunting sister. Chloe was making a pitiful face and patting the seat beside her. "Please join me, Rosey. Our sisters are a complete bore!"

Rose laughed with a suspicious look. "You mean so that you can humiliate me for entertainment like usual?"

"Yes, of course. What else are sisters for?"

Ignoring Chloe's jibe, Rose resumed untangling her hair, which was more like torture. Regardless, after a few minutes, she started analyzing her life. Her sister's teasing seemed to have gotten under her skin. Tears began to well in her eyes, as her frustration started brewing inside. Suddenly, just as another tooth in the comb broke and fell to the floor, Rose slammed the comb down in frustration.

"I've had it with this stupid comb...and...and last night's spell-breaking flop and —my ridiculously lonely life!!"

Last night, the sisters had hired another well-known sorcerer, Noel Spellgem of Holly Oak, to fix Rose's curse. The three nymph sisters were unaware of how to cure dark magic. Thus, they were forever hiring sorcerers for help.

Rose pulled her emotions together, picked up her invisibility cloak, and descended a spiraling staircase within her treehouse before exiting a doorway at the trunk. She joined her sisters and placed her special cloak on a chair beside Chloe. "Could you pass the tea, please," Rose mumbled.

"Sorry about last night, Rosey dear," Her sister Chloe said, making a pouty face and pouring Rose some tea into a tiny delicate cup."I guess Noel is unlucky sorcerer number six."

Sitting across the table from Rose and Chloe was Zoe, who was giggling and slapping her leg as she read a story in the newspaper. The raven-haired beauty suddenly finished reading, folded the paper, and placed it on the table.

"Sorry about Noel not breaking the curse, Rosy dear," Zoe apologized sympathetically.

Rose nodded, acknowledging her comment, then sat quietly, trying not to cry. Rose's chestnut-haired sister, Reeva, was sitting across the table too, half-listening as she read her book, 'Remedies for the Cursed' by Cleodore Finch.

"Sorry, I can't talk yet," Reeva said, making a disagree-able face. "I'm a brute until I've had a full cup. But I'm looking for a cure!" After taking another sip, she nodded before refocusing on her book. "I'll let you know when I find it."

Rose was thankful for Reeva's efforts. However, now that the sisters were together, Zoe cleared her throat loudly like she had a big announcement. The sisters knew it was a big one and shifted in their seats nervously.

"Rosy dear," Zoe said softly, "I have to tell you some-thing important." Zoe could hardly look at her sister be-cause of what she was about to say.

Rose smiled sweetly, sipping tea and eating a pastry. "What is it?"

Clearing her throat again nervously, Zoe announced, "Your sisters and I were talking earlier this morning, and we all agreed that … ah, we aren't going to hire more sor-cerers to try to break your curse. Because…. ah, we don't believe you have one."

Rose's jaw hung open in shock. Fighting her emotions back, she wanted to punish her sisters somehow, like turn-ing them into warty frogs, or worse, making them —unat-tractive. But Rose would need magic to do such a thing. As her hands shook and her eyes rolled up into her head, Rose kicked a stone with anger. After it flew into the woods, she moaned and grabbed her foot, hurting her own toe instead.

"Sorry, Rosey. At least you have your magic cloak! Let's look at the positives. Let's see. Umm, Can I make you a brush? Didn't you lose your brush? I can make one for you. Wouldn't that be delightful?" Zoe snapped her fingers, and a brush appeared in her hand. She tried handing it to Rose. But as if fate had other plans, the brush slipped from her grasp, clipped the edge of a nearby cup, tumbled into the jelly, then landed in the dirt below. Zoe felt embarrassed about the calamity. "How about some crazy 8's? What do you say, Rosey? Do you want to play a game?" Zoe was trying her best to move on from the subject, so she snapped her fingers, and a deck of cards appeared in her palm.

Looking frustrated by endless lousy luck, Rose grumbled, "You want to give me a brush after months of torture. And then play cards with me when my future is at stake? You don't CARE if I must live with this curse —forever!"

"No, we *do* care," Zoe said, adjusting her dress like she was fussing with it nervously, adding, "but there is simply nothing we can do about it anymore. Clearly, I've made enough mistakes in my lifetime to know that six sorcerer failures are enough."

Rose's face was on fire. So full of emotion, she thought about how much she hated her sisters for this decision and wished they weren't her sisters —at a*ll! How could they do this to me? I thought they loved me.* Rose thought.

Chapter Two

The raven-haired sister started playing a card game with Chloe while Reeva hid behind a new book, hoping Rose wouldn't confront her about the subject. The three sisters had moved on from the curse drama and hoped Rose would, too.

"Fine," Rose barked, forcing a smile that looked like she accepted the decision.

Startled by Rose's answer but happy to be off the hook, Zoe blurted out, "My brave sister!"

Chloe added, "I can't believe it! She's finally maturing after 205 years."

Reeva put her book down and chimed in. "Isn't she just top-notch!"

Keeping her phony smile up briefly, Rose grabbed her magic cloak and stormed off towards the woods.

"They think my problem is a joke," she said to a nearby squirrel who was following her, intrigued by her beauty. "They don't know what it's like being invisible all the time, never making friends, worried today could be my last, or that I could be kidnapped and sold on the dark market like most enchanted creatures are." She was thinking about the screaming birds that morning and feeling like she might be next if she didn't figure out a solution to her problem.

Plucking an apple off a tree, Rose was about to take a bite when she locked eyes with a squirrel on a branch. Being the kind-hearted nymph she was, she handed the apple to the squirrel and watched it scurry off in a hurry.

Chloe chased after Rose. "Are you okay, Rosey? What are you up to?"

As she pulled her invisibility cloak from her basket, Rose answered, "I have a plan."

"Really?" Chloe looked curious as to what it was.

Beaming confidently, Rose announced, "I'm going to look for lost treasures, collect a small fortune, and trade it for a sorcerer's magic."

Chloe giggled.

Rose sneered. "I'm on a mission to break my curse! I refuse to be lonely forever…and...and...no one else cares, so I'm taking charge of myself."

Feeling guilty, Chloe said, "You hold onto whatever dream is tugging at your heart, but don't tell Reeva and Zoe I told you that. I have my mean sister's reputation to keep up."

Unsure that she could prove her sisters wrong but willing to try. Rose gave Chloe a fake smile before whipping her invisibility cloak around her body and disappearing, at least from sight. Heading up a narrow path into Everwood, Rose thought of a particular spot to start her treasure hunt. As she pushed through the brush, she veered onto an overgrown path but noticed some flowers, electric orange, scarlet red, and oddly shaped. Petals that looked less like flowers and more like a species from outer space. They were blooming in the shadows of a tree as if they didn't need light to grow. After all, in a mystical forest, anything was possible. Rose thought. *Extraordinary. This could be something. Flowers have importance in specific antidotes. I'm sure a sorcerer will love these fantastic beauties.*

The nymph was convinced the vibrantly unique flowers were special and wanted to do the unthinkable—pick some. Reaching under the limbs, she pulled several flowers up from the earth. As dirt trickled down, a sudden burst of light scattered from the tops of the petals. Rose jumped back—surprised. Still, under her invisibility cloak, she backed away slowly as the light scattered into several tinier lights. They spiraled around in circles before taking off into the dark forest, all except one. The little light flitted and floated about. Suddenly, it transformed into a being as tiny as a child with luminous wings, sparkling skin, and holding a small book with a feather quill sticking out of it.

"Hello? Is anybody there?" The fairy squeaked. The shimmering markings on her body matched her pink crystal hair. As her eyes darted back and forth, she looked for whoever had just plucked the unusual flowers. The curious faye chewed on the end of her white feather quill, then scribbled something important into her book. Rose knew the fairy was looking for her.

"Whoever you are, these flowers are precious! Please stop!" The tiny fairy squeaked.

Still, Rose stayed silent. *She's a deviant reporter, and I can see mischief in her almond-shaped eyes.*

The nymph was forever hurt by the crazy stories fairies would write about her in the newspaper. Rose thought. *She's probably the very fairy who wrote I'm a monster with warts on my cheeks and foul breath. Now, if I had powers like my sisters, why would I make myself look and smell — like that? I mean, really! Fairies are ridiculous!*

The sparkling faye scribbled more in her book, then covered the remaining precious flowers with dried leaves like she feared Rose might pluck some more. Once satisfied that the flowers were safe, the fairy transformed into a sparkling pinpoint of light and flew off into Everwood like a shooting star.

You are valuable. Rose thought, as she inspected the flowers before placing them in her basket.

The nymph was already feeling successful when she eventually made it to a large clearing near Blackwood Road. It was the spot she'd been thinking about exploring for treasures. Several deer were grazing in the center, unaware of Rose's presence. Patches of snowdrops, violets, and daffodils were blooming, a sign that spring had arrived. While the nymph was investigating in the brush, one deer lifted its head. As voices in the distance became louder, the group of deer scattered.

Two figures with tricorn hats, longbows, and a cage between them, were walking through the meadow.

Chapter Two

Pirates! Rose thought, pulling her invisibility cloak tighter while keeping her distance.

"I bet we'll get a fortune for this birdie!" Two-fingered Tex belted out.

"Why don't ya tell the whole world we caught a golden birdie, ya numskull!" Baxter whispered angrily.

Once the two babbling pirates were closer, Rose could see a golden starling inside their cage.

How dreadful. I better get out of here before I'm next. Rose thought. But a sense of relief washed over her, as the pirates hurried away. She took a deep breath, trying to calm her racing heart. "That was too close for comfort," she whispered. The golden starling in the cage had sparked her curiosity. Carefully, she moved through the clearing, her steps light and silent. As the wind was beginning to pick up, carrying with it the scent of fresh earth and blooming flowers, Rose's thoughts flickered back to the golden bird. As she moved deeper into the clearing, she noticed animals whispering amongst themselves, sharing gossip about the two scallywags sudden appearance.

Rose paused, looking toward the hill where the pirates had descended, considering her next move. She had originally come here to explore for treasures, but now there was something else on her mind. *What if there were more pirates?* Rose followed the scallywags at a distance, keeping to the shadows and making sure they didn't hear her. She adjusted her cloak and set off silently, moving deeper into the forest, her mind already working out the best way to approach.

As she followed curiously, the two pirates descended a hill at the edge of the clearing. Bracing herself against a tree, she spied through branches, following their every move, when there was a loud crack.

Tex and Baxter were joking about how much the golden starling was worth when they heard something. An unidentifiable object, tumbling towards them down an embankment, finally stopped and unfolded on the path before them.

"What the…?" Baxter was tongue-tied by the sight.

"Is that what I think I see?" Two-fingered Tex gasped, then looked at Baxter, who was still standing with his jaw hanging open.

For only a few seconds, the platinum-haired nymph beauty was sprawled out on the ground in front of them with her invisibility cloak by her side. Known to eat her enemies alive, as reported in *The Fairy Tale Times*, the two pirates stood like statues, staring at the beauty as she hurried to her feet.

"Excuse me!" Rose bumbled. At lightning speed, she wrapped her invisibility cloak around her body and disappeared, at least from sight. Some squirrels were so stunned by the appearance of the nymph they dropped their acorns. Birds were chirping wildly like they were gossiping about the sudden discovery of the phantom nymph. A herd of fairies hiding in the brush burst into the air like firecrackers had gone off. Rubbing his eyes in disbelief, Tex stammered, "I can't believe it. Did we just see the nymph… or…or were we dreamn' ?"

Baxter shook his head, slapping Tex on the back. "We saw the white-haired demon! We did! We did! I can't believe it!"

"We didn't get swallowed up whole by her either!" Tex bragged stupidly.

"That was close," the one-eyed pirate shook his head in disbelief. "We need to get back to the ship before the captain finds out we're missin'. Hurry up! Get our horses!"

Chapter Three

Miss Dazzle-Dust Saves The Day

At the port of Bellefont, a massive pirate ship arrived in the middle of the night, seemingly unnoticed. With a sign that read 'The Revenge' prominently displayed on its bow and a worn-out-looking black flag with criss-crossed daggers hanging from its mast, the townspeople would soon know the notorious Captain McSly had arrived.

Stealing valuables and persuading children to join their team of vagabonds were McSly's pirate crew's daily chores. Of course, they did it all for their overly suspicious leader, Captain Corbin 'Peg-leg' McSly. Rich yet paranoid, McSly was forever accusing his crew of stealing from him, yet they probably were. Nonetheless, his troublemaking hoodlums had to be careful because their captain had a pirate fairy as an assistant.

Captain McSly was sitting at the head of the long, splintered table in the ship's dimly lit war room. His eyes darted back and forth between the faces of his crew, while his wooden leg tapped impatiently against the floor.

WANT TO BE A PIRATE?
FREE ROOM AND BOARD
FAME, FORTUNE, AND
A COOL NICKNAME
GUARANTEED!
OIN US ON "THE REVENG
TONIGHT AT SIX

"Which one of yah scoundrels stole my ruby compass?" he growled, his voice as sharp as a dagger.

The crew exchanged nervous glances, no one daring to meet McSly's gaze. Vivienne was by his side like a devious pet. She smirked and waved her hand, causing the candles to flare brighter. "Should I start zappin' 'em one by one, Cap'n?" she asked sweetly, her voice like mischief.

Vivienne Dazzledust Dior, like all fairies, possessed minimal but effective magic, which made her powerful enough to torment the crew in the blink of an eye, by the captain's orders, of course.

"Not yet, my Vivi," McSly said, leaning forward. "But mark my words, the thief is in this room. And when I find 'em, they'll wish they'd been marooned on an island instead!"

Outside on the docks, stray cats were weaving between crates, watchmen were patrolling the ships, and some children were roaming the streets, when a pirate from McSly's ship exited a ramp and posted a sign next to the Revenge. It read: Want to be a Pirate? Free room and board, fame, fortune, and a cool nickname guaranteed! Join us on The Revenge tonight!" Some boys saw the pirate posting the sign and walked over to investigate. As they read the details of the enticing offer, they heard someone shout,"You can eat candy all day if you join up!" Bubba 'The Bull,' a sizable pirate with a big tricorn hat and pistols strapped across his chest, had posted the signup sheet. As Bubba tried to persuade some boys to join, a crowd of townsfolk had gathered, whispering and pointing at the tattered black flag with daggers on it.

"Pirates," muttered the blacksmith, his hands tightening into fists. "First they steal our goods. Now they're trying to take our children!"

Near the docks, Bubba was still shouting promises of candy and fame, oblivious to the brewing anger. However, as he bantered back and forth with his pirate recruits about what it would be like to live on a pirate ship with a piece of red licorice dangling from his mouth, Baxter and Tex arrived from magical creature hunting. After freeing their horses, Baxter and Tex quietly hid behind some barrels and waited for the perfect moment to sneak back on board the Revenge. Thanks to blabbering Bubba, the two criminals crept back into an entrance on the other side with their new golden starling prize, unnoticed. After they descended below deck, Baxter and Tex entered a room where they and eight other pirate mates slept. The crew's den was supposed to be big enough for ten men to sleep in. Filled with hammocks lined up within inches of each other, it regularly smelled like mildew and stinky underwear.

"Where should we put it?" Tex asked, nervously scanning the room in a panic. "We are as good as dead if anyone sees us—"

"Put it under your blanket next to your stuff," Baxter ordered, pointing confidently towards Tex's hammock,

"just till we figure out a plan."

"Right… of course," Tex said, setting the cage down next to his hammock and covering it with his blanket. As they looked around curiously to ensure no one was watching, Baxter whispered,

"Let's go on deck… act normal…then go to The Salty Parrot and see when the next auction is."

"Sounds good," Tex whispered.

The golden starling chirped softly within its makeshift cage, its feathers glowing faintly in the dim light.

"Are you sure this bird is worth alot?" Tex whispered, glancing nervously at the blanket hiding the cage.

"It's not *just* a bird, you idiot" Baxter hissed. "I heard it's the key to unlocking treasures—like an old sea king's treasure chest hidden under the sea. Big things are going to happen for us, buddy."

"I sure hope the Cap doesn't find out—"

Baxter interrupted, grinning slyly. "Not if we sell it at the dark market first. That's the plan —buddy boy. Then we'll be rich. We'll have enough gold to buy our freedom."

But neither pirate noticed the faint shimmer of magic that trailed from the starling's feathers.

"Right..its magical…got it," Tex whispered back, "I'm in!"

"Let's go Tex!"

The two pirates grinned confidently at each other before disappearing out the door with their plan.

That same morning, inside the captain's quarters, wearing a black silk robe adorned with a large M on the front pocket, was Captain McSly. He quietly ate a bowl of his favorite breakfast, Krusty Puffs. It consisted of the most scrum-dilly-iscous sugary-flavored letters. And it was the most popular cereal around. McSly and his crew could not live without them. Because of this obsession, he and his pirate scoundrels stopped in Bellefont to fill up on a month's supply, among other things.

McSly was happily eating his bowl of Krusty Puffs when a particular letter, which he despised greatly, caught his eye. Yelling obscenities in a rage, the captain banged his fist against the table and threw his bowl of cereal across the room like a spoiled baby, smashing the bowl into pieces against the wall.

"Is there something wrong, Captain?" asked a tall young pirate with curly blonde hair.

Langford 'Loose-Lips' was Captain McSly's personal servant. This meant that if the captain wanted something, Lang was expected to get it—no matter what. Lang's specialty was talking too much, which the captain disliked but put up with. The captain held a small letter between his fingers. "You half-wit! There's an 'n' in my Krustys! How could this be?"

Lang stood at attention, with his dirty blonde hair covering half his face. The letter McSly was holding was a upside down letter 'u'.

"It reminds me of that nymph beast! Nymph begins with a 'n'. Lang, I DESPISE that nymph beast!"

Krusty Puff cereal was made out of the letters that spelled Krusty Puffs, go figure.

"Yes, Sir...Sorry sir, I must have missed one— it won't happen again!" Lang mumbled, just before the captain grabbed Lang's throat. The babbling pirate knew not to accuse the captain of 'being wrong'. He learned to accept the blame for everything or he'd be 'done in'.

"Do you not hear that sound, you idiot? The thump of my wooden leg? Every day, it reminds me of the nymph beast who devoured my foot like a hors d'oeuvre! Get this 'n' out of my sight," the captain growled, then threw the puff across the room.

There was a tinkling sound of the lone Krusty Puff bouncing off the wooden floor, when the captain's front door banged open. McSly's pet monkey Smokey, entered wearing a blanket wrapped around his head inscribed with "Property of Two-fingered Tex."

"What the—" The Captain was startled. The tiny monkey pirate also had Baxter's oversized eyepatch strapped across his little eye. Behind him, he was dragging the pirate's dilapidated cage like a two-year-old who had just found some toys to play with. The captain could see the gleaming golden starling inside. It was obvious McSly's two devious crewmen had captured a magical creature *without* the captain's knowledge. McSly exploded. "Get me Baxter and Tex! Now!"

Little Smokey, McSly's notorious pet monkey, was a small little devil with a mischievous glint in his golden eyes. He was usually adorned with a miniature skull and crossbones bandana, his trademark cigar hanging from his lips, and wearing frayed jacket with pockets stuffed with stolen trinkets.

After Lang rushed out the door to get the guilty culprits, Smokey sat on the floor and played with his newfound toys. The irritated captain picked up the cage, slammed it on his desk, and exited the room with his devious monkey pet. Moments later, the Captain and Smokey re-entered, both dressed in matching pirate hats with feathery plumes and gold trimmed jackets. As McSly admired himself in a mirror in the far corner of the room, Smokey played with his cigar, acting like an elegant man.

"Can I cheer you up with a charm to make your smile brighter?" Sitting on a chair in the corner of the room was Vivienne, twirling her dark raven hair around her finger. Her hypnotic blue eyes and tiny sparkling wings accented her shimmering dress. Vivienne noticed the captain's brown smoke-stained teeth as he smiled at himself in the mirror.

"Of course— Vivie," McSly answered, "of course!"

Vivienne winked twice, casting a charm, and magically changed the color of his teeth from brown to pearly bright white.

"Thank you, my little Vivie—you are so talented," Captain McSly said, blowing a kiss to her from across the room. She smiled back at him and winked, delighted to have made her captain so happy.

Vivienne enjoyed helping McSly with her fairy charms. A fairy turning to the dark side, such as pirating, was not unusual. If a fairy *wasn't* writing for the newspaper, they were considered mischievous and not to be trusted. Nevertheless, whether good or bad, fairies on the isle had magic, minimal but useful. The captain was admiring himself in the mirror when the cabin door opened, and Lang escorted the two guilty pirates in. With stringy black hair hidden under a charcoal headscarf, Baxter's shifty dark eyes scanned the room. He yelped quietly to himself when he saw the cage, elbowing Tex, who looked just as shocked with eyes like saucers. The golden prize was sleeping in its cage on the captain's desk. Next to it was Tex's blanket and Baxter's eyepatch.

"Captain," Lang announced, "Baxter and Tex are here. Delivered as requested."

Chapter Three

The Captain turned and acknowledged them as they stood in front of his desk, looking petrified.

"I see you two have been busy," McSly growled with one eyebrow lifted.

"Yes, Captain, we stole some horses and went hunting this morning, Captain Sir. We ended up catch'n this golden beaut for ya too," Baxter said, trying to sound sincere instead of a liar. "I see you found it! We hoped to present it to ya after ya finished your breakfast, Cap."

McSly pulled a dagger from his boot with a glint in his eye and a greasy smile. His black tangled hair frizzed as his temper grew. Looking more like a madman now, he walked closer to the two scallywags, as he pretended to admire the daggers' craftsmanship in order to stifle his rage. "Yes…but I believe you and Two-fingered Tex were going to KEEP this magical creature for yourselves, *weren't* you?"

"No, Cap, we were gonna surprise ya. We covered the birdie so none of our mates would steal it, of course." Baxter's face was perfectly placed in his lie. He smiled at Tex and nodded. Tex nodded back in agreement but was shaking, fearing for his life. The captain looked at the dagger in his hand like he had an uncontrollable urge to strike someone with it.

"I know you're lying —you idiots!" McSly grumbled. "You two are going to be shark bait!"

Chewing on a cigar butt like his master, Smokey jumped up and down, making squeaky monkey sounds like he was excited to see what was going to happen next. Just then, there was a knock on the door. Lang walked over to the small window on the heavy wooden door and slid it open with a creak. Bubba leaned in, his voice barely a whisper as he exchanged secretive words with Lang. With a sharp *crack*, Lang slid the window shut, his expression unreadable as he turned and crossed the room. Lang leaned in close to the Captain, his voice low and clear

"The Devil's Dagger and The Angel of Doom just docked."

McSly's lip curled into a snarl, his face darkening. "Ah, so Wolfgang and Razor Face Cutter have graced us with their presence. The question is... *why*?" He raised an eye-brow, his piercing gaze locking onto nothing in particular. "Not for the blasted Spring Fair?"

Lang shook his head emphatically 'no' towards the Captain, confirming his suspicion."Of course not," McSly muttered, scornfully. "No, it's something far more pre-cious." He stroked his chin, his scarred fingers dragged over his stubbly chin, as his eyes narrowed in thought. Baxter stepped forward hesitantly, sweat beads on his brow. His voice was trembling, but desperation pushed him to speak.

"Captain, I… I have some information you might find —useful." McSly's gaze snapped to Baxter like a striking snake.

"Well? Out with it!" McSly barked, his tone razor-sharp. "Unless you'd rather take a stroll off the plank."

"While Tex and I were capturing this golden starling for ya — we saw the phantom nymph!"

"WHAT?" McSly threw the dagger he was holding at the wall. With a loud thump, the blade sunk into the wood like butter. The captain had a stunned yet excited look on his face, but with a slight sneer. Baxter and Tex both gulped, fearing for their lives. McSly's mind had switched gears and was now focused on —the nymph. "You idiots saw where that white-haired ugly nymph lives?" McSly snarled, looking outraged by the mention of the nymph's existence. Storming up to Tex, he put his face so close. They touched noses.

The two pirates jumped, "Because if you don't know where she lives— you'll be in the water with the sharks!"

Feeling doomed if they didn't, they agreed to lie.

"We know! We know…I mean, we know where the ugly white nymph lives!" Tex lied, "we swear!"

"We do, Cap," Black-eyed Baxter confirmed the lie, elbowing Tex.

Just then, there was a knock on the door. Lang slid the small window open again. A rolled-up paper came through the opening and fell to the floor. It read:

> "*The Fairy Tale Times*. Special report: The Phantom Nymph is real!"

"This is incredible!" Captain McSly shouted with delight. Picking it up in a hurry, he shook the paper and read the front page:

> "Fairy reporter Thicket Moonmist writes A Special Report: The Phantom Nymph is real. It's not a myth anymore! Having spotted the platinum-haired creature, Mr. Moonmist reports, "I was just minding my own business, playing cards with my friends Cirrus and Flax, when we all heard a crash. We jumped up to see the commotion and saw this beautiful lady on the ground!" Thicket reports, "She had twigs, leaves, and tree remnants in her hair," Flax reports, "I saw her pretty snake eyes... and tongue...metallic little symbols over each eyebrow...like little buttons, but they didn't stick out like buttons. She was as tall as the trees with a tail, too." For two hundred years, the nymph has been considered just a myth. Now, the citizens of Lumiere know— she's real!" Cirrus reports, "I can say this... we only saw her for a few minutes, but that nymph is a powerful beauty because she disappeared— just like that!" Continued on page 3.

McSly crumpled the newspaper in his fists like he was strangling an enemy. With a snarl, he slammed it onto the desk."I want her first!" he barked, jabbing a finger at Baxter and Tex."Everyone will read this—Wilhelm, Machado, *everyone*! They're coming for her, that ugly, white-haired *BEAST*! That's why those ships are here! She'll regret the day she crossed me. That beast will *pay*!" His face twisted with rage as he leaned closer, eyes blazing. "Go, you imbeciles! GO NOW! Make me a map—or you're *shark bait*!"

"Don't worry, cap," Baxter lied, "we'll be right back with a map!"

Baxter and Tex bolted from the room, bumping into each other on the way out.

Smokey jumped on top of the cage with the golden starling and beat his chest like he had conquered something.

"Yes— Smokey," McSly said, "the golden starling will be our good luck charm for finding the wretched beast!"

"Sir," Lang noted, "a nymph is a powerful being. She is the daughter of Poseidon, the God of the Sea. She's one of the most powerful God-like creatures on this island. Why don't we embrace that power — not kill it?"

McSly turned on Lang, his teeth clenched and his eyes full of venom. "I don't care who her father is. I want to rip her to shreds for what she's done to me!" He turned abruptly, his gaze falling on Vivienne, who lounged in the corner, filing her nails and twirling a strand of hair as if none of it concerned her.

“Vivie? What do you think? Kill or capture?”

The fairy pirate smirked, pretending to mull it over. Finally, she spoke, her tone sharp with envy. “As a magical being myself, I’m jealous of the nymph’s power. I say, with a golden starling in our possession, we have luck on our side. Let’s capture her — and rule the world with her power!”

McSly’s expression shifted, a wicked grin spreading across his face. "Fair point," he said, his voice with sinister glee.

Smokey took the golden bird out of the cage and held it up like a trophy, cigar clenched between his teeth, earning a laugh from McSly.

“Give me one of those,”McSly barked, snapping his fingers.

Smokey ran and grabbed a cigar for his master.

“Wolfgang and Razor-Face must have read the news too—why else would they be in town?” Lang said, his voice sharp. “Why don’t we sharpen our knives, gather our guns, and hunt down that ugly nymph beast at dawn? We’ll beat them to it—capture her before she even wakes up!”

McSly leaned back in his chair, puffing thoughtfully on his cigar. “Hmmmm… I like it. Let’s move fast and take what’s ours!”

Chapter Three

On deck, the crew gathered, when Lang called. Their chanting thundered through the ship, fists raised high: "Sly! Sly! Sly!"

The captain burst from his quarters, a manic grin stretched across his face. "My scoundrels and hoodlums! I have great news!" he bellowed, the crew falling silent. "We know where the nymph beast lives!"

A cheer erupted like cannon fire.

"HURRAY!!"

McSly raised a hand to quiet them down, his voice carrying over the uproar. "Today, we sharpen our blades and gather our guns. Tomorrow, at dawn, we capture that wretched nymph beast—and make her regret the day she crossed Captain McSly!"

The crew roared their approval, stomping and chanting louder than ever, "Sly! Sly! Sly!"

Meanwhile, Baxter and Tex, still without a map, lurked in the shadows at the edge of the deck. They flinched as Lang stormed over, his eyes narrowing.

"Ya boyz better have something for the captain," Lang hissed. "The whole island's buzzing about the nymph beast now. Tick-tock!"

Baxter, trembling, forced a nervous smile. "We were just on our way to the loo. Don't worry, we'll be right back...with a map. Of course."

Lang added,"Make it quick. I wouldn't want to be in your boots if you come back empty-handed." He stormed off, leaving the two of them huddled in a corner.

"What now?" Tex muttered, his voice low and desperate.

Baxter's face lit up with sudden inspiration. "Let's ask Vivienne!" he blurted out.

"Vivienne?!" Tex stared at him like he'd lost his mind.

"She helped Gilly Mudpie that time the captain shredded his laundry!" Baxter said, his voice climbing with desperation. "Remember? He tried to blow the dirt off with *gunpowder*! Nearly took the whole ship with him!"

Before Tex could argue, a sudden swirl of dust and glittering light filled the air. Out of the shimmer stepped Vivienne, in a silver jacket and dress, her dagger strapped elegantly across her chest. Her dark hair draped down her back like a waterfall of night, and her iridescent wings shimmered in the faint light.

Startled by her sudden appearance, both pirates jumped back, nearly tripping over each other.

"You called?" she asked, her lips curling into a sly smirk.

"Vivie, we need your help!" Baxter said, his voice trembling with panic.

She raised an arched brow, folding her arms. "This better be good."

"Of course," she smiled, as she knew already, then added, "for a fee."

Baxter had a look of desperation on his face. "How much?"

Vivie played with her hair, then checked her nails obnoxiously, as if thinking of a price for her services. "Four *gold* doubloon's will do— I suppose."

After whining momentarily about the amount, Tex and Baxter agreed.

"So, now what?" Baxter grumbled.

"Now, here's the plan. I have to investigate first. Meet me at the tiger lilies along the Brandywine River in thirty minutes. And bring the gold! Or no deal! Got it?" Vivie snarled, looking at Tex and Baxter like they were idiots, which they were.

Tex gulped under her glare and nodded. "Got it. That's on the other side of the isle—where we saw the phantom nymph."

Vivie raised a brow, unimpressed. "Then you'd better hurry, hadn't you?"

Tex grabbed Baxter's arm. "Let's go, Bax! Vivie's our only shot at *not* getting turned into 'shishkebobs' by the Cap!"

The two scoundrels bolted, muttering plans to find horses as they disappeared into the shadows.

Vivie watched them go with mild amusement, then gave a small, satisfied sigh. In another swirl of dust and light, she vanished as suddenly as she had appeared.

Chapter Four

Plan B

The Isle of Lumiere shimmered under the morning sun. Its dew-drenched meadows dotted with flowers glowed faintly in the light. However, as ancient trees loo-med with roots curled like fingers, Blackwood Road cut through the middle of Everwood like a dark scar. It went from one end of the isle to the other, and everyone from kings and queens to diabolical fiends traveled down it, making it the obvious first choice to explore. But being an extremely lengthy road, the question was posed: *Where on Blackwood were the best spots to find treasures?* Ironi-cally, Rose had recently read Kasper Tig's article: 'Ha-zards on Blackwood' in *The Fairy Tale Times*.

> "At the crossroads of Blackwood and River, there is a pothole so big you could fit six fat cats inside—beware! Travel by the intersection of River Road at your own risk!"

So, after reading that, River and Blackwood became the next spot the nymph decided to explore.

Eventually reaching the landmark, she thought the pothole looked even more prominent than she had ever envisioned, so she felt hopeful that carriages may have lost some goods. As sunlight filled the meadow generously, the nymph noticed something right away. It was long, thin, and near the edge of the woods.

"Hmmm, perfect!" she exclaimed, picking up her prize with a grin and swishing it through the air like a sword. "Yes, sir, this is absolutely splendid—the *ideal* treasure-hunting stick!" she announced with excitement.

Feeling a spark of luck, she began poking around the bushes at the edge of the clearing—perhaps a bit too enthusiastically. Her exuberance stirred up a group of pixiaries. The tiny glowing orbs were tired of watching grass grow and more interested in their unexpected visitor, so they flitted closer.

Rose, however, was no stranger to these luminous beings. Her sisters had told her plenty about pixiaries.They were harmless and inquisitive, unlike the mischief-making fairies that often caused trouble. The radiant spheres hovered around her, as if somehow able to perceive the nymph behind her invisibility cloak.

Remembering her manners, Rose greeted them with a polite nod. The pixiaries lingered only for a moment before darting away, their movements purposeful, as though late for some unseen gathering.

Satisfied that she hadn't caused any trouble, Rose resumed her search. A glint of something caught her eye in the dirt. She crouched down and carefully unearthed it, a tiny book, no larger than the palm of her hand. Holding it up to the light, she turned it over, curiously. As she studied it closely, she saw an inscription faintly written in the center: Teena Cloverleaf: Reporter for The Fairy Tale Times.

"A fairy's journal…ahhhh! I wonder what untruths this gossipy fiend is writing about now."

A fairy's life's purpose on the Isle of Lumiere was to fill their journals with observations and report their findings to the island paper, The Fairy Tale Times. But to Rose, the mischievous fairies wrote lies. That's right— lies. For two hundred and five years, they have described the phantom nymph as a ghostly fire-breathing monster girl with buckteeth, sometimes an albino-finned serpent girl with bulging eyes, and even a snake-eyed girl with oddly hairy nostrils. It went without saying that since Rose had no powers to transform into anything, these were insults, so Rose was skeptical of anything they reported.

However, after randomly opening the journal, she was pleasantly surprised. A row of bunny butts with cotton ball tails was drawn in burnt umber ink, and a charcoal drawing of a miniature man with a bald head, large ears, and a tiny chin, presumably a goblin, was in the top corner. *Ahhh, nicely done!* The nymph admired the delicate lines of the sketches. Swirly cursive notes in cerulean and emerald ink filled almost every page. *Hmm, intriguing.* Rose decided to read more:

> "While searching for some Challiwoohoo blossoms in a clearing near Blackwood, I spotted two pirates hunting with longbows and a cage. They successfully captured a golden starling. The helpless magic bird looked like its luck just ran out!"

How sad. Rose thought, *but believable. Golden starlings are captured all the time. Anyway, I'm sure there's some perfectly horrible gossip about me somewhere in here.*

The nymph closed and opened the fairy book again to another page.

> It read: "After three days of experiencing never-ending dizziness, upset stomach, and extreme anger… I believe I have Fairy Flu."

She stopped reading immediately. *Maybe I've been too harsh. Clearly, this fairy is innocent of anything devious. The lines were delicate, almost trembling, as if the fairy's hand had been unsteady.* Rose wondered if the fae had drawn this while ill. She suddenly felt a flicker of pity. Rose decided to read more.

> "Thankfully, I met a sorceress, Belladonna Barbosa. After I agreed to give her some fairy dust in exchange for the antidote for my Fairy flu from her Book of Remedies, I must eat challiwoohoo

flower petals and two drops of juice from the Spanglepangle orange every day for thirty days, but my chances of survival are slim. Good Luck!"

Out of nowhere, a light zoomed by Rose's nose like a shooting star. A tiny wisp of a being snatched the fairy's journal from Rose's hand and hovered before her. The owner of the fairy book was caked in mud and rambling on in a high-pitched tone with the challiwoohoo flower petals in each hand. After yelling 'fairy obscenities' at Rose, the sickly fairy zoomed off.

"Sorry!" the nymph cried out, staring into Everwood. But Rose felt more forgiving of fairies than before she found the fairy's journal, at least for a few of them.

As the nymph disappeared under her cloak again, she gathered her basket and continued her search for treasures. Spotting a bush of oversized blackberries, Rose couldn't resist filling her basket and mouth with some.

"Dewishes!" She slurred.

The morning sun was higher above the trees now, illuminating a patch of grass filled with daisies and violets near Blackwood Road. While filling her mouth with berries, she noticed a lump in the grass. Walking closer to investigate, she poked around it with her stick, smelling a not-so-agreeable odor. "*Ew—Rotten apples!* "She groaned. And to make the discovery even worse, a fly landed on her nose. Rose repeatedly swung at it but failed to 'do the fly in.'

"Annoying—Aren't you!" She snarled.

As she did her best to ignore the fly poking and prodding at her under her cloak, she continued rummaging by River Road, only to uncover a worthless overnight bag, a stinky old boot, and a chewed stuffed toy bear.

"That's it! I'm a foolish dreamer, a complete treasure-hunting failure, stuck with a curse forever, and now—an annoying fly!"

After removing her invisibility cloak, Rose hid in some nearby ferns, feeling defeated, when a miracle happened.

The irritating fly went away.

"Good riddance, little Devil!" She snapped.

With her invisibility cloak by her side, she closed her eyes and relaxed in the tall grass. She was loving the sudden cool breeze, freedom from her cloak, and disappearance of the annoying fly, when she heard a bird break out in song in the distance. She listened to the tweeting of its beautiful melody, soothing and peaceful. Rose was almost asleep when an incredibly off-key voice sang out.

"She's the cutest fairy girl I've ever seen… oh yeah—the cutest!"

Rose jumped to her feet in a hurry, diving into the brush. As she scanned the area for the source of the singing, her gaze landed on a boy with soap suds foaming atop his head like a makeshift hat. Nearby, a pair of pants hung on a branch, shimmering as tiny sparkles trickled from its pockets.

"He's definitely enchanted," she muttered under her breath, her heart racing with curiosity.

Just as Rose reached for her magic cloak to investigate the mysterious boy, a sudden flash of light froze her in place. Before she could react, he was standing above her, glaring with a disagreeable expression.

Rose shrank deeper into the bush, her cheeks flushed. "Hello," she squeaked.

"Hello, spy!" The boy with wet hair and pointy ears grumbled, as he was buttoning his pants around his waist.

"I—I'm not a spy!" Rose stammered, fumbling for words.

"Not a spy?" His voice was sharp with suspicion. "You're in Elflin without permission, sneaking about. That *sounds* like a spy to me."

Rose swallowed hard, flustered. "I didn't know I was in Elflin—what is it, exactly?"

The boy crossed his arms, his wet hair dripping onto his shirt. "Elflin is the heart of Everwood, where the elves dwell. And intruders—especially spies—don't leave without proving themselves."

"Proving myself?" Rose echoed nervously.

He raised an eyebrow, a sly grin curling on his lips. "Answer my riddle, or you'll face the consequences."

Before Rose could protest, he lifted a flute that dangled around his neck like a pendant. He played a soft melody that echoed through the trees, causing unseen creatures in the shadows to giggle and whisper.

“Silence!” he barked, shooting a glare into the darkness. The laughter ceased instantly.

He turned back to Rose, his expression serious. “Here’s your riddle: I have no lungs, but I need air. I have no mouth, but water kills me. What am I?”

Rose’s mind raced, her thoughts tumbling over one another. She was still fumbling for an answer when she heard a faint voice in her head.

“I can help you,” it whispered.

The nymph looked around the woods for the mysterious voice's owner but saw nothing in the ferns or the brush, just the angry elf in front of her. Then, the voice was louder.

"I can help you,” said a whispering voice. It sounded like a angel, soft and calming. Rose sensed that it was in her head, but didn't want to confess the strangeness of it.

“Did you hear that?” She asked the elf, "that voice.”

“What?…Ah…no,” the elf remarked with one brow raised like she was kooky.

“Close your eyes.” the voice said this time.

Rose closed her eyes. And in the darkness of her mind, a vision appeared—a crimson-orange flame danced vividly, burning as if it were real. Her eyes snapped open. She blurted out, “Fire! The answer is—fire?” She saw the elf’s face, which looked stunned.

"No. No..Noooo!" He shouted angrily, jumping and hollering, then kicking the dirt. "How did you know?... RATS! Who—*are you*, oh smart one?" The boy inquired. "Are you an evil sorceress?" Poised with sparkling crystals like he held a weapon, he was ready to strike her, if she tried anything funny.

"Of course not!" Rose snapped, crossing her arms.

His eyes narrowed. "Then... are you a *beardless pirate*?"

"What?!" Rose groaned. "No!"

"Well, *what* are you then?" he demanded, still hovering, ready to toss the crystal dust at the slightest move.

Rose sighed, stepping out from behind the brush. "Some would say..." she began, meeting his suspicious gaze, "I'm a nymph."

Several birds flew overhead and settled on a nearby branch, their heads tilting curiously as they observed the radiant girl below. Her every move seemed to hold them spellbound. The gold markings above her brow shimmered in the sunlight like tiny jewels, while a gentle breeze lifted strands of her hair, making her appear ethereal and glowing. The birds remained transfixed, caught in awe of her beauty.

Rose adjusted the daisy crown aroun her forehead, holding her hair back like a delicate headband, emphasizing her enchanted features. She noticed the elf watching her, intrigued. Clearly, he hadn't seen the papers—her face had been on them every day.

"Do you not read *The Fairy Tale Times*?" she asked with a sly smile.

"I think the paper is a bore!" the elf replied bluntly.

Rose laughed, her eyes widening in disbelief. "Really? How could anyone be so rebellious? The paper is a bore?"

"Absolutely," the elf said, his tone firm yet teasing. "Except for the comic section and the cake and candy recipes, I don't bother with it."

Natts eyed her carefully, noting her innocence. Satisfied she was no threat, he discreetly returned the magic dust to his pocket. Then, with his hands on his hips, he tilted his head at her. "But tell me, are you a spy, Miss Nymph? I do say. Can't an elf get a little privacy while taking a bath?" Some voices were giggling in the brush.

The nymph laughed, too. "I'm sorry. Please forgive me."

"Well, I suppose—just this time" the elf said, reaching out with his hand to help her up. "I'm Natts Soto."

Observing him curiously, the nymph realized she had never met anyone in Everwood.

"No need to be frightened," the elf said, noticing her hesitation. "I'm an elf. And elves are harmless...mostly." He straightened, placing his hands on his hips. "But don't forget—I have powers! I can transform and bewitch!" His tone was proud, yet playful.

Rose bent to retrieve her invisibility cloak and basket, then curtsied gracefully. “I’m Rose,” she said, her voice soft.

He could sense her unease. “Nice to meet you, Miss Rose,” he said with a courteous bow. “Now tell me—are you a regular spy, or is there some important reason for wandering Everwood alone this fine morning?”

Rose felt herself relax. His cheeky smile and polite manner put her at ease. “No,” she replied with a small laugh. “I’m not a spy. I’m just gathering berries...among other things.”

Natts tilted his head curiously. “Are you lost?”

“Not at all.”A fly suddenly buzzed by and landed inside Rose’s basket. She tried to wave it away repeatedly.

“Where are you from?” Natts asked, watching her with interest.

“I live at the Shallows with my sisters.”

“The Shallows?” he repeated, intrigued. “I don’t think I’ve ever heard of it. How long have you lived there?”

“Hundreds of years,” Rose replied casually, as though it were the most natural thing in the world.

Natts blinked in disbelief, mumbling under his breath. *Hundreds of years? She looked no older than twelve.* He had never met a nymph before, and despite his efforts to hide his astonishment, his gaze lingered on the shimmering gold markings on her brow.

"Fascinating," he muttered, then cleared his throat. "I can't say I've ever heard of the Shallows..." He trailed off, his curiosity growing.

"It's a secret place," Rose said softly. "We don't ever have visitors. It's for protection—against pirates or villainous immortals, of course."

"Oh...of course," Natts replied, a little too quickly, his gaze fixed on her. He couldn't help it—she was mesmerizing. The gold markings above her brilliant blue eyes caught the sunlight, gleaming like precious metal. "But I'm sure it's delightful to live there."

Rose smiled politely, uncertain how to respond. "Yes, it's... lovely," she said, hesitating before adding, "It's truly breathtaking. We have a pond surrounded by the most beautiful flora you can imagine."

Natts nodded, though his thoughts were elsewhere. He still hadn't put the pieces together—he had no idea he was speaking to *the phantom nymph*, the whispered legend of Everwood.

The annoying fly reemerged, buzzing out of Rose's basket to land on a daisy in her flower crown.

"It sounds enchanting," Natts said, struggling to sound casual and not like an admirer entranced by every word she spoke.

Rose's heart fluttered. *Was it fear? Or was it the unfamiliar thrill of speaking to someone new?* Decades had passed since anyone outside her family had seen her. She felt the weight of her curse. Yet she couldn't help herself—she wanted to impress him. She wanted to take the risk.

"Oh, it *is* enchanting," Rose said, her voice brightening. "We have the finest berry bushes around the entrance—the best on the island, I'd say. At least, I've never tasted better in all my travels. You should visit sometime. You could pick some yourself."

The fly returned. As Rose swatted at it furiously, forcing it to flee.

"Annoying fiends, those flies!" she exclaimed, her delicate features momentarily twisted with frustration.

"Yes,… those flies surely are!" Natts agreed.

Trying to summon the courage to ask him for help, she picked a berry out of her basket and silently stared at it. After seeing the sparkling crystal in his pockets, she wondered if he had the powers of a sorcerer.

"So," Natts asked curiously, "do you have a magical disguise, Miss Rose? Most of us magical creature types do."

Rose's eyes darted back and forth, unsure what to say, wondering if she should expose her weakness.

"I transform into a dragonfly," he said, looking proud.

"That is very clever. I must say," Rose commented.

"And you, Miss Rose? What is your disguise?"

Rose's expression wavered. "Unfortunately," she mumbled, her voice barely above a whisper, "I have a...a curse."

She glanced away quickly, as though ashamed, her hands tightening around the handle of her basket.

"A curse?" Natts repeated, his brows furrowing. "That sounds dreadful! What kind of curse?"

Before she could answer, a loud chirping erupted from Natts' wrist. A tiny bird on his sundial watch flapped its wings frantically like an alarm.

"Oh no!" Natts exclaimed. "It's quarter past—I'm late! I'm so sorry, but I have to go." He reached into his pocket, grabbing a handful of sparkling dust. "I don't mean to be rude, but I've got an important date. Can we meet later?"

"Of course," Rose replied, disappointment flickering in her eyes. She hadn't yet asked him about fixing her curse, and now the moment was slipping away.

"So, I can visit you at the Shallows, then—*spy girl*?" Rose was excited about the possibility of a new friend, she didn't hesitate to give him directions, forgetting for a moment of the consequences.

"I'd like that," she said eagerly. "From here, go down Blackwood for about twenty-five paces. Then turn right and walk another twenty paces until you see two enormous lilac bushes. That's where we live—at least, that's where our secret entrance is."

"Got it!" Natts said, tapping his temple with a wink. "I'll remember, I promise."

"Goodbye, *spy girl*!" he teased again, turning to leave.

Rose waved back, her emotions swirling as she watched him toss the sparkling dust into the air. He mumbled a few words under his breath, and within moments, a brilliant swirl of golden light surrounded him. In a flash, he was gone, leaving only a cascade of shimmering sparkles drifting to the ground.

Rose stood there for a moment, staring at the sunlight catching the glittering particles as the elf flew away like a shooting star.

It was late morning when Two-Fingered Tex and Black-Eyed Baxter crouched in the bushes near the vibrant Tiger Lilies along the Brandywine River, just as instructed. The Brandywine stretched several miles across the isle and was about five horse lengths wide. Usually it was busy with islanders swimming, but today it was eerily quiet—perfect for a secret pirate meeting.

Baxter puckered his lips and whistled a melodic trill of a bird, a signal meant for someone—or something.

Moments later, a fly zipped through the trees and landed on the mossy ground before them. Without warning, leaves and twigs swirled into a tiny whirlwind, spinning faster and faster until the funnel dissolved, revealing a fairy pirate.

"Ah, Vivie," Baxter cackled nervously. "Got good news for us, eh?

"Are you going to keep your promise and pay me the gold?" She hissed. The sinister young fairy had a glint in her eye like an angry cat. She quickly pulled out her dagger and held it towards Baxter's throat.

"I swear… I've got it! Relax." He pulled out a small velvet bag that jingled with the sound of coins and dropped it in Vivie's hand.

The fairy dumped the content into her palm and counted it swiftly. Satisfied that her full payment was there, she quickly returned the gold coins to the bag and tucked it away in her jacket, announcing, "I saw her! I saw the phantom nymph!"

"Excellent! Excellent, Vivie!" Baxter shouted, "This is great news!"

"Not so fast," Vivie interrupted. "She wears an invisibility cloak. I can see her, but you—" She sneered. "Forget it."

"She's invisible? Oh no!" Tex moaned. "Weez as good as dead!" He slapped his leg in frustration. "Weez supposed tah lead the crew to the phantom nymph's lair tomorrow morn. If we don't find her today, weez 'done in' on Cap's sword. Shishgabobbed, as they say!"

Baxter's mouth hung open as he considered an alternative plan. "He's right," he noted, "but what should we do?"

Baxter's brow furrowed as his mind raced. "He's right," he muttered. "If we don't deliver, it's our necks on the line. But what now?"

"Stay put," Vivie snapped. "Hide in the bushes and don't move."

In a swirl of leaves, dirt, and twigs, the fairy pirate transformed into a fly again and took off. Before they could even say a word, she was back. As the funnel died down, Vivienne appeared.

"Well?" Baxter asked.

With arms crossed, Vivie announced plan b. "The phantom nymph has befriended an elf. He's in the clearing about five jackrabbit leaps from here."

Tex asked stupidly, "An elf?"

"Yes, and an elf named Natts," Vivie confirmed.

"Why should we care about an elf? Baxter asked.

"Because the nymph told the elf directions to where she lives! You imbecile!"

"Okay…okay," Baxter adjusted his jacket and scarf. "What does he look like?"

Vivie growled, clearly running out of patience. "He has hair the color of lemons and pants as dark as grapes." She leaned closer, her voice dropping to a venomous whisper. "The nymph mentioned something about the Shallows. That's her hideout. You'll need to trick the elf into giving up the location. Get him to draw a map, and once he does — Vivie smiled like the sinister fairy she was.

She slashed her hand across her throat with a cruel smile. "Kill him."

Baxter blinked, his face pale. “Kill him?” he echoed nervously, as though hoping he’d misheard.

“Yes, kill him,” Vivie snarled. “We have no use for him once we have the map. If he lives, he’ll only help the nymph escape. Do I make myself clear?”

“Kill the elf—got it!” Tex said with a delighted cackle, already rubbing his hands together.

“You’ll need disguises,” Vivie continued, her tone icy. She whispered a spell under her breath, and in a flash of light, a bundle of clothes appeared on the ground before them.

Baxter bent down, lifting one piece of fabric with suspicion. “Right. Trick the elf, get the map, kill him,” he muttered, as if committing it to memory.

Vivie’s wings buzzed as a sudden funnel of leaves and twigs spiraled around her. “Now go,” she shouted over the rising wind. “Before he slips away!” In an instant, she was gone, the swirling debris falling back to the earth.

Baxter straightened up, pulling on his disguise. “Come on, Tex,” he said. “We’ve got work to do.”

Tex smirked, slipping on his new clothes. “Work I can handle. Let’s go find us an elf.”

Chapter Five

The Imposters

Not far from River Road was Buttercup Lane and Blackwood, another notorious intersection for mishaps and catastrophes. Although Buttercup Lane sounded like a sweet and innocent path, like the hundreds of teenie-tiny sunny yellow blooms near the road, it was anything but. There were rocks the size of small elephants along the lane's edges as well as several craters as wide as two fat cats. The devilish region was known to make carriages bounce like bunnies, which made things fly from their backends. Because of this, Rose thought this would be her next treasure-hunting spot.

Although feeling a bit depressed Rose was trying her best to be positive. Yet as the down-and-out nymph daydreamed about finding a lost jewelry box, something caught her eye. Hoping it wasn't an underground wasp nest or napping monster, she moved closer to investigate. She held her breath and carefully reached out with the tip of her stick into the mass of darkish unknown beneath the grass. To her surprise, it was a travel bag. Although flat tened like a pancake, she lifted what looked like a flap with her stick so she could see inside. Immediately recognizing something, she pulled out the object and held it up like a trophy.

"A letter! Why, it's in perfect shape, too!" Wanting to inspect her first fascinating prize, she looked around the meadow again for anything suspicious. When she saw the coast was clear, she let her invisibility cloak fall back off her head. "Now, what do I have here?" Caressing the smooth paper with her fingertips, she admired the amber-colored seal resembling a thick coin of candle wax. Although looking stuck in the center of the envelope like a lock, the seal was broken in half. "This letter has been read but kept for some reason." After studying the intricately embossed letter B in the middle, she flipped it over only to discover swirls of rich umber ink expertly written by hand. She read: To Miss Winifred Brown, Thirty-Six Waters Street in Archmere, and on the top left corner, it read: Mr and Mrs Winston Brown of 7 Horseshoe Lane in Devonshire. "Hmmm, I'll look at this later."

Refocusing on the possibility of more treasures, she looked inside the squashed travel bag again. Seeing two dots of light inside the bag staring back, Rose hoped it wasn't a wild animal or worse, a snake. However, she felt courageous and decided to reach in.

"A brush! After years of using a torturous comb, my hair thanks you for coming into my life!"

Chapter Five

After tucking the brush and letter into her basket, she felt fortunate. She secured her invisibility cloak again and got to her feet. As Rose picked up her treasure-hunting stick, she noticed the morning sun had risen higher over the trees. And although she grabbed a slithering snake, escaped the bite of a fly, and smelled gag-awful smelly apples, the cursed nymph still felt better. She realized her mission to restore her magical power was worth risking her life for, even though it made her sad to think her happiness was unimportant to her family. At least, that was what she felt.

Ready to return home, Rose turned off of Buttercup Lane and headed into the woods towards the shallows. Dragging her stick through a pile of leaves, she clumsily lost hold of it. It tumbled through the air, bounced off a nearby rock, then landed in the grass. When she bent down to pick it up, she noticed something. Sitting on a leaf, like a present on a tray, was a round and lustrous object.

"I think the Gods are pitying me? Could this be gold?"

Picking it up in a hurry, she examined it curiously. The gold button was worn around the edges, slightly dented, and in the center was an elegantly etched letter W. Rose was so excited, her mind was racing. It was another sign of luck. "A seaman…or a pirate…or maybe even a king wore this!" She clutched it in her hand, thinking about what it meant."I shall wear it like a lucky charm." Sitting on a nearby branch was an entourage of bird groupies that had been following Rose around Everwood. As they watched her inspect her newfound miracle, they chatted intensely. "So what if it's a button!" the nymph barked, "It's gold, and it's… it's—better than rotten apples!" The birds scattered, screeching wildly, sensing Rose's frustration. The nymph immediately attached her new lucky button to a necklace she was wearing, feeling happier.

With a kick in her step, she disappeared from view under her cloak and headed for home. But when she spotted some irresistible blackberries along the way, she couldn't resist and dropped to the ground to fill her basket with some. However, just as she popped one in her mouth, she heard people talking. Quickly securing her invisibility cloak, she followed the voices. Within yards of where she was standing, she spied two elderly-looking fairies talking to a small boy.

"Tilly and I are so thankful for yee map, Me fine fellow!" said a colossal fairy.

Spying through the trees, Rose could see the boy— was Natts. But she had no idea who the fairies were. Observing the woman's bushy eyebrows and long dark hair, Rose wondered. "She's mysteriously hideous. But there were a lot of unique creatures on the island, so I suppose this is normal."

The hideous fairy with long dark hair continued, "We must pick zee best and plumpest berries for our jams. We want to win the jam and jelly contest at zee Spring Fair.

But we heard —the Shallows is da best place to find them."

Rose sat there dumbfounded by what she just heard. "How could these women know of —the shallows?"

Feeling compelled to impress the elderly fairies like he was under a spell, Natts immediately wanted to fix their problem like a hero. "It must be fate! I was just told how to get to the shallows! I know exactly how to get to the finest berry bushes around." Tilly, the other large fairy woman with wings, squeaked in a high-pitched voice, "If Berty and I are goin' to win, we need to find de Shallows. Please, little Natts! Can yuz help us?

"Don't worry! I've got this!" After pulling out some elf dust from his pocket, he chanted, "Dim dim Bing bing Tah Tah!" There was a sudden burst of light, and a map fell to the ground.

Rose looked on— stunned.

"There, that should be good enough. Just follow the map, and when you get to the lilac bushes, you're there."

Natts looked proud to have helped the two elderly fairies. "There's a path next to—" Falling back surprised, Natts looked like he saw a ghost. After pulling their hair off...yes— hair, like the two imposters that they were, the scoundrels laughed out loud before throwing their wigs to the ground. Within seconds, Tex held a dagger to Natts's throat.

"The map to the nymph beast's liar is ours! Captain McSly, thanks ya too," crackled Baxter.

"It's all ours! We iz gonna be rich Bax!"

"The caps' gonna reward us! I'zz sure of it Tex!"

Frantically thinking of a survival plan, the elf begged, "I want to kill the nymph beast, too! How do I join your crew—"

"Shut up, ya stinkin' liar! I'm the only one that's supposed to be talk'n now." Pushing the dagger into the elf's throat, Tex made Natts grimace with pain.

"But we can talk about it on da way, dare, little elf." Baxter growled, "Now take off ya— magic pants!"

Stripped of his only power, Natts stood shaking in his undershorts.

"Hurry up!" the one-eyed pirate barked. With a sparkling trail behind them, the scoundrel pirates and their elf prisoner disappeared into Everwood.

Stunned by what just happened, the nymph barely knew Natts but felt compelled to do something. Securing her magic cloak in a hurry, she took off. Horrified that her friend may be doomed, she ran as fast as she could, listening for their voices. *This is all my fault. I shouldn't have told him where the shallows were.* Running out of energy, she stopped to catch her breath and sat down on a fallen tree. She pulled off her boot and watched an annoying pebble fall to the ground. As she sat silently staring at the small stone, tears began to well.

"This is all my fault."Rose mumbled, then wept silently. But as the nymph slipped her boot back on, a dragonfly buzzed by. Its luminous wings were glistening, making her stop and wonder. It circled her several times before finally resting on her hand. Wiping tears from her eyes to see more clearly, she asked, "Natts? Is it you?"

In a flash, the dragonfly transformed into a ball of energy—emerald and gold light spiraled before morphing into a boy with pointy ears and lemon-yellow hair. Natts stood there boldly, elf dust spilling from his pockets.

"Hello again, Miss Rose!"

He bowed like a gentleman before the nymph leaped towards her elf friend, hugging him tight. "I thought you were —dead."

"Spying on me again, Miss Nymph?"

"Yes, but… but…I was so *worried*!"

"Cleverness is my middle name, Miss Rose!" Natts declared, puffing out his chest. "Do you think I'd let a couple of scurvy pirates outsmart me? Ha! I always keep a stash of elf dust in my…er, most secret of pockets." He winked, tapping the waistband of his undershorts. "They'd have to strip me bare before they could catch me—and even then, good luck!"

"I'm so glad you're all right."

With the magic cloak by her side, animals gathered, spellbound by her beauty. The elf observed her curiously. The gold markings above her eyes were glistening.

"You look like...," the elf muttered to himself. "Are you—the phantom nymph Miss Rose?"

"I am," she sniffled, still sad about what happened.

"Can't believe it. You're the phantom nymph! I should have known. So it was you they were after?"

Shrugging her shoulders, she was unsure of what to say.

"How could I give those pirates directions to —-" The elf kicked a stone angrily, shooting it into the brush. "I'm such an idiot."

Rose put her hand on his shoulder, trying to comfort him.

"The ugly hags had hair on their chins! I should have known they were pirates!" Natts whimpered, feeling guilty, "I can't believe I didn't figure it out," Natt's face suddenly changed. "I could intercept the map before McSly gets it."

"You could?"

"Why not? Magic Natts has what it takes!" The elf gloated shamelessly about himself.

Natts smiled. "Let's go together! You could use your invisibility cloak— Yup...*you* have magical talents!" He reached into his pocket and grabbed a handful of elf dust. "Now, hold my hand—"

"Wait!" Rose interrupted,"—I have to think about this a minute," She muttered, her voice barely above a whisper. "My sisters have warned me a thousand times not to meddle with humans—or pirates." She said, glancing at Natts. "But really... my sisters don't understand." She bit her lip as she was rethinking things. Her gold marks were flickering with an otherworldly glow. "I'm feeling lost about everything. Oh, I…I think I'm not sure what to do, Natts."

The elf tilted his head, studying her. "You don't seem lost to me, Miss Rose. I think you're just waiting for the right moment to shine."

Rose smiled. "My sisters think hiding in the woods will solve everything. But.. but I need answers. That's right—answers! I can't stay invisible forever. I've made my decision. I want to go. I might even meet a sorcerer along the way!" Rose muttered, clutching her cloak tighter. "Ever since I was born, they've told me not to take risks. But sitting around waiting for someone to rescue me hasn't worked either!"

"Look, I don't want to get you in trouble. It might be dangerous. But don't worry.—You got magic Natts with you."

Rose suddenly looked delighted to go on the adventure. "I don't think this basket will be easy to hide. Will we be returning here? To this spot?"

"We can if you'd like."

"I'll put my things in these shrubs, about ten jackrabbit leaps from Blackwood and Buttercup Lane" Rose stuffed her stick and basket under a bush. "That should be safe."

"Looks perfectly hidden to me," Natts confirmed with a half smile. "Now— let's go! We have to hurry. I heard the scallywags say they were going to the Revenge. That's McSly's ship, which is always at the port of Bellefont."

"Of course," Rose was holding her special cloak, feeling nervous and excited at the same time.

"Miss Rose," the elf insisted, "please hold my hand, and whatever you do, don't let go. Okay?"

Nervously biting her lip, she nodded yes to her instructions.

Natts threw some dust from his pocket in the air, then whispered a chant.

A swirl of golden light wrapped around them, lifting leaves and twigs into the air. As the magic enveloped Rose and Natts, her heart raced with fear and excitement.

"Hold on tight!" Natts shouted, his hand gripping hers firmly. The world around them dissolved into a blur of color and light, and with a final burst of sparkling energy, they were gone—leaving only silence behind.

Chapter Six

The Krusty Puffs Taste Test

Colorful awnings, oversized flags, and boldly painted signs were creating a stir as the townspeople of Bellefont anticipated the upcoming Spring Fair, which was just days away. However, behind a wall of stacked barrels, hidden from view, were Natts and Rose. They had just successfully rematerialized out of thin air by elf magic.

"That was unbelievable!" Rose announced, holding her head like she was mind-blown from the experience.

"Okay, good…good—I'm glad," The elf said, chuckled at her, then made a strange face. As Rose observed the elf's strange behavior, she realized she may have overlooked his odd personality before placing her life in his hands. But she decided to ignore it.

The two peered through the stacked barrels at all the activities at the port when the elf spotted the sign 'The Revenge' prominently displayed on a nearby vessel.

"We're in the right spot," he mumbled, pointing towards McSly's ship. "See, I know what I'm doing! Magic Natts has it all under control."

The worried-looking nymph commented, "I hope so."

A few yards from where they were hiding, a group of pirates had just exited a diner in town. They were dressed in worn-out clothes with a logo patch on their sleeves. It had a swirly letter M with a skull and bones symbol for McSly's crew. Rose had heard the captain's name before and observed them as they chatted away. As the pirates picked their teeth and scratched their butts like dogs with fleas, they were bragging about how great they were when the smallest one in the group let out a belch that sounded like a monster roaring from out of the abyss. It was so loud and scary that several stray cats screeched in horror and ran.

"You know what that belch means?" Natts said, watching the rude scoundrels.

Rose looked at him, appalled by the pirate's disgusting behavior with a look of shock.

"It's the sign of a good meal!" Natts growled

"Ridiculously gross," she remarked back at Natts with an unbelieving expression like she had just seen a ghost.

After the horrendously foul scallywags moved on, two gremlins were talking nearby. Like all gremlins, the two workers looked creepy, with green skin and ears like bat wings. Their enormous tricorn hats and navy jackets adorned with KP logo's made them stand out. One was holding a piece of paper and giving orders as if he were in charge.

"Krusty Puff delivery men," the elf whispered as if making an astute observation.

"Obviously," Rose noted with sarcasm in her voice.

The gremlin, receiving orders from the bossy one, had ears that looked like they were dipped in something purplish. The boss had extra plumes on his hat to show his seniority. He shouted, "Zin!" The grem with weird purplish ears stood at attention. "Take these barrels onto the Revenge. McSly's crew will show you where to take them. And remember, Captain McSly will expect you to deliver his supply personally."

The boss removed his hat and wiped the sweat from his brow. "That McSly is so obsessed. I heard he got a Krusty Puff's tattoo!"

As Zin waited for his two barrels to take onto the Revenge, Natts got an idea.

"I'm going to become that gremlin delivery guy," the elf whispered excitedly.

"Perfect disguise!" Rose answered back, "Then what?"

He pressed his hand over her mouth. "Shhh! I'll pretend to be the delivery guy. You'll follow me under your cloak, your perfect disguise. Then, we'll make our way onto the ship and into the captain's quarters to deliver his supply of Krusty Puffs. Then I'll distract McSly with a taste test while you locate the map, sneak it under your cloak, and change the directions to the shallows. It's perfect!"

"I guess I could do that," Rose said weakly.

"You guess? What's wrong with you? You guess! What?! You have your magic boyfriend, Natts, to protect you. What else do you need? Come on now, sabotaging this map will be a piece of cake!"

Pulling out some dust, he snapped his fingers. In an instant, a stick of charcoal appeared in his hand. He offered it to the nymph. She reluctantly took the charcoal from his hand, smiling like the plan to sabotage the map was destined to go sideways. After covering himself with elf dust, within seconds, Natts transformed himself into the same gremlin as the delivery guy, but with purple on the tips of his ears.

"You look perfectly horrid," Rose remarked teasingly. As she covered herself with her invisibility cloak, they waited patiently for the Krusty Puff delivery gremlin to pass. As planned, Natts threw some elf dust with a chant on his target, and after an overzealous sneeze into the air, Zin collapsed.

"Disgusting!" Recoiling from the sudden shower of phlegm that landed on her from his sneeze, Rose wanted to quit immediately. But the elf quickly pushed the gremlin into a barrel and locked it shut with a wink.

"Come on! Are you ready?"

"Piece of cake!" Rose lied.

Natts and Rose approached the only entry they could see onto The Revenge with the two barrels on a cart.

Bubba 'The Bull' was manning the entry.

KRUSTY PUTTS
CEREAL
KP

"What's wrong with your ears?" The giant pirate snickered.

"I thought grape brought out the color of my eyes."The disguised elf joked.

With nostrils flared like his nickname, Bubba pulled out his pistols. "Very funny, ya slimy Grem. What's the password?"

"How about Krusty's rule?"

The giant pirate grinned, showing his lack of dental care. "Nope."

Natts asked again, "How about no Krusty's for pirates forever?"

After Natts pointed out the two barrels on a cart with the Krusty Puffs logo of a smart looking pirate pug, Bubba suddenly realized his favorite sugary cereal would be compromised, if he didn't let the purple-eared Gremlin on the ship.

"That's good enough!" Bubba snarled before shoving his pistol back in its holster.

"Thanks, jolly green giant." Natts teased.

Wearing an emerald jacket, which fit the description perfectly, the oversized Bubba snort-laughed, which sounded terrifying.

Natts ignored the pirate and pushed the cart with the two barrels up the ramp before the pirate guard changed his mind. The pair emerged onto the deck, which loomed vast and intimidating. The dark, umber planks creaked faintly underfoot, emitting a strange, musky odor of salt, damp wood, and stale rum. Ropes coiled like serpents were strewn everywhere, adding to the chaotic atmosphere of the ship.

Rose's gaze darted around nervously, while Natts took in the scene. Several crew members were huddled near the center of the deck, engrossed in a lively card game. 'Slippery' Sammy, a wiry man dressed in dark clothes with a red sash tied around his waist, dominated the table with a sly grin. His sash held his trademark weapons—playing cards marked for cheating and a pair of pistols gleaming faintly in the light. Opposite him sat Billy Blade, whose wild, dagger-like hair jutted upward as if ready to strike. They were locked in a heated round of Crazy 8's, a game that seemed to be a favorite among the crew. Shifty Hassler, a lanky pirate with a permanently suspicious look etched on his face, leaned casually against the mast, watching the game with a crooked smirk. His sharp eyes caught sight of Natt's in his gremlin disguise. Noticing Natts's pointed ears, he nudged the pirate next to him and muttered loud enough for others to hear, "That grem looks like a clown."

A ripple of laughter spread among the pirates, but Natts kept his head down, his hands tightening on the cart. Rose instinctively moved closer to him. Her cloak shifted slightly as she scanned the crew under her cloak.

"Ignore the bullying, Natts," Rose muttered quietly so only Natts could hear.

"I could change that bully into something unpleasant in a snap!" He whispered scornfully.

"That's right," Rose whispered back, trying to calm the elf down. "Please contain your temper," she added. Natts pushed the cart with the barrels forward to the center of the deck.

Rose whispered. "I can't believe we haven't gotten caught yet."

"Pull yourself together! Magic Natts is on your side. Shhhhush!"

As they waited in the middle of the deck, a pirate with a sinister cackle approached. He stopped before the elf and stuck his bulging eye in his face. Natts choked on the smell of his breath.

"I'll take one of these from here." He said, referring to the barrel.

The cyclops-looking pirate took a barrel of Krusty Puffs and rolled it towards the corner of the deck, where he and the barrel suddenly disappeared through an opening in the floor.

The doors to the captain's quarters unlocked, and an arm waved toward Natts to enter. As the elf approached, Rose was close behind under her invisibility cloak. But as they aproached, she noticed Two-fingered Tex and Black-eyed Baxter rattling coins in the shadows.

"McSly has the map," she whispered. "I see the two pirates from the woods counting their gold coins. McSly must have rewarded them for it."

When they entered the captain's quarters, the room was dimly lit by several candles throughout. Their flickering flames casting dancing shadows on the walls, highlighting the woodwork on the walls which was intricate and beautiful. Large windows in the far corner, typically a source of sunlight, were now obscured by heavy, dark curtains. The room carried an air of secrecy, thick with the faint scent of wax, wood polish, and salt. The captain sat at a broad, weathered desk in the center of the room, hunched intently over his latest prize: a map to the phantom nymph's lair. Rumored to be home to the most powerful being ever known, McSly ran a gloved finger across the parchment, tracing its fresh markings, his eyes gleaming with a mixture of excitement and greed. Though the captain was typically a neurotic man—especially with rumors of spies and betrayal likely to spread now that the map's existence was known—at this moment, his suspicions were forgotten. All his focus was fixed on the mysterious document before him. In the dim, candlelit quarters, it seemed as though the map itself pulsed with a faint energy, as if it carried its own secrets, waiting to be unraveled.

As Lang babbled away about nothing important while helping the gremlin roll the barrel through the two doors,

Captain McSly momentarily lifted his nose from the map with a glare.

"What a great day it is, Your Highness!" Natts bellowed nervously before bowing to the captain.

"You can call me—Captain McSly." The captain was confused by why the gremlin was even talking to him —at all. Because McSly doesn't usually converse with grems, which is short for gremlin.

"My superior, Captain Shu'gar, instructed me to have you taste test this barrel of Krusty Puffs before I left. He wanted me to make sure your supply was perfect!"

Captain McSly leaned back in his massive wooden chair, eyeing Natts with suspicion. His fingers drummed against the table, where the map lay flat, corners weighed down by small, ornate daggers. His angular features were shadowed by the flickering candlelight, but his smirk gave away his condescending attitude.

"Taste test Krusty Puffs, you say?" McSly drawled, his voice sarcastic. "Since when did Shu'gar care about perfection?"

Natts fumbled with his words, bowing again as he tried to maintain the façade. "Oh, Captain Shu'gar, he's very particular, sir. He insists on... quality assurance."

McSly chuckled darkly, his piercing eyes moving from Natts to the barrel. He gestured lazily toward it. McSly grumbled, "Then open it. Let's see if these 'Krusty Puffs' are worthy of my attention."

Natts swallowed hard. Rose stayed perfectly still under her invisibility cloak. Natts gripped the lid of the barrel tightly. The plan was straightforward: get the captain distracted while Rose locates the map, slips it out undetected, and returns it to the desk in its new sabotaged state. With McSly's full attention on him, the plan felt like it might work.

With a loud pop, the barrel opened, revealing a heap of golden, crispy treats. The smell of sugar drifted through the room. McSly's nose twitched, and he leaned forward, intrigued despite himself.

Natts bowed, hoping McSly fell for his plan.

The captain chuckled, but his amusement quickly faded as his gaze shifted back to the map. "Enough of this nonsense," he growled. "Leave the barrel and go. I've got more important matters to attend to."

Natts smiled like the great actor that he was. "But Captain Shu'gar won't accept *no* as an answer, Sir. He insists you have the best Krusty Puffs supply we have."

Obsessed with the map to the phantom nymph's lair, the captain was anxious to get the grem out of the cabin.

"How else will I get you to leave but to do it," The captain remarked.

McSly's pirate fairy, Vivie, was out running an errand and not around to help him decide. "Let's have it then… hurry up," the captain grumbled, deciding to go through with the taste test. "Anything to get you out of here."

As the captain walked around the desk, he narrowly missed bumping into Rose under her cloak. As the irritated McSly looked in another direction, the nymph saw her chance to make a move. Rose carefully slipped past McSly's desk, her eyes darting to the map. It was detailed, with strange symbols and landmarks, all pointing to the fabled Phantom Nymph's Lair. If she didn't act fast, the captain would secure the map and begin his quest to — do her, and her sisters, in.

In a flash, she slipped the map under her invisibility cloak and scribbled all over the directions to the shallows— as fast as possible. Natts continued to fiddle with the cereal, trying to give the nymph more time to create charcoal spirals on the map. As Natts focused McSly's attention on him, he felt sure everything was going as planned. But the unthinkable happened.

Little Smokey woke up.

Unbeknownst to Rose and Natts, the monkey troublemaker had been napping in the corner of the room. So, as Rose was attempting to make a charcoal disaster on the map, the devil monkey climbed onto the captain's desk, grabbed a cigar, and sat watching his master taste-test the cereal like he was today's entertainment.

Needing to go to the bathroom, Lang babbled out loud that he would be back shortly as if someone was listening, but they weren't, so he left the room.

"Well, come on with it!" McSly snapped at Natts. The gremlin imposter handed McSly some puffs.

"Is it crispy?" the elf asked stupidly.

Crunching loudly, McSly, obsessed with the sugary treats, smiled.

"Yes….OF COURSE!" The captain barked.

Then, disaster was about to happen. Smokey noticed a mysterious object on the floor and pounced onto it like a cat. He wanted it badly, even if he didn't know what it was. Thankfully, the captain ignored Smokey, as he usually did. Natts gave McSly a fake smile, trying to keep the captain focused on tasting the cereal he was so obsessed with. But the mysterious blue object that was wiggling on the floor was Rose's dress. It was peeking out from under her invisibility cloak. The mischevous monkey finally took hold of it and pulled.

"Is it sweet enough?" Natts asked, trying to keep McSly focused on the cereal.

But as McSly thought about the savory taste he loved so much with his eyes closed, Rose battled Smokey in a tug-of-war over her dress. However, in the silent struggle, the nymph accidentally knocked over a burning candle on the table —which landed on the map. Within seconds flames hungrily devoured the map's edges. The smoke spiraled out like a living thing, curling through the air and forcing everyone to cover their mouths and squint through watering eyes.

"Fire! Quick! My map!" McSly yelled. "Everyone, get some water!" Smokey was jumping, screaming like a lost child, making things worse as dark smoke filled the cabin. McSy pushed the doors open, shouting, "Fire!" McSly stormed onto the deck, his face red with anger. "The ship will be ash if we don't act faster!" He grabbed a bucket from one of the pirates and stormed back into the smoky cabin. Lang returned from the bathroom, frantically grabbed pitchers, and threw water on the flames as fast as possible. Natts and Rose hurried through the open doors that led onto the deck as pirates scurried in with more buckets.

Crowds on the docks were gawking at the billowing smoke, probably wondering if The Revenge would go up in flames, which made it easy for Natts and Rose to escape unnoticed, at least until Rose bumped into someone. It was Vivie. She had been shopping for supplies in town when she saw the fire chaos on The Revenge and returned in a hurry. Natts prayed to the gods that the cloaked stranger didn't follow. But, of course, they did.

"I'll circle the docks." he whispered to Rose, who was still under her magic cloak, "That cloaked person is a woman, and she smells like trouble," Natts mumbled to Rose.

"What do you mean? How do you know?" the nymph asked.

"She smells like perfume and gunpowder, kind of trouble." Natts said, "which means she's a pirate fairy—for sure."

"Oh…that kind of trouble," Rose whispered. She wasn't sure what he meant since she'd never met a pirate fairy, but she didn't question him and followed his orders. After pushing the invisible Rose behind stacked Krusty Puff barrels where they had initially materialized at Bellefont, he took off in a hurry.

While waiting for Natts to return, Rose observed the townspeople walking by. Looking through the space between the barrels, in one direction, she could see a few men with tall top hats and wearing long-tailed coats hovered together in a group. They were talking so intensely that they sounded like muffled chaos because no one was listening to what the other was saying. "Such a common human trait…no one likes to listen." In the opposite direction, closer to the town of Bellefont, Rose noticed a mother gazing at shoes in a store window. Unfortunately, the mother was so delighted to be looking at shoes that she had no idea her small child was pulling out food from her basket and throwing it on the ground. A stray dog couldn't eat the falling food fast enough. "Tough luck. I wonder how anyone gets anything accomplished around here," Rose thought.

Several minutes had passed when she heard, "Hey! Grape lollipop ears is back!"

Sparkle fell to the ground as the gremlin transformed back into an elf in a swirl of light. “That’s one thing we can stop worrying about. The cloaked stranger was not following us. I guess I was being paranoid.”

“Fantastic,” Rose remarked as she slid her cloak off in front of Natts. The elf smiled at the sudden appearance of his friend.

“You look radiant, even after you battled an obnoxious smoking monkey and set a pirate ship on fire.”

“It was an accident, of course,” the nymph smiled, looking embarrassed. Natts chirped.

“Yes, but we don’t need to be bothered about anyone finding the shallows. The map is burnt toast!” He flung his arm into the air like they had won the battle.

Rose smiled. “Thanks to you, Natts. My sisters won't kill me now for opening my big mouth!”

The elf reached out his hand towards the nymph. “I’m glad the map is no more for your sake, too, my lady,” Natts confirmed, smiling brightly at her with a wink.

Rose smiled back. “I still feel like a helpless child who constantly needed assistance.”

The elf said nothing and held out his hand, gesturing to hold on. “Now, let’s go home, Miss Glum!”

Natts whispered words before she took his hand, and they disappeared in a flash of sparkling light.

Chapter Seven

Sister Love

Moxie Jingle Pop The Great was on his way to Bellefont for the Spring Fair on Blackwood when he saw a sign to his right that read, "Devilishly Large Boulders Beware." Nervous but confident, he suddenly recalled these rocks near the intersection at Buttercup and Blackwood, but if he could pass them again without crashing was a mystery. As he approached the dangerous intersection, he directed his horse towards the opposite edge of the road expertly, avoiding the large boulders and prevented his carriage from tipping over like a hero. But as Moxie pulled to the side of the road to check on his horse, he noticed a squirrel nearby eating a cookie. Although thinking it was odd, he ignored the furry-tailed rodent.

However, the cookie-eating squirrel did not ignore Moxie. The furry-tailed cookie eater had discovered Rose's basket and desired to catch a few more prizes popping out the backend of Moxie's carriage. So when nothing happened, he threw down his cookie with disgust. Another squirrel with big eyes threw its tiny arms in the air and joined his buddy, grumbling with disappointment. The big eyed squirrel pulled another cookie from Rose's basket and handed it to his buddy.

But as the two prize-snatching squirrels started arguing about whose turn it was to hold the basket, Rose and Natts appeared. Out of the sudden swirl of sparkling mist, the elf and nymph suddenly rematerialized from their map-sabotaging adventure. The sudden swirl of magic spooked the two squirrels, and they simultaneously let go of the basket. It sailed through the air, where it crashed against the sizable boxy carriage with 'Moxie Jingle Pop the Great: Where Normal is an Illusion' was inscribed on its side. A top hat, pink shoe, broken Bingo cookies, odd-looking red-orange flowers, smooshed blackberries, a dirty silver brush, and a lovely old letter all scattered into the meadow.

"Hey, watch it," snapped Moxi. But the magician did a double take when he saw Natts and Rose. Recognizing them as both magical beings, he didn't want trouble, so he got back in his carriage and traveled onto Bellefont for the Spring Fair.

The elf and the nymph crouched behind a large tree and thick shrubs, their breaths shallow as they watched the line of carriages rumble past. The forest around them was quiet, except for the distant creak of wheels and the occasional neigh of horses. They waited in silence, tense and still, until Rose suddenly blurted out, her voice tinged with guilt,"I'm a villain! I mean, I'm burning ships! I think this curse has made me… kinda evil."

Monsie Jingle Pop The Great

The elf stifled a laugh. "I call the ship-burning incident a casualty of war, Miss Rose," he said lightly. But when he glanced at her, he noticed the worry etched on her face. "What's troubling you? Afraid a family deity might come down and punish you for causing such a mess?"

"Of course," Rose muttered, fiddling with the hem of her dress. "My parents are Gods. I'm held to a higher standard because of it."

Natts brushed some dirt off his trousers and leaned back against the tree trunk. "You know," he said thoughtfully, "it was actually good luck if you ask me. The Gods might have been helping you. Life isn't perfect, Miss Rose, and sometimes you have to fight to survive. That smoking monkey was about to expose you to McSly, and if he'd seen who you were—well, you wouldn't be sitting here talking to me right now."

Rose's shoulders slumped a little, and she frowned. "I guess."

"Not to mention," Natts continued with a sly grin, "I don't think the fire hurt anyone, if that's what's eating you. And anyway, I'm the one who created the map they were using! If you think about it, none of this would've happened without me."

Rose glanced at him, her expression softening. "I suppose you're right," she admitted, a faint smile tugging at her lips.

"Of course I'm right." Natts leaned over, placing a hand on her shoulder. "So, will you forgive me for getting us into this mess, Miss Rose?"

Rose laughed, shaking her head. "Of course."

The elf rose to his feet and gave her a playful bow. "I'm glad the map is burnt toast now," he declared, grinning. "That's one less problem to worry about!"

Rose rolled her eyes but couldn't suppress a chuckle. "Let's hope you're right about that."

After some more carriages passed by, Rose and Natts stepped out from the shrubs. The nymph was gathering her things that were scattered in the grass when Natt's watch alarm started tweeting.

"I've got to go, my lady."

After a few more carriages rolled past, Rose and Natts emerged from the shrubs. As the nymph crouched to gather her belongings scattered across the grass, Natts's watch alarm let out a sharp, birdlike tweet.

"I've got to go, my lady," he said, glancing at the device.

Though Natts had brought chaos to Rose's life in true elven fashion, she couldn't deny she enjoyed his company. The map-burning fiasco alone had been exhilarating, and the thought of him leaving left her with an unexpected feeling of disappointment.

Natts silenced the alarm with a quick press of a button. He had a look of regret on his face. "I'm not sure when we'll meet again, but it's been a delight, truly!" He took her hand, brushing a kiss across her knuckles. "I have a meeting with a fairy friend," he added, smoothing his hair.

Rose tilted her head. "A fairy friend?"

"Yes, Teenie—uh, Teenie Lightshimmer," he replied, as though plucking the name from thin air. "We met near the daisies by River Road."

Rose forced a smile, though her heart wasn't in it. "How lovely. She must be special. What's she like?"

"She's… sparkly," Natts said, fidgeting. "But enough about her—I'll miss you, spy nymph. I hope we cross paths again soon."

"I'll be watching for you," Rose said with a playful grin.

With one last hug, Natts stepped back and, in a shimmer of magic, transformed into a dragonfly. He darted into the sky, leaving a sparkling trail behind him like a fleeting comet. Rose stood there, watching him vanish.

After gathering her things, Rose held her basket close, whipped her cloak around her body, and disappeared from view before setting off for home.

"There's no question I'm going to keep the morning's map-burning-drama to myself. Why would I tell my sisters that their lives were momentarily in danger of being 'done in' by McSly and his pirate crew? Now that the map is burnt, that would've been their doom. I feel more relaxed. Everything seems — back to normal." Rose mumbled.

Finally arriving at the secret entrance to the shallows, she stood between two gigantic lilac bushes and pushed down a branch like a lever. Leaves, flowers, and twigs swirled before the secret doorway appeared. Rose entered with her special cloak still on, observing geese floating quietly in the far corner of the pond, enjoying the warmth of the afternoon sun. When she pulled her cloak off, Zoe noticed her sister reappearing out of nowhere.

"How nice of you to make an appearance, Rosey!" Zoe joked as she admired herself in an unusual dress before an elegant tree-like mirror. Rose sat down at the table where her sisters were gathered.

"Isn't this sort of late to be picking out dresses for the Spring Fair—tomorrow?"

Zoe admired herself in the mirror. "what else is there for us to do while we're home," she remarked, contemplating her feelings about the dress.

"You look like a party on top and a funeral down below," Chloe teased, "—part cupcake…part casket, and your gold markings are showing too! Do you want everyone to know you are a nymph?"

"Oh dear," Zoe remarked, looking at the gold mark on her shoulders and stomach, small delicate symbols, beautiful and elegant. All the sisters had them. Rose was the only one with it on her forehead. Suddenly, Zoe snapped her fingers, and a new dress appeared on her body, while the cupcake-funeral dress popped up in a pile marked 'Makes you look ridiculous.'

After a day of the sisters picking outfits, the shallows looked like a bomb had gone off. Piles of dresses were everywhere, in fact, hundreds of them. Some were labeled 'Makes you look too old,' another, 'Just okay,' another, 'Makes you look reptilian in a scary way,' and another, 'Almost Perfect.'

"Where have you been all day, Rosey?" her sister Ree-va asked, looking alarmed.

"What does it matter," Rose answered, reluctantly.

Reeva could sense Rose's anger, adding, "We're glad you're safe at home now anyway. Oh my gosh—Rose! You're lucky you didn't get kidnapped!"

"How about that, Reeva," Rose snapped, "I must have magic to avoid such a thing. Oh, that's right — I don't have any!" The platinum-haired beauty picked up a pastry and took a ferocious bite out of it as her sisters stared in wonderment at her attitude. Zoe, Reeva, and Chloe were curious about what mischief Rose had been involved in. Reeva, a chestnut hair beauty, picked up a paper on the table and flopped it down in front of Rose.

"You're on the front page of the news."

"I am?" Rose acted stunned but assumed the fire calamity would be in the news.

> *The Fairy Tale Times*: A Special Report by Pyro Muddybug: "Fire on The Revenge! McSly's pet monkey, Smokey, is taking the fall as the fire starter for the recent burning on The Revenge. Over half of the captain's quarters, even a map to the phantom nymph's lair, went up in smoke while McSly taste-tested some Krusty Puffs cereal." Pyro reports, "I was flying near all the smoke and ash when I saw Smokey. He stood yelling frantically with a cloth on his head. Could the cloth be mimicking long white hair? Could the 'Phantom nymph' be the reason for the fire?"

"A cigar-smoking monkey with a name, no less," Chloe laughed. "Apparently, a map was created to show where you live!?"

"It burned up when the ship caught on fire. There's no need to worry," Rose confirmed.

Chloe growled, "Where have you been, Rosey?"

Rose narrowed her eyes. "Why do you ask, Chloe? Last I checked, you're not my mother."

"This is true," Zoe interjected calmly. "Thankfully, the map is no more—or so the papers say. But as your magical guardians *and* your loving sisters, we're concerned for your safety... and ours."

"Loving?" Rose thought bitterly. "More like *my abandoning sisters*," she muttered under her breath, her words tinged with anger. Still, she took in their expressions: Zoe's worried pout, Reeva's tentative half-smile, and Chloe's knowing wink. Their concern felt genuine, though it only made Rose's guilt twist deeper.

"I suppose you're right," Rose said, feeling bad for being mad at her sister—but kinda not. "Fine," she relented, her tone softening. "You're right. I guess I shouldn't have gone off alone."

Chloe leaned in, her voice sharp. "Did you... tell someone where we live?"

"Of course not," Rose lied.

Zoe crossed her arms. "Rose..."

It was apparent she had. "Well...maybe....an elf," Rose mumbled, heat rising in her cheeks.

"Better an elf than a countless number of pirates." Chloe chimed in.

Reeva, the worrier, construed the worst possible scenario in her mind."Now, whoever you told might be tortured for information. They will tell mortals and or fairies, and they'll tell another fairy, then they'll tell someone who knows a pirate, and then all pirates will know where 'the Shallows' are!" Reeva babbled crazily, annoyed by her sister's big mouth.

"I can fix that," Zoe replied, "I'll let you know later where our new entrance will be." Zoe confirmed, "Now, back to picking my dress."

The sisters felt relieved that Zoe was handling the problem and returned to helping her.

As the sisters ate lemon cakes and sipped tea, Chloe, Reeva, and Zoe were already satisfied with their dress choices and focused on Rose.

"We'll come on now, Rosey," Chloe said, "stand up, and we'll find a dress for you— be quick with it."

"I won't need a dress for this…. gala, Will I? After all, I am the invisible one, right?"

"How about this then," Reeva said, changing Rose's outfit into a pirate's jacket, a tricorn hat, and big black boots with a wave of her hand.

"Very clever," Rose commented with a fake smile.

The sisters all laughed, except for Rose, of course.

"Exactly," Reeva teased, "you need to stop believing that you're going to find a sorcerer to break the curse, a curse that doesn't exist! I might add."

"One day, Reeva, we'll both remember this moment."

Reeva shook her head like Rose was a fool.

"Till you walk in my shoes, dear sister, you'll never know what it's like to live in fear of being 'done in' any day by a pirate."

Reeva wiggled her nose again and returned her sister to her favored look. The invisibility cloak draped over Rose's arm was now on the ground.

"I feel happiest when I have hope. It's who I am." Rose mumbled, picking up her cloak off the ground.

"Let Rose do what she wants," Zoe said, defending her sister.

"If you want to be a fool, so be it," Reeva remarked, sticking her tongue out at Rose.

As the sisters tried on more dresses, Rose sat back, watching them banter with each other.

"Maybe a prince will come to the Spring Fair," Reeva said, striking a pose in front of the mirror in a new gown, her voice teasing.

"I'm sure a prince would be shocked if he chose *you* as his bride," Chloe remarked with a sly smile, "especially when he finds out you're a 232-year-old nymph!"

All the sisters laughed. Reeva winked at her reflection, running a hand through her long chestnut hair. Her flawless skin gave her the appearance of a 16-year-old.

"I still got it at 232." She joked, stroking her long chestnut hair and admiring herself in the mirror, "But enough about me. The shallows is a mess." Dirty dishes were stacked, linens stained, hundreds of dresses were piled everywhere, and some were even floating in the pond. Before cleaning up, Zoe admired herself in the intricately carved mirror one more time before waving her arms. The mirror instantly transformed into a tree, which looked oddly similar to the mirror it once was. Reeva looked out over the mess of dresses and snapped her fingers with a command. In an instant, each dress, except for the ones marked 'Perfect in every way,' exploded into the air before morphing into an array of different colored birds.

Rose climbed a tree to observe Chloe. Her obnoxious sister's blue eyes sparkled as her arms waved back and forth, creating spell after spell. An unseen force cleared the dining table, stacked the dishes, and made the stains on the linens disappear.

Rose watched, admiring her sister's talents.

"Well done, Chloe!" She sounded envious but proud. She wished she had the gift of magic like her sister, but she didn't.

"Don't let go of whatever is tugging at your heart, Rosey."

"Thanks, Chloe."

Rose jumped down from the tree. Chloe put her hand on Rose's shoulder, adding, "Someday, you'll be as magically talented as me," then winked.

"It sure is a mild sort of punishment to live here with you, Chloe," Rose said jokingly, pinching her sister's arm, hoping to inflict pain.

They both laughed.

Chapter Eight

The Spring Fair

Zoe announced, "Blenda is conceiving a spell to create a Wheeler this morning."

Blenda was a nickname Zoe called Reeva because she always came up with ideas from books on how the sisters could 'blend in' as mortals.

After collecting elements for her wheeler charm all morning, Reeva stood next to the new secret entry and exit point to the shallows, two gardenia bushes. As the chestnut-haired nymph sister snapped her fingers, within seconds, white chunks appeared on a plate in her hand.

"Cheese for my volunteers!" Reeva announced. The other sisters, unsure of how to respond, clapped politely, while hiding their giggling behind delicate fingers. Reeva set the cheese plate on the dirt path, right next to a polished jewelry box. Mice and squirrels crept closer, their noses twitching as they sniffed the air. They hesitated only a moment before pouncing on the treat, devouring everything on the plate."Perfect—two mice, two squirrels. Just

what I need!" Reeva said, brushing her hands together. She straightened, closed her eyes, and stretched out her arms, focusing her energy.

A sudden breeze swept through the meadow, spinning fallen leaves into a swirling dance. The air seemed alive, choosing and gathering leaves with purpose. They swarmed over the small animals like miniature whirlwinds, wrapping around each volunteer. When the spell subsided, the transformation was complete. The two mice now stood as tall groomsmen, dressed sharply in dark jackets and boots. The squirrels had become magnificent chestnut horses, their coats gleaming in the sun. Even the plain wooden jewelry box had changed, now a sleek black carriage polished to perfection.

"Wow, Reeva," Chloe commented, "Now that's — a Wheeler!! I love it!" Zoe laughed, adding, "After our sister read an advertisement, I decided we need to have one."

"The Wheeler looks very nice!" Rose shouted. "I approve!"

"There," Reeva remarked, smoothing her dress, "is everyone ready?"

"May I help you, my lady?" The coachman with burnt umber hair and a fancy goatee bowed to Reeva. "I'm Mouch, and he's Mugsy." A curly blonde-haired coachman bowed and extended his hand as if gesturing to help her onboard the carriage.

"They're splendid!" Chloe smiled happily, so impressed with the two groomsman's manners.

After loading their bags, Mouch and Mugsy helped the nymph sisters onto the carriage, and— they were off.

After several unscheduled stops in the woods—thanks to an overindulgence in morning tea—the sisters finally arrived at the bustling port of Bellefont for the much-anticipated Spring Fair. Through the carriage windows, they glimpsed a world alive with color and activity. Towering ships dominated the harbor, their sails snapping in the sea breeze, while oversized tents and vibrant flags transformed the cobbled streets into a festive maze. Tables piled high with goods for sale tempted passersby, and extravagant decorations hung from every awning. Visitors swarmed the streets, their laughter and chatter filled the air.

When the sister's carriage came to a halt in front of the Bellefont Inn, a grand establishment buzzing with guests for the fair. The sisters left Mouch and Mugsy to stand watch over their fancy wheeler carriage and hurried inside to check in to their rooms.

By sea or by land, whether they were welcomed or not, mortals, pirates, and disguised magical creatures were roaming the village for the celebration. Some traded their true form for clever disquises. The Grey sisters were no exception.

They wore their mortal diguises with ease, covering their golden marks which revealed their deity status. Though suspicion from a stranger did happen, for such moments, they relied on their simplest enchantment—a *forget-me* spell, quick and effective.

Rose, however, required a little more effort to be inconspicuous. She wore a veil with her tophat which covered the markings on her brow, gloves covered the intricate gold markings on her hands. Because of this, the cursed nymph— was unrecognizable.

As two men admired Reeva's unusual dress, Zoe pulled Chloe and Rose aside where no one would notice them. She snapped her fingers, and a satin bag instantly appeared in her hand.

"Here are some gold coins for you, my dear." Zoe jingled the bag slightly before dropping it in Rose's hand. "Don't spend it all in one place."

"Of course I will!" She joked," But thank you, Zoe."

"Unfortunately, your deplorable sister will be your escort today."

"Don't worry," Chloe said smartly. "I'll take care of my favorite beast."

Rose made a disappointed face."You do get such pleasure out of being rude to me."

Chloe smiled as she hugged her sister.

"Okay then," Zoe waved for Reeva to join them.

Chapter Eight

"We'll meet you in front of Godmother's," Zoe said, looking at her watch. "At five o'clock."

"Agreed!" Chloe wrapped her arm around Rose and pushed her forward. "We'll see you later."

Reeva and Zoe exited towards a street where dresses, jackets, and hats were heavily displayed, while the overly excited Chloe and Rose headed down a street they nicknamed 'Sugar Heaven.'

Towering cakes, billowing muffins, and cookies as large as plates were covering the first table they encountered. A sign in front of the table read Coco Sugarbutton's Bakery.

"Look at these," Rose said excitedly, "Gigantor cookies."

Chloe laughed hysterically at her sister, who was holding two jumbo cookies decorated with spiral designs in front of her eyes, which made her look ridiculous.

Unbeknownst to Rose, a boy, standing behind her, pushed her hard in an attempt to make her fall. She fell forward slightly but caught her balance

"Excuse me," Rose said, thinking she was in his way. Chloe noticed the boy's attempt at injuring her sister or exposing her identity. She wasn't sure which, but his rude behavior angered her. Chloe blinked her eyes twice. In an instant, a mysterious force squeezed the back of the menacing boy's neck, making him yelp.

"There…there, "She said in a snarky tone, grinning at the boy with a fake smile. He stormed off, looking back at Chloe with a sneer.

"Thank you," Rose said, acknowledging her sister's action.

"I'm just watching out for you," Chloe mumbled. Feeling hungry, Rose waved to the woman at the bakery table.

"Can I help you, Miss?" said the peculiar-looking woman. She was wearing an explosion of violet and cobolt tinsel on her hat. Miss Coco Sugarbutton's hat was quirky but pretty.

"I'd like two Dragonfly pies, two Pink-a-delic cupcakes, and two Coco Loco cookies, please," Rose said, pointing at her selections.

The obnoxious boy was back, standing next to Rose. He didn't scare off easily, as Chloe had hoped, and this time he had two friends with him. The trio looked like trouble, their smirks promising mischief.

Coco, who had been nervously smiling, shifted uncomfortably as the boy leaned closer to whisper to his friends.

"Her name should be—Loco Coco," he said with a mocking grin. He made a face like Coco was crazy, rolling his eyes in circles. Coco smiled nervously.

Everyone heard it, even Coco. His friends, who called him "Wolfy," snickered in approval of his cruel joke. Coco kept packing cakes into a box, pretending she didn't hear them, though she could feel Wolfy's gaze on her, scanning her outfit with suspicion. Rose ignored the obnoxious boy and waited patiently for her box when Wolfy tugged at her sleeve. Rose, unfazed by the boy's antics, stood quietly waiting for Coco to fill her order. Wolfy, determined to bother her, tugged impatiently at Rose's sleeve.

"Excuse me, miss," he sneered.

Chloe, standing behind Rose, narrowed her eyes suspiciously at the three boys.

"Yes?" Rose responded.

Suppressing his laughter, Wolfy leaned in closer, in a sacastic tone. "Are you pretty or ugly under that veil?"

His two friends snickered.

"Excuse me?" Rose was stunned, caught off guard by his rude question.

Wolfy's friends laughed harder, egging him on. "Maybe you're both?" Wolfy added with a smirk. "Pretty ugly!"

He and his friends cackled, their laughter cutting through the air like nails on a chalkboard. Rose stayed silent, too stunned to respond. Chloe, on the other hand, felt her anger rising.

"I mean," Wolfy continued, "why else would someone wear a veil? You're hiding something."

People waiting behind Rose were whispering. Feeling humiliated by the boy, she wanted to rip off her veil and punish him with magic, but she had none, and he had a point.

This hiding thing makes me feel like a coward. Rose thought. *He's right.*

Chloe could feel Rose's frustration, her thoughts loud in her mind. "Stop thinking that way," Chloe whispered, reading her thoughts. She grinned, her eyes sparking with mischief. "You know I'm here to watch over you." Chloe said, wiggling her nose, which cast a magical force. Her magic took shape within seconds. As Wolfy and his friends continued to laugh, a sudden stream of soap suds spewed from Wolfy's mouth.

Chloe leaned down next to Wolfy, who was now choking on soap suds.

"Did you say your name was Wolfy or Big Mouth?"

Furious and embarrassed, Wolfy bolted into the crowd. His friends followed.

The crowd of onlookers whispered and wondered who the mysterious woman was. Rose stayed quiet, trying not to draw attention to herself. Chloe could tell she was feeling awkward in her outfit, so she took Rose's arm and went off through the crowd.

"Don't worry about that bum, Rose," Chloe whispered so no one could hear. "I took care of him for you. I think 'the big mouth' learned his lesson." Chloe remarked. "Don't make fun of a nymph if you know what's good for you."

"I'm not feeling very well."

"Now, let's not overreact."

Chapter Eight

As they walked through the crowd, Rose felt sick to her stomach with anxiety. Chloe wrapped her arm around her sister's shoulders.

"Please don't worry." She said softly, her voice reassuring.

Rose gave her a grateful smile, although she felt a storm inside. "Thanks, Chloe." She whispered, leaning into her sister.

The fair was buzzing with more energy now. The sisters kept close, cautious of Wolfy and his friends, but there was no sign of them.

"Look at this table—it's gorgeous! It smells wonderful too, doesn't it?" Chloe, still with her arm around Rose's shoulders, led her to a booth labeled *Belladonna's Lotions and Potions*. Behind the table stood a young woman with raven-black hair, tiny white flowers woven through out. A hawk, scarred across its face and chest, perched on a lush topiary urn. The table was a riot of color, with neatly stacked bottles and jars filled with brightly hued lotions and soaps.

"Hello, ladies! My name is Belladonna," the young woman greeted them, her voice warm and inviting. "Let me know if I can help you with anything."

Rose gently stroked the scarred hawk on its head. It looked at her and gave a soft screech, as if thanking her for the attention. Meanwhile, Chloe picked up a small glass jar filled with something pink.

Belladonna studied Rose's outfit with a faint, curious smile, clearly wondering about what was hidden beneath the veil, much like Wolfy had.

"Please, try this delightful lip balm. It's called *Dragonfly Kisses*," Belladonna said. "There's a jar for you to sample."

Chloe quickly found the sample and applied it to her lips. "This is delicious… it tastes just like watermelon!"

Feeling a little awkward, Rose stepped back, reluctant to try it herself. She hoped Belladonna wouldn't press her.

Chloe winked and whispered, "Don't worry, I've got this. You just relax."

But at the neighboring table, Captain McSly was shopping with Vivienne for a new pirate hat, after the fire had reduced her last one to ashes. Smokey, the mischievous pirate monkey, was trailing behind them. Bored and unpredictable, Smokey wandered off, just as he had a habit of doing. Predictably, he found his way to Belladonna's table. Intrigued by the colorful lotions, he took particular interest in Rose's mysterious outfit.

"Great, just my luck," Rose muttered to her sister, nudging her. "The pirate monkey's here."

"I've got him under control," Chloe whispered back. "Don't worry about it."

But as Chloe became absorbed in the beautiful packaging of the lip balms, Smokey, with his tricorn hat and cigar stub, winked at Rose.

"Oh no," Rose mumbled, a nervous smile crossing her face.

Belladonna, noticing the monkey's antics, grabbed a broom from behind the table and marched toward Smokey, shooing him into the crowd. He squealed as the broom poked him, and he scrambled away, disappearing into the crowd.

"Thank you so much," Rose said with relief. "I'm not fond of monkeys."

"Not a problem, my dear," Belladonna replied, her tone still cheerful. "Would you like to try this *Stellaberry* lotion?"

She picked up a turquoise bottle wrapped in elegant ribbons and gestured to Rose's arm, offering to apply it. Chloe, seeing what was about to unfold, quickly stepped in.

"My sister is allergic to everything—thus the outfit," Chloe remarked, sounding more like a lie.

Ignoring her, like all persistent sales ladies, Belladonna attempted to push back Rose's sleeve. Chloe quickly wiggled her nose, casting an unseen force. The hawk noticed the gesture and screeched. The bottle of Stellaberry lotion in Belladonna's hand slipped from her grasp and fell to the ground, splattering everywhere. With a forced smile, Chloe tried to clean up the mess."Did I mention my sister is a klutz!"

Belladonna raised an eyebrow, clearly suspicious of something unusual happening.

Before anyone could react, another bottle of lotion shattered on the ground. Unseen by the women, Smokey had climbed onto a shelf and, with a mischievous grin, started tossing bottles to the floor, creating a chaotic mess.

Belladonna, furious now, shouted at the monkey, but Smokey, undeterred, simply ignored her.

Panicking, Chloe grabbed Rose's arm, ready to push her into the crowd to escape the chaos, when a hand suddenly grabbed Rose's other arm.

"I'm sorry, my lady," a deep, gravelly voice cut through the commotion.

A tall man stepped into Belladonna's booth, his presence commanding attention. He wore a dignified ebony jacket trimmed in gold, the fabric glinting in the light, and an oversized tricorn hat perched jauntily atop his head. His eyes, sharp and calculating, roved over Rose's outfit with an unsettling intensity, as though peeling back her secrets.

"I trust my little Smokey hasn't caused you any harm?" he rasped, each word slow and deliberate. His eyes were looking at her outfit with suspicion. Vivienne was standing behind him. Belladonna's reaction was no less dramatic. She blinked, her usual composure slipping as she gawked at the unexpected arrival.

"No, Sir," Rose answered, petrified beyond belief.

Like everyone else, McSly was puzzled by Rose's mysterious outfit. It was apparent— she was hiding her identity. Smokey was still sitting on a shelf, acting like a naughty devil, uninterested in Rose.

"SMOKEY!" McSly roared. The rude monkey imediately jumped off the shelf and landed next to the captain, taking his master's hand like a small child obeying his parent's orders. "Ladies," McSly began, bowing with a sly grin. "I apologies for my pet's behavior. He takes after my less civilized crew, I fear. Allow me to compensate."

He dropped a velvet bag into Belladonna's hand."I will pay for any damage Smokey has caused."

"Thank you, Sir," Belladonna nodded.

McSly cleared his throat, then bowed. "I'm Captain McSly, my ladies. And who might you two be?"

Chloe's pulse raced as she gently tugged Rose's arm. "We're fine, really. No harm done." Her tone was light, but her grip tightened. "Come, sister."

But before they could slip away, Smokey struck again. With a triumphant screech, he snatched Rose's veil, her platinum hair tumbling free like liquid light. Rose's identity was exposed. Her gold markings were gleaming in the sun, and her distinct platinum hair almost touched McSly in the face.

Time slowed. Chloe barely registered the gasps from Belladonna or the captain's sharp intake of breath. Her hand shot out, nose twitching in a precise flick. The "get yourself together" spell hummed through the air. Veil and hat snapped back into place, as if nothing had happened.

Neither Vivie nor the captain— saw her.

"It's been a pleasure," McSly bowed.

The troublemaking monkey had a cigar hanging from his mouth. He jumped from the shelf to the ground and took hold of his master's hand, winking at Rose. Vivie was looming in the background behind McSly, looking suspiciously at Rose and Chloe, obviously suspecting them to be immortals.

The sisters rushed through the crowded market, weaving between merchant booths and shoppers, their goal clear —escape.

"We need to get out of here," Rose murmured, her voice tight with anxiety. "I'm sure they're following us."

"They are," Chloe replied, her eyes scanning the crowd behind them. She nudged Rose forward, urging her to keep moving. "I can see them. We don't have much time."

Thankfully the crowd was busy, prodding and poking at possible things to buy. As the nymphs pushed their way through as fast as they could, they knocked into people, making packages fall.

"I feel sick." Rose was feeling the anxiety.

"I've tried my best," Chloe barked, rolling her eyes."But it's just one spell after another trying to protect you! Don't worry, I'm sending you home."

Rose held Chloe's arm as a gesture of thanks.

"I'm handling this. You'll be fine. I'll become you, temporarily, just to make sure Captain McSly doesn't follow you in the carriage. I'll distract him."

"Whatever you want to do." Rose didn't want to argue with her sister. She just wanted to get home.

They pushed through the last of the crowd, finally reaching the Bellefont Inn. Chloe quickly gave instructions to Mouch, the coachman, to bring Rose's bag down from her room.

"Take her to the shallows, then come back right away. Mugsy, stay here and keep watch over our things," Chloe ordered, before turning to Rose. "I'll fill Reeva and Zoe in on everything. We'll be back in a couple of days. I'm sorry you're not staying."

As Rose climbed into the carriage, a familiar bird landed on the roof with a soft flutter. There was the faint rustle of feathers making her look upward. A scar-faced hawk descended with a soft, deliberate flutter. It perched on the roof of Rose's carriage as though it owned it. She recognized it immediately—it was the same bird from Belledonna's table.

"Go on, birdie," Chloe commanded. But the hawk ignored her. Stay hidden inside until you're home," Chloe urged, scanning the area one last time, making sure no mortals were in sight.

Chloe snapped her fingers, and an invisible wave of energy surrounded the carriage. The hawk shot into the sky, as if something had pricked its talons.

"There," Chloe said, satisfied. "The carriage is protected now. You're safe as long as you don't step or reach outside."

"If you say so," Rose replied, giving Chloe a relieved smile. Rose waved goodbye to Chloe as the carriage door closed behind her, finally feeling a little bit of peace as she started her journey home.

Chapter Nine

The Dark Market

Now that Rose was comfortably settled in the carriage bound for the shallows, the nagging ache in her stomach seemed to have subsided. The rhythmic clopping of the horses' hooves and the creaking of the wheels on the dirt road lulled her into a drowsy haze. Staring out the window, her gaze wandered aimlessly over the endless stretch of trees. Suddenly, a bird appeared, its silhouette stark against the pale sky.

Was it the hawk from Belladonna's table?

Intrigued, Rose fixed her eyes on it, hoping that it would swoop closer. But no matter how much she squinted, wished, and waited, the bird remained distant. Eventually, the hypnotic sounds of the squeaky carriage wheels and the steady rhythm of the road lulled her to sleep.

In her dream, Rose found herself walking through Everwood under the cover of night. Strangely, although the forest was shrouded in darkness, she could see everything. How was that possible? She wasn't sure. But then again,

dreams rarely made sense. And yet, as we all know, dreams can be complicated, unexplainable, and strange.

Feeling for her magic cloak on her shoulders, Rose panicked when she couldn't find it. Searching for it in the shrubs, she saw nothing. But to her surprise, out of the shadows, a herd of pixiaries emerged from the brush instead. As they surrounded her, she remembered the familiar little creatures and greeted them with a smile. Rose's worries melted and a warm smile spread across her face as the tiny, luminous creatures flitted around her. One of the pixiaries floated closer, its glow intensifying as it hovered inches from her face. The light shifted, morphed, and suddenly, it transformed into a tiny girl. She wore a shimmering emerald dress, and her ebony hair floated as if suspended in water, moving gently like a invisible current.

"Shine your light," the tiny pixiary said in a squeaky voice. The nymph thanked the little girl with a nod and a smile but was clueless about what she meant by 'shining her light.'

Did she not get the note that I have no magical powers?

The small girl morphed back into a globe and rejoin her tribe of pixiaries, before they disappeared into the shadows. Still in a dream, Rose blinked her eyes again and was suddenly home at the shallows. Looking towards the familiar spot by the pond, she saw a man in dark clothes, wearing a tricorn hat and sitting at their favorite table. His back was towards her, so she wasn't sure who it was. But a man at the shallows was highly unusual, as no one ever visited, let alone a man.

"Hello, Rose," he said in a low, raspy voice.

"Captain McSly?" Rose stood frozen.

"How are you doing, Rose?"

Her mind was spinning in a panic. *I thought the map was burnt to ashes! I scribbled heavy black marks...I mean... how could this be possible!*

Rose looked around, expecting more pirates to come out of the woods and take her hostage or 'do her in' like pirates do. This was a dream, of course. And dreams, as we all know —are unexplainable. McSly got up from the table and ran straight for Rose. In a panic, the nymph cried out for help, but no one appeared. No sister...No Natts...Nobody came to help. McSly laughed with delight, waving his sword around like a madman. The platinum-haired beauty screamed. Everything went dark. And she woke up with a start.

"Oh, Thank God it was just a weird dream."

After stretching and yawning until her whole body trembled, the nymph tried to shake off the strangely unsettling dream that lingered in her mind. She glanced out the window, searching for something familiar, when a savory scent of beef stew lingered through the air. Her stomach growled, reminding her how hungry she was. Spotting her box of chocolate-covered Coco Loco cookies, she opened it eagerly and devoured one.

Tapping on the small door that led to the coachman's seat, she called out, "Mouch! Do you want a cookie?"

Hearing no reply, she knocked again, louder this time. "Mouch? Are you there?"

A little door slid open, revealing Mouch's whiskered face.

"Thank you, Miss, but I'd rather have some cheese." He smiled sheepishly, then hesitated, his ears twitching. "Actually, that's silly of me. I'd love a cookie. Thank you for your generosity."

Rose smiled, handing him a cookie, which he accepted graciously.

"We'll be at the Shallows soon, Miss Rose," Mouch said as he nibbled.

"Thank you, Mouch." After shutting the little door again to the grooms, she leaned back and popped another cookie into her mouth. But before she could enjoy the next bite, the carriage came to a jarring stop.

Peering through a gap in the curtain, she saw a cloaked figure standing near the horses. "The blasted mouse has lost his mind!" she muttered.

The stranger moved toward the carriage, tapping a walking stick against the road. The carriage door creaked open, and Mouch leaned inside with an apologetic look.

"She was standing in the middle of the road, Miss. I couldn't just run her over!"

Rose glared at him, exasperated. "Mouch, of course you can't *run her over*! I just—" She trailed off, suddenly uneasy. "I don't want to give her a ride. It might be a trap."

Her words were interrupted by the stranger's voice, warm and melodic. "My dear, thank you for stopping."

Rose sank back into her seat, her unease— growing.

The cloaked figure's voice was strange and unsettling. Through the window, Rose caught a glimpse of silvery hair spilling from beneath the hood and piercing green eyes that seemed to glow faintly. The old woman sniffled, her voice trembling. "I'm so sorry to bother you... but I must have stepped into a hole and hurt my ankle. If you could take me home, I'll pay you handsomely." She pointed at her ankle.

Rose inspected the woman through the carriage window, her eyes narrowing. The stranger's sharp, equine features were unsettling, almost grotesque. *She looks like a horse in a terrifying way—probably a witch.*

The woman shifted her weight and pulled a bag from her cloak. Tilting it toward Rose, she let several gold coins slip through her fingers like she had gobs of it. "I can give you this," she said, her voice coaxing, "if you could take me home."

Rose's mouth fell open. *Is it my birthday?* she wondered, her gaze fixed on the bag. *How much could that be worth?*

Rose felt a strange compulsion, as if a spell had woven itself into her thoughts. It tugged at her reason, replacing caution with the sudden need to help.

"Well?" Mooch repeated, his voice low, almost cautious.

Rose hesitated before whispering, "Okay… okay. We'll help her."

Mooch nodded, stepping out of the carriage. "As you wish, Miss Rose."

The woman's thin lips curved into a smile as she extended the bag toward Rose. The nymph hesitated but finally reached through the open door to accept it. Chloe's protective spell, meant to shield Rose, dissolved the moment the bag dropped into her hand.

As soon as her fingers closed around the bag, a strange sensation rippled through Rose. Above her, Belladonna's scarred hawk screeched, diving from the trees. It clawed at the bag, desperate to snatch it, but it was too late. Rose yanked it into the carriage, her grip firm.

"Miss Rose?" Mooch's voice trembled with concern. "Are you alright?"

But Rose had already slumped into the corner of the carriage, unconscious. Gold coins spilled from the bewitched bag, clattering onto the floor.

The hawk shrieked, its wings flapping furiously as it dove towards the old woman. Horse-face swung her walking stick with surprising force, striking the bird and sending it tumbling into the woods. A dark energy began to swirl around her. Within seconds, the frail old woman transformed, her appearance shifting like a storm. The disguise melted away, revealing Silvia Obsidian. Her long coat was covered with weapons—daggers, pistols—and her sinister grin promised trouble.

"I'll take it from here," Silvia purred, stepping toward Mooch. Her hand rose, casting a spell. "You'll remember nothing of today. When asked about your journey, you'll say, Everything went well. Everything went well."

Mooch stood frozen, his expression vacant as the spell took hold.

From the shadows of Everwood, three figures emerged: Wolfy, Sid, and Dean, a trio of troublemakers from the Spring Fair.

"Excellent work, Silvia!" Wolfy barked, his voice filled with self-importance. Sid and Dean smirked behind him, whispering ideas to each other like scheming schoolboys.

Before Wolfy could continue, a sharp *thwack* echoed. He stumbled forward, clutching the back of his head.

"Enough."

From the shadows, a tall man stepped forward, dressed in a long coat with a wide-brimmed hat adorned by a single white feather. Captain Wolfgang Wilhelm, Wolfy's father, loomed like a storm on the horizon. His striking blue eyes, framed by a mischievous goatee, gleamed with menace.

"I give Silvia orders, not you," Wolfgang growled, leaning close to his son.

Wolfgang put his face up close to his son.

"Understand?"

"But I thought you'd be proud of me for recognizing her," Wolfy grumbled, rubbing his head. "I'm the one who spotted her at the fair."

"I am, dear boy. I am." Wolfgang held his son's face like he had an important thing to say. Wolfy smiled at his father, wishing to be respected by him instead of punished.

Captain Wolfgang Wilhelm, Wolfy's pop, was the infamously handsome, hot-tempered pirate who was a legend for trapping magical creatures and playing a mean game of Crazy Eights. The captain was adjusting his jacket when he noticed a missing gold button from the cuff of his coat.

"Pop?" Wolfy distracted him.

"Yes, my son," Wolfgang refocused. "Let's take a look at our prize… shall we?"

"Yes…yes," Wolfy waved toward his buddies to come closer.

Wolfgang and his crew leaned inside the carriage, observing the nymph as she lay there passed out. The gold disc markings on her forehead were an obvious sign she had been birthed from a God. "Definitely the nymph," Wolfy remarked.

"Yup— she's the one," Sid chimed in.

"Nymph!" Dean belted out. Wolfgang sneered at the trio's idiocy.

"Of course, she's the nymph, you fools!" His amber-stained teeth glinted as he turned back to Rose, his smile as rotten as his soul.

"Wolfy," he ordered, his tone cold, "take her to Bellefont. Now!"

Having a table at the Spring Fair for the next four days meant Belladonna Barbosa needed a room at the Bellefont Inn. To feel at home, she brought along her cherished possessions: a crystal ball, Juniper—her black cat, Berwick—her hawk, and her collection of sacred lotions and potions books.

Settling into her room, Belladonna sat before the crystal ball, attempting to locate her missing hawk. Her brows furrowed as swirling images began to form in the orb's glassy depths. Suddenly, the scene came into focus, and she gasped.

"So *that's* where my Berwick went—he's chasing a *guuurl!*"

Her voice rose with delight as she leaned closer to her glowing crystal ball. Watching the vision unfold, she threw back her head and cackled.

"Is that guuurl… who I *think* she is?" Belladonna shot out of her chair, her excitement electrifying the room. She clapped her hands together as she watched Captain Wilhelm lift a platinum-haired beauty onto Wolfy's horse.

"She's more than just a guuurl... she's a *nymph*—the *phantom nymph!*" Belladonna shouted, spinning in circles like a child celebrating a wicked idea. "McSly has obsessed over her for years!"

Juniper, lounging nearby, leapt onto a chair and pressed his curious nose against the crystal ball. The black cat's green eyes narrowed as she studied the glowing vision.

"What's so great about this *guuurl,* master?" Juniper asked.

"She's *exactly* what I need, Juni," Belladonna said with a gleeful laugh, stroking her pet's sleek fur. "She's no ordinary girl—she's a nymph, and nymphs, Juni darling, live *forever!*"

Juniper—formerly a Werecat before Belladonna had stripped her of her powers—blinked in surprise. Though once able to shift into human form, she was now just a cat, a situation she begrudgingly endured.

"Oh wow," Juniper said, her tail twitching. "She's *immortal!*"

Belladonna's grin widened. "Yes! And I shall buy her at the dark market, where they're taking her. I'm sure of it."

Rubbing her hands together, she began to pace, her wicked plan taking shape in her mind.

"Then," she whispered, her eyes gleaming, "I'll drain her life force out of her body and—*in-to-mine!*"

Her dark laughter filled the room. Juniper gulped, her fur fluffing. *What if her next idea involves killing little cats, too?* She wondered nervously.

Trying to calm her, Juniper hopped down and rubbed against her leg, purring sweetly. Belladonna, in turn, patted her head affectionately.

"Juni darling," she said with a cunning smile, draping a cloak over her shoulders, "I'll be right back!"

With that, she swept out of the room, leaving the crystal ball glowing ominously in her absence. Juniper watched her go. "This will not end well," Juniper thought, her tail flicking anxiously

Rose woke to a boy with pointy ears and wide, curious eyes staring down at her.

"Welcome to the dark market," he said cheerfully, flashing a grin that made her headache worse.

Blinking hard, she half-hoped this was some kind of dream. But no. The ache in her head and the cold stone beneath her hands were very real. Groaning, she sat up and took in her surroundings: three grim stone walls, a barred window too small to crawl through, and shadows that stretched into corners she couldn't quite see.

"I'm Pippin," the boy whispered.

She tried for a smile but failed. "Do you know what happened to me?"

"Nope," Pippin said, flopping down beside her with an annoying lack of concern. "But you were dragged in by Captain Wilhelm's son."

"Wolfy?"

"I guess you know more than me. I don't know the boy's name." The elf sat down next to her.

"Are we really in the dark market, Pippin?"

The elf looked at her like she was kidding, "Yup…And we are the new goods."

Even if I had my magic cloak now, I'm still helpless. Rose pulled her ripped jacket around her body tighter and her skirt over her legs for warmth. She felt her pulse quicken as she reached for the collar around her neck. Her fingers brushed over cold metal and jagged crystals embedded in the band.

"What's this?" she asked, her voice cracking.

"Oh, that?" Pippin leaned back, his wiry frame silhouetted by the dim light filtering through the barred window. "That's a s*imilatra choker*. Pretty, huh? The crystals are enchanted—designed to keep people like us in line."

"People like us?" Rose echoed, panic rising in her chest.

Pippin gestured at his pointed ears, then at her. "You're not exactly ordinary, are you?" He didn't wait for her to answer. Instead, he pointed toward the far corner of the cell, where a girl slumped against the wall. Even in the low light, Rose could see the shimmer of iridescent wings curling around the girl's small frame.

"She's Nerin," Pippin explained. "Fairy. Not much of a talker. Don't blame her, though. Being caged like this will mess with your head."

Rose hugged her knees, shivering in her torn clothes. "And the boy outside?" she asked, nodding toward the pirate-looking figure just beyond the cell.

"Gorman," Pippin said with a sneer. "One of Wolfgang Wilhelm's goons. Thinks he's a real piece of work. He's been laughing at the same joke in that paper for hours."

Rose squinted at the elf in the shabby scarf and gold earrings. His laugh was sharp and joyless, more like a bird caw than anything human. He seemed oblivious to their conversation—or maybe he just didn't care.

"Gorman. He works for Wolfgang Wilhelm. We are all Wolfgang's prisoners. This isn't *exactly* Hades, but if you're waiting for someone to save you, don't bother. We're in the Dark Market now. We're merchandise."

"Right," Rose said, slumping back against the wall and pulling her coat tighter, feeling defeated.

Chapter Ten

Mad Dog Bart To The Rescue

The Salty Parrot Tavern was the favored spot for most pirates, scallywags, and hoodlums to hang out at. Reeking of spilled ale, burnt tobacco, and the unwashed bodies of scoundrels, the dimly lit room was alive with the clatter of card games and drunken laughter. Pirates swapped stories. Their voices rising and falling like the tide. In the corner, a pistol cracked—a warning shot from a sore loser at a card table.

By the door, Rocky, the tavern's infamous parrot, squawked loud enough to rival the noise.

"The nymph is here! The phantom nymph! And she's a looker—squawk!"

"Shut it, Rocky!" Hugo bellowed, chucking a half-empty mug at the bird. The parrot dodged it with ease, cackling.

"Rocky knows all! Rocky knows all!"

Sitting at a table with Wolfgang was Hugo. As he adjusted his oversized tricorn hat, Hugo grinned and scribbled a list of names with his quill on a piece of parchment.

"Tomorrow's auction will be the biggest we've ever *seen*," he muttered to Wolfgang, seated across from him.

Captain Wilhelm scratched his bearded chin, flakes of dirt fell onto the table.

"Biggest day, eh? I'll drink to that." He laughed, loud and menacing, then sniffed sharply, the sound echoing like a foghorn.

A group of scallywags were playing cards in the corner, when suddenly, one of them shot off his pistol at a fellow pirate for cheating, as usual.

But on this particular day, there was buzzing about the phantom nymph. Rocky, of course, wouldn't shut up about it. Several pirate men and women were laughing at the bar whispering, "…the shallows…the nymph girl…the ghost has been caught." Pirates were stunned that the rumor of the ghost nymph existing was even *true*, plus no one could *believe* the nymph was imprisoned below their feet in the Dark Market. Yes, just below the tavern was a dark and ominous prison where captured beings were contained. It seemed a bit surreal to the bounty hunters on Lumiere about the Phantom Nymph. They'd been reading about sightings in *The Fairy Tale Times* for years. But now—she'd been caught. The most enormous bounty for any magical creature *ever* would happen tomorrow.

Hugo, who owned the Salty Parrot, was in charge of running the seedy Dark Market. As he adjusted his tricorn hat—a gesture Hugo made whenever his nerves got the

better of him, he scribbled more names furiously. "I'll send notices to Captain McSly and Captain Shu'gar, of course." He grinned with a smile, showing his gold teeth, as he wrote more notes. "And Stinky McDoogle, Captain Brownpants, Captain Machado, and..."

"Can't wait to see how much she goes for," Wolfgang interrupted, then laughed obnoxiously with a nod as he scratched the scruff on his chin.

Gorman, the elf forman who monitored the dark market prisoners, suddenly showed. Hugo waved him over. He leaned in next to Hugo's ear and whispered something secretly.

"What is it, you rude imbecile? Can't you see we're in a meeting?" Wolfgang sneered.

Wolfgang's twitchy fingers betrayed his eagerness to profit, but his sunken eyes darted nervously at the crowd, wary of anyone who might challenge him.

"Sorry, Sir," Gorman studdered nervously.

"He informed me that Captain Shugar had requested to see the nymph. He's sending gremlins to see the Phantom Nymph girl. They'll be here tomorrow."

"Ha! Shugar!" Wolfgang laughed happily but still sounded scary. "More money for me! I welcome the interest!"

The captain spotted a mouse carrying a gold coin across the floor. He quickly pulled out his pistol.

"No one steals from me!" Wolfgang shot at it twice. The mouse miraculously dodged his bullets, dropped the coin, and narrowly escaped into a hole in the wall. He crackled, "Not even a blasted mouse! Hahahahahaaa!"

The next morning, two gremlins with spiked, rockstar hair stood gawking at Rose through the bars of her cell. Candlelight flickered against the walls, casting twisted shadows over the dark market chambers. Gorman was acting like an irritating salesperson to anyone that visited.

"The beast nymph needs a bit of fixing up, mister," Gorman sniffled, flashing his toothless grin. "But once she's polished, I guarantee she'll be the most expensive creature ever sold. Captain Shu'gar will be more than satisfied—you'll see."

The gremlins, their pockets embroidered with "KP" for Krusty Puff, nodded eagerly. Basher and Torch, employees of the notorious Captain Samson Winkfield Shu'gar, had been sent to scout the legendary phantom nymph. The phantom nymph was supposed to be beautiful beyond words and powerful like a god—Shu'gar wanted to ensure Rose lived up to her reputation before buying her as both bride and weapon. He planned to sweep her off her feet, marry, and then rule the world with her as his second in command, whether she wanted to or not, of course.

Gorman jabbed a finger through the bars. "Hey! Wake up, nymph girl!"

Rose lay motionless beneath her makeshift jacket blanket, every muscle taut. *Stay calm. Endure.* Rose thought.

"Show your face!" Gorman barked, jabbing her again.

When Rose finally sat up, the flickering candlelight revealed her striking features—platinum hair, soft blue eyes, and metallic marks on her forehead that shimmered like molten gold.

"She's a cute one!" Torch exclaimed, his beady eyes gleaming. Next to Torch was Basher, another gremlin with a club strapped to his back.

"Yeah," Basher said, looking enamored with her magnificent looks."She's incredible!" Basher said, with ogling eyes."Extraordinary," He added, gawking.

Torch slapped him. "Focus!"

Their sinister laughter echoed as Rose clenched her fists beneath her coat.

"She's extraordinary!" Torch whispered, his beady eyes gleaming. "Captain Shu'gar will pay a fortune for her."

Gorman nodded his head in agreement.

Torch slapped Basher in the face. "Get a hold of yourself!"

Basher laughed like a hyena in a sinister way. Torch joined in.

Pippin remarked."I feel like we are going to be——sold to idiots that laugh like hyenas," Nerin growled, finally saying something after being silent for hours.

After the two gremlin visitors were satisfied with their findings, Gorman led them down the hall and out a doorway. Moments later, one side of the cell moved. Floors rumbled, and walls shifted.

"What's happening?" Rose whispered. "Are we going to die?"

The walls slid apart, unveiling another caged wall, through which mortals and creatures suddenly observed the three of them.

"We're on display," Nerin said, "the dark market is open."

Halls lit by candles, the dark market lived up to its reputation— dim, gloomy, and filled with criminals. Creatures of all kinds were there, immortal and mortal, and all were looking to buy illegal things at the event. Characters were observing Rose, Pippin, and Nerin like animals on display at a store.

"I feel so ridiculous," Rose mumbled.

"Me too," Pippin added.

A cloaked woman, holding a small child's hand, approached. The woman was reading the sign with their credentials near their cage.

"She's the one, sweetie."

The small child pushed his hood back. It was a boy with large eyes and ears like he was part gremlin.

"It's the phantom nymph," the creepy woman said in a froggy voice. "She's the one I read you stories about in *The Fairy Tale Times*."

Rose grimaced at seeing the Demi-gem (short for half-gremlin and half-mortal).

"Supposedly, she has large fangs and devours people whole if she doesn't like them."

The boy stepped closer to the cell, inspecting Rose. He smiled, showing his razor-sharp teeth. Rose, Nerin, and Pippin stared at him intensely, wishing he would go away.

"Mother," the boy growled like a gremlin, which sounded scary. "I hope you buy — her!" The young boy pointed at Rose. The nymph immediately wrapped herself up tight, wishing she was invisible. Then cried out, "— hope not!"

The mother revealed her pointy fangs like a threat, grabbed her son's arm, and moved on.

Pirates were crowding the cage, daydreaming about the possibilities. Not only did they want the beautiful Rose but also Nerin. The fairy was an extraordinary beauty. Her hair was dark as the night with an emerald shimmer, and her long indigo dress accentuated her figure.

"We could rule the ocean together, you and me," said a toothless pirate named Mickey, who made kissing sounds at poor Nerin. She wanted to punch him in the face but couldn't.

Rose, Nerin, and Pippin were poked and prodded like food at a grocery store. They had limited space to escape the annoying —magical slave shoppers. A cloaked sorcerer walked up close and started yelling.

"How much for the three of them?"

The elf in charge heard the man's question, so he exited a door and was now outside in the dark market. He answered the mortal's question.

"Sir," Gorman announced," There is an auction at two pm sharp in the Salty Parrot Tavern in approximately thirty minutes."

The crowd in front of Rose, Pippin, and Nerin's cell was larger. Evil mortals, sorcerers, and other curious pirates crowded around them, making rude comments and asking redundant questions. A pirate with an eye patch, long lemon hair, and a tricorn pirate hat whispered to Rose.

"Hello there," the pirate said in an obvious fake accent.

Rose's eyes popped.

"Natts?" she whispered, "is that you?"

"No," he shushed her angrily. "I'm Mad Dog Bart!" Rose was so happy to see Natts, she cried and laughed at the same time.

Nerin distracted the onlookers so that the nymph could talk to her friend. Rose stood with Natts towards the corner of the cell, trying to talk to him unnoticed.

"I can get you out when you go upstairs to be auctioned off. I'll be in the ceiling looking down on you. When the time is right, I'll throw elf dust down. Then you reach up and grab my hand."

"Okay," Rose mumbled, teary-eyed. She was missing home and wondering if she would ever make it out—alive.

"In the meantime…pretend you have the power of magic. Just give excuses if they ask you to actually prove it. Just…Just convince them you have it!"

"Right!" She smiled at him with tears in her eyes. "Maybe… you could find my sister Chloe at the Bellefont Inn?"

"Don't worry, my dear," Natts whispered, "I will save you. Trust me."

"Okay," Rose whispered, "I trust you."

"Who are *you*?" Gorman, the cell monitor, pulled Natts backwards with a thrust.

Rose's heart skipped a beat from fright, as she watch Natts being dragged away. His fake mustache had fallen to the ground. A boy picked it up and laughed at it, showing it to his mother.

Rose pulled her jacket back over her head, wanting to hide. She felt like the escape plan was already going sideways. *Natts is a prisoner now too! This is just perfect!* She crouched in the corner of the cell, as tears ran down her cheeks.

She felt the fragile threads of hope slipping through her fingers. Now clenching her fists, the plan had just fallen apart in her mind.

Rose had to find a new one—fast!

Chapter Eleven

The Dark Market Fiasco

Godmother's at The Bellefont Inn was the nymph sister's favorite eating spot. The food was so unbelievably exquisite that townspeople believed the owner, Wanda Dinglespark, must be a magical being, because customers had reported feeling pleasantly hypnotized by their meals. However, whether Wanda Dinglespark was a magical being and had something to do with this phenomenon remains uncertain.

As planned, Chloe was waiting in front of Godmother's restaurant at five o'clock when her sisters arrived.

"And where is Rose?" Reeva asked. As she and her sisters piled their packages in Mugsy's arms

"I'll take these to your rooms, my ladies."

Chloe cleared her throat, which sounded more like a lie was about to spill out."Rose's fine. I sent her home in the carriage with Mouch." She put her arm around Zoe like the manipulating sister that she was. "We had a pirate and monkey issue, but I fixed it, and everything's fine now!"

"What?" Zoe snapped.

GODMOTHER'S
RESTAURANT

"I'll give you more details when we sit down," Chloe quickly pushed her sister into the restaurant to avoid more unnecessary questioning.

When they entered Godmother's, several heads turned. After all, the nymph sisters were exceptionally beautiful.

"Ah… Zoe Grey," Winston said with a bow.

"Good to see you too, Winston."

A table full of men stared, winking and nodding with approval. Another table of four women sneered at the sisters with piercing eyes and pursed lips. One woman whispered something horrible to another woman at the table then laughed like a cackling witch. Chloe had the powers to hear the woman's insult.

"I swear that woman hates us with her whole black heart," Chloe commented."If she could just make me slip so that I look thoroughly ridiculous…oh dear … wait. I'm afraid that I'm the one with that power."

So, as soon as one of the cackling evil women got up from the table, Chloe blinked her eyes and made her fall into a not-so-agreeable position. "Oh dear, bad luck for you, I'm afraid. Chloe said in a snarky tone towards the lady.

Winston, the Maître d', was unaware of the fallen woman and directed the sisters toward the balcony.

"If this table will be suitable, Ladies, your server will be with you shortly."

"This is perfect," Zoe said excitedly. "Thank you, Winston!" She dropped several gold coins in his hand.

"Thank —you, indeed, my lady."

After being on their feet for several hours, the sisters were relieved to sit down.

"Now, tell us what is going on! Where is she?"

Chloe explained everything that had happened to Rose. "When shopping for lotions, the sales lady was pushy to put it on Rose's arm. A monkey was suddenly there causing havoc, and then McSly showed up, which is why I had sent her home."

"McSly?" Reeva responded, "this is a bad omen, Zoe," Reeva commented.

"The monkey was McSly's pet. But it's okay…I handled it. Everything fine! I distracted McSly after I sent Rose home."

Chloe looked confident with her decision. "Besides, Rose pleaded with me to go, so there you go— end of story."

"I see," Reeva said, looking at Zoe with a look of concern, questioning Chloe's decision. Reeva added, "should we go home tonight? This sounds serious."

"I think Rose would rather be by herself and look for found treasures in the bushes of Everwood than be here," Chloe growled, "she doesn't like being looked over like we are her mothers."

"I see your point," Zoe said, thinking. "You're right. She'd rather be at home."

"I hope Rosey is happy," Reeva said, looking at Chloe like she should know.

"She's scratching little bunnies under their chins, as she collects fallen jewelry boxes in the bushes of Everwood," Chloe exclaimed sarcastically, "I don't know…I'm guessing our sister dreams about being as powerful as us someday." Chloe stuffed a piece of bread into her mouth, then made a stupid face at Reeva.

"Don't be such a pompous patootie," Zoe snapped.

Chloe laughed, "I'm only joking! Don't be so serious all the time, *Zoe!* I love our sister, probably more than you!"

"Thinking like that will get you into trouble," Zoe said, staring at her obnoxious sister.

"I hope it does!" Chloe remarked, laughing, "I could use a little excitement in my life."

Reeva was busy looking at the menu, licking her lips.

"You both need to decide what you want for dinner." Reeva rubbed her hands together, "I know what I want. So please— hurry up! I'm starving."

The Spring Fair was still buzzing with townspeople. Near the balcony where they were sitting, they could see some high-fashion-looking ladies trying on hats and children throwing balls at a target, hoping to win stuffed animal prizes. Moxie Jingle-Pop was performing close by, too. He had just made half of a lady disappear. The crowd cheered.

"Nobody cheers for us when we ensure their water supply isn't poisoned," Zoe commented.

"Mortals take things for granted sometimes," Reeva said.

"I'm just kidding, Reeva." Zoe said.

"I know that," Reeva said with a wink.

Zoe noticed Mouch arrive back from taking their sister home. Jumping up from her seat, Zoe announced, "Mouch is back. I'm curious how his trip went. I'll be right back with a report."

Standing by the carriage, Mugsy and Mouch ate cheese like there was no tomorrow.

"Thank you for delivering our poor sister Rose home safely," Zoe said, "I hope there wasn't any trouble along the way."

Some cheese chunks fell out of Mouch's mouth. "Everything went well, my lady," Mouch said. "Everything went well."

"Okay then," Zoe said, feeling awkward. She decided to look in the carriage curiously. Opening the carriage door, she looked inside but saw nothing unusual but a gold coin on the floor. "Finders keepers, losers weepers." She picked it up and slid it into her pocket. "Thank you, Mouch and Mugsy."

"We'll see you in the morning, my lady."

Zoe returned to the table, where Chloe and Reeva were still waiting for food.

"What's the report? How is our Rose?" Reeva asked.

"Mouch said that everything went well!"

"There," Chloe nodded. "She's safe."

"I guess I'm being overprotective of our sister, but I swear. I'm feeling like something is not quite right." Zoe said, shaking her head.

There was hooting and hollering from The Salty Parrot Tavern. The sisters witnessed Bubba fly out the tavern's front door, pull a pistol from his pants, and rush back in.

"Pirates!" Zoe chuckled, "Sounds like the whole tavern is fighting." Zoe pointed out, feeling annoyed by it.

Chloe laughed, "I wonder what's going on in there? Sounds exciting!"

The Salty Parrot was packed, filled with pirates, low life's, maggots, and cheats of all kinds. Excitement was building. The most important prize of the day was just downstairs, the myth, the legend, the one and only —Phantom Nymph.

The highly anticipated moment was finally here for Captain McSly. He and some of his crew, Langford, Bubba, Black-eyed Baxter, and Two-fingered Tex, were in one corner, smartly dressed and anxiously waiting for the nymph beasts' arrival.

Chapter Eleven

Captain Samson Winkfield Shu'gar, the mastermind behind the tastiest cereal and the wealthiest pirate on the island, was standing close to the auction block holding his pet pug, Krusty. Dressed in a dashing long jacket with pistols on each hip, he scratched Krusty's head, while listening to Torch and Basher update him with intel.

"This nymph," Torch mumbled,"is beyond belief gorgeous, Captain but a bit wild. I believe the fairy Nerin is more suitable as a wife, Sir. We heard the nymph girl has a reputation of being— deadly."

Captain Shu'gar glared at Torch. "I am aware of her reputation, Torch. I read the Fairy Tale Times— you idiot."

"Oh…Yes, Sir, Captain Shu'gar," Torch stumbled over his words as the captain's stare burned a hole through the bumbling gremlin.

Basher nudged Torch. "Don't be so stupid, or you'll get us both killed."

The three magical creature prisoners were led up from the dungeons with similatra crystal chokers around their necks and chains around their ankles. Little did Pippin, Nerin, and Rose know their magical powers would be tested in the next few minutes. Pippin was the first to be auctioned off. Gormer led him up on the auction block so everyone could see him.

"They are all wearing crystal neck braces, preventing them from performing magic." Gormer announced to the room, "there's no need to be worried."

Standing next to the stage, Hugo unfurled a scroll and started reading information on all the victims for auction. "Known for his dastardly heinous deeds and powerful elf magic, Pippin stands at three jackrabbit lengths tall, with beady little eyes and dashing good looks. He could be yours — for the right price!" After cheers for Pippin's credentials, Wolfy brought out a tiny fairy girl.

"Maggot elf boy, you perform magic for all the mortals here to see and believe, or we will kill your fairy friend, Octavia Twink," Wolfy said, sneering like he had no heart. "We'll run her through in a blink of an eye."

"Kill The Twink! Kill The Twink," Rocky squawked.

The tiny fairy was petrified as several pirates held knives toward her tiny face, which was only the size of a coin.

"Please… don't hurt my little Twink!" Tears began to well in Pippin's eyes."I'll do as you say," he whispered.

After Pippin's neck brace was removed, elf dust was placed in his palm. He chanted something that no one understood but made everyone listen curiously.

"Shim dim Shim dim… Boo bee Doo bee Wha!"

Within seconds, Pippin created a decadent feast. Lamb, fruit, croissants, and desserts were displayed on a table where several gremlins sat.

"Wow," the gremlins shouted, devouring the feast happily like they hadn't eaten in days.

Several bids for Pippin were shouted out immediately by an older woman cloaked in the back of the room, Captain Shu'gar, and the sorcerer, Noel Spellgem.

Captain Shu'gar won the bidding war easily. His gremlins replaced the crystal neck brace and held Pippin until the auction ended.

Nerin, the fairy, was next.

"She's a beauty…she's a beauty" Rocky squawked.

Men whistled and cheered.

When asked to perform magic, Nerin was threatened with the death of her dog, Speckle. Her smidgeon of a dog with a cute little bow on her head was surrounded by pistols. With tears in her eyes, she snapped her fingers. The food table now had piles of diamonds.

A bidding war for Nerin began immediately.

Cloaked inconspicuously in the back of the room was Belladonna. She raised her hand, shouting, "Ten gold Onzas!"

As everyone might *not* know, Ten Onzas was the equivalent of ten ounces of gold or ten thousand dollars. Although Belladonna came for the Phantom Nymph, she decided—a fairy would suffice. But to everyone's misfortune, Captain Shu'gar won again with Twenty Onzas. The room went wild.

But the pirates around the room were all wondering what was going to happen next, especially since Captain McSly's main obsession, the nymph girl, was next.

It was Rose's turn. When her name was announced, pirates howled and whistled, torn between admiration and fear.

"She's a smoke show…she's a smoke show…Hot! Hot! Hot!' Rocky squawked.

I'm going to look like a fool. Rose worried about faking her magic skills as Natts instructed. Looking out into the crowd, she wondered. *What possessed these God-forsaken fools to want to pay money to own someone against their will. Bunch of creeps!* As Rose ascended the platform, she brushed past Captain Shu'gar. His hand brushed hers, and a cold shiver ran up his spine. He stared at her, awestruck.

"I have to have her…" Shu'gar whispered to himself, his obsession ignited. Her beauty was like nothing he'd ever seen. On the other hand, Rose barely noticed, thinking it was just a bug bite.

As she reached the stage, the crowd's chaos intensified.

"She's magnificent!" Tex shouted.

"She's the Phantom!" Bubba fainted, overwhelmed.

The room erupted in noise as Gormer removed Rose's neck brace.

Wolfy hissed, "Perform magic, or we'll kill your hawk friend."

Rose's heart sank. Her hawk, scarred and loyal, was at the mercy of the pirates.

With a deep breath, Rose fought to remain calm. "What shall I do to prove my power?" Pretending to be confident, she asked outloud. "Shall I set you all on fire? Or turn into a serpent and swallow you whole?" A spark of genuine courage ignited within her as she leaned in, her gaze locking onto Bubba's. "I can do it all." Rose hissed. Her voice rising with every word. The room fell silent in fear. Some pirates nervously drew their pistols.

"Stop her! She'll kill us all!" Billy Blade growled, eyeing her suspiciously. Nervous murmurs rippled through the gathered pirates, some hastily drawing pistols, their hands trembling. In the confusion, McSly's voice rang out, demanding attention.

McSly shouted, his seething hatred was undeniable. "I want this beast, the one who took my leg! A hundred gold onzas and—she's mine!" The crowd went wild, cheering, fighting, shouting.

Captain Shu'gar raised his hand, his voice cool but firm. "One hundred and fifty gold onzas!"

The bidding war was fierce, but McSly's rage reached a boiling point. "You should have told me to bring more *gold*, Lang!" McSly yelled, his fury uncontained. With a swift motion, he shot his assistant—dead.

"You're mine now, Bubba!" McSly shouted, pointing his pistol at the pirate who had fainted on the floor.

With no more gold to add, McSly held his arm in the air, shouting, "Kill the beast, now! I want her dead or alive!"

Chaos exploded. Pirates fought, shouted, and shot wildly. But amidst the madness, Natts' voice rose above the clamor.

"Look up! Look up!"

Elf dust fell from above, showering Rose in sparkling light. She vanished in an instant, escaping into the chaos.

"The nymph has escaped!" Gormer shouted.

"The nymph flew the coop! The nymph flew the coop!" Rocky squawked.

The doors burst open, and McSly's crew rushed inside with an urgent message. "A large serpent is attacking the Revenge!"

McSly's blood boiled. For years, rumors had circulated that the Phantom Nymph could transform into an emerald serpent. It seemed the myth had been true all along.

"We must kill her! Kill the serpent!" McSly roared.

The tavern was left in disarray—tables overturned, chairs scattered, and Wolfy's lifeless body on the floor. His father, Wolfgang, knelt beside him, tears streaming down his face. "Who did this to you?" he sobbed, his voice breaking.

With his dying breath, Wolfy whispered, "The phantom… nymph."

A sob echoed from Wolfgang as he cradled his son's body. "How could she?" he whispered, overcome with rage. "I will make her pay. I will make her suffer for this."

Wolfy's eyes closed. He was dead.

"How could she!" Captain Wilhelm screamed in agony, outraged by this injustice.

He threw chairs against the walls. Pirates scattered.

"I will 'do her in' through for this! My son is dead! I will make that nymph girl pay for what she's done. I will make her suffer like I am now!"

Chapter Twelve

The Betrayal

Everyone on the island seemed to be at the Spring Fair, indulging in food, shopping, and perhaps even dancing for at least another three days. But by late afternoon, near the shallows, a sudden screech of several grey geese broke the silence. They honked in unison, alarmed by an unusual energy swirling near the pond. The mysterious light twisted and spiraled for several minutes before the startled birds fluttered away from the water, only to stop short. To their surprise, two figures materialized from a mysterious haze— Rose and Natts.

They had just escaped the chaos of the Salty Parrot Tavern, arriving by elf dust thanks to Natt's clever plan. When the geese recognized the travelers, they relaxed, and returned to the water—but not without eyeing the nymph and the elf with curiosity. Rose's once-beautiful indigo dress was now in tatters, its fabric torn and dirtied. Natts, too, looked every bit as disheveled, his pirate disguise barely holding together.

Chapter Twelve

Rose stumbled forward as she fully materialized, too exhausted to stay upright. After she collapsed to the ground, Natts quickly helped her to her feet.

"Miss Rose, please… lean on me."

Having gone days without rest, the elf guided her toward her treehouse. Together, they ascended the spiral staircase slowly, each step deliberate. Rose's tired eyes drifted over the walls, lit by enchanted candles. The shadows from the flames flickered, casting ghostly silhouettes on the walls.

Finally, as she sank into bed, her head hit the pillow and she fell into a deep sleep.

Natts decided to stay and watch over her for a while. Settling into a comfy chair in the corner, he scanned for pirates with his oversized telescope. After hours of watching from the corner window, he was sure they were safe. He pulled out a *Fairy Tale Times* from his pocket. Flipping through it, his eyes landed on the "Sweet Delights" section.

"Ahhhh! How to Make Lemon Tea Cakes by Tina Twerp. Sounds delish!" He whispered to himself. After reading the recipe, an overwhelming urge to make them hit him. "Zing zing, butt butt—boobee doobee," he muttered, and with a swish of his hand, a table appeared, covered with yellow mini muffin cakes topped with a glaze. Beside them sat a pot of warm tea and two teacups. "That's better!"

Chapter Twelve

The aroma of the cakes filled the air, enticing the sleepy nymph awake.

"Oooooo," she cooed, eyes fluttering open, "What is that?"

"Lemon tea cakes. Try one! They're delish," Natts said, licking his fingers. She swung her feet over the edge of the bed, looking dazed.

"What day is it?"

"It's your first day of freedom from the dark market dungeons, my lady," Natts replied, taking a hearty bite from a lemon cake. "I'm very proud of you. You had them all duped. But then again, pirates can be easily fooled!"

Now more awake, Rose eyed the lemony treats and popped one into her mouth.

"They thought you were going to set them on fire," Natts chuckled, slapping his leg. "Naturally, there's a story about it in the paper." He folded the *Fairy Tale Times* with care and held it up for her to see. It read:

> "Riot at Salty Parrot Tavern by Legendary Phantom Special Report: The legendary nymph strikes again, causing chaos at Belefont's local tavern, The Salty Parrot. Captain McSly and his crew saved the tavern from ruin and are now chasing after the menacing demon. The village of Belefont thanks Captain McSly and his crew for risking their lives to destroy the dangerous beast and

protect the innocent people of Lumiere. Thank you, Captain McSly!"

Rose slumped back against the bed. "Oh no, I'm a fugitive for something I never even did. What next?"

"Can you believe it? The town is thanking him!" The elf laughed, popping another cake into his mouth.

"Not funny."

"I know what you're thinking," Natts responded gleefully, "but you bluffed your way out of a catastrophe. Incredible performance! I think you're more powerful than you realize." Rose frowned, still skeptical and shot him a fierce look before inspecting the scrapes on her body from the kidnapping.

After a moment of thought, she sighed. "I'm not sure about my power, but I know I'm lucky to have you as a friend," she said, her voice shaking with emotion. "I'd probably be—dead without you."

Natts sat beside her on the bed, wrapping his arm around her shoulders.

"You're very much alive," he reassured her. "Bad people are rarely clever. You were outstanding. You had them all believing you had magic! The look on Bubba's face was priceless! I couldn't stop laughing."

Rose's eyes began to well up, and she hunched over, feeling a sharp pang in her stomach.

"What's wrong? Are you okay?" Natts asked, concerned.

"Yes," Rose whispered. "I just feel sad about everything. That's all."

Natts hugged her gently. Rose suddenly remembered something. "My… my invisibility cloak!" she stammered, panic creeping into her voice. "I don't know where it is?"

"Invisibility cloak? Oh—*no*!"

"My invisibility cloak… it must still be with my bag in the carriage."

"Don't worry—magic Natts is here," he said, trying to calm her. "I'll look into it."

"Who knows what's happened to it? What if Wolfy took it? What should I do?"

"Just stay here—I'll be right back." With a whispered chant, Natts disappeared in a swirl of sparkling light.

Rose slumped back onto the bed, waiting. The trees rattled outside, their branches clanging against the treehouse walls, making it hard to relax. So, she grabbed Natts's newspaper and decided to read by the pond. After descending the spiraling stairs, she exited her treehouse through the secret passageway, and sat at the table beside the water. It was a sunny spring morning, but a stronger-than-usual breeze swirling around her. Unbeknownst to Rose, the winds were gathering debris from the ground as she read a funny article in the paper. Minutes later, a colorful swirl—like a tornado—rose into the air. A giant mobile of flower petals, leaves, and twigs surrounded her.

"Odd," Rose thought, taking in the phenomenon. Laughing, she held out her arms, and for a brief moment she pretended to feel the power. The swirling debris eventually drifted upward, as if it had completed its task. When the wind died down, birds began chirping again.

Strange Rose thought, before returning her attention to the paper. The peacefulness of the pond returned—no flower tornadoes, no strange occurrences, no weird phenomena. Rose felt safe.

"There's nothing like home," she thought, gazing into the trees and enjoying the soft breeze against her face. She stopped reading for a moment, savoring the warmth and serenity of the day. That's when a voice shouted from the treehouse window.

"I found it!"

Natts was back.

Rose's heart raced as she sprinted up the spiral stairs of her treehouse, her pulse quickening with excitement. Her invisibility cloak and Natts—her loyal companion—were waiting for her like old friends, ready for their next adventure. Her fingers trembled as she grabbed the cloak, wrapping it tightly around her, feeling the soft, familiar fabric against her skin. It was a gift from her sisters, and she never thought she'd find herself so grateful for it. But today, it felt priceless.

"Thank you for finding it, Natts!" she said, with a sigh of relief.

Natts beamed at her."It was in your carriage, tucked away in a hidden compartment. Magic Natts always comes through for you, Miss Rose. I told you I'd find it. A little dust, a little whisper, and—voilà! There it was."

Rose couldn't help herself. She swept Natts into a hug, squeezing him tightly. "Thank you so much."

He laughed and patted her back. "You're welcome, of course."

With that, he flopped into the cushioned chair by the window, his legs dangling over the edge, picking up a plate of tea cakes and a folded newspaper. Rose's eyes wandered to the bag she had placed on the floor, already feeling lighter knowing it contained the things she'd thought she'd lost. She pulled out a dress Chloe had given her before they'd left for the fair. It was simple, yet stunning—white linen, soft and flowing, with intricate stitched designs along the hem. It was similar to the one she was wearing now, and for a moment, she was reminded of Chloe.

Suddenly, Natts's voice broke the quiet. "I've got some bad news."

Rose was barely listening, too caught up in the excitement of having her belongings back. She untied the string around her package, revealing the treats she had brought back from the Spring Fair—delicious dragonfly pies, their golden crusts promising sweetness. She took a bite eagerly, savoring the bite with her mouth full. "Hmm? What?"

Natts's face, usually bright with mischief, looked sad. He unfolded the paper slowly, revealing the headline. "Wolfy's dead. This obituary says *you* killed him during the tavern fight."

Rose froze, the bite of pie halfway to her mouth, as the words sank in. The world seemed to slow, her stomach twisting painfully. It was as if the air had been sucked out of the room.

"What? Wolfy's dead?" Her voice was a whisper, fragile with disbelief. "But I didn't do ANYTHING!"

She collapsed onto the bed, her head spinning. The familiar ache in her stomach returned, this time gnawing at her insides like a wild thing.

Natts's voice was cool."Wolfgang's got to blame someone. That's how it works. A good story sells papers, and nothing sells like scandal."

He casually tossed the *Fairy Tale Times* onto the bed next to her, the paper crinkling as it landed with a soft thud. Rose didn't hear him. Her eyes were already scanning the article, her heart pounding in her chest.

> "Phantom Nymph Escapes the Dark Market, but was seen murdering an innocent boy before transforming into a serpent at the docks of Bellefont."

Her blood ran cold as the words danced before her eyes. Her throat tightened, and a wave of anger rose in her chest. “This is ridiculous! I’m being blamed for everything—even Wolfy’s death?”

Natts sighed, running a hand through his hair. He was watching her closely, waiting for her to react. “Sorry to leave you like this, but…”

Rose’s voice cracked with frustration as she shot him a look. “So now I’m a murdering outlaw? Great! My parents will be thrilled.”

She flung herself back onto the bed, her body sinking into the soft blankets, the weight of it all pressing down on her.

“I know,” Natts murmured, his voice softer now. “It’s ridiculous.”

There was a long pause before he pulled something from his pocket—a tiny vial, delicate and shimmering. It caught the light like a star trapped in glass. He held it out to her, the sparkling golden and white dust inside catching the sun. Rose’s eyes widened in awe as she reached for it.

“This is for you,” Natts said quietly. “Just in case of an emergency.”

Rose’s fingers trembled slightly as she took the vial, admiring the way the dust shimmered within.“Elf dust for me?”

Natts’s eyes twinkled with a mix of mischief and sincerity. “Sprinkle a little on yourself, think about where you want to go, and you’ll be there faster than you can blink. You’ll be safe, Rose.”

She held it between her fingers, marveling at the sparkling dust. "Thank you."

Natts gave her a small, crooked smile. "Now, please say goodbye. I've got to go."

With a swirl of shimmering dust and a soft incantation, Natts disappeared, leaving behind a faint scent of something sweet in the air.

Rose stood there for a moment, holding the vial close to her chest, before tying it to her necklace beside the luck gold button. "Ahhh, I'm feeling better already. No one's going to catch me now."

The weight of the vial against her skin, the cloak around her shoulders, the button around her neck—all of it combined to make her feel invincible, like the luckiest person alive. She smiled, a fierce determination rising within her. She wouldn't be stopped.

Her stomach growled, reminding her of the treats in her bag. She approached the hidden compartment in the tree, opening it to reveal her stash of emergency snacks: Gobbers, Dilly Bitters, Ting Tings, and Flipper-do's—muffins filled with creams, jellies, jams, and juices. Rose's mouth watered at the sight. She grabbed a handful of Gobbers, feeling their crunchy sweetness fill her mouth as she settled herself on the edge of the pond, preparing to relax.

But just as she was about to take another bite, a hawk screeched overhead, its sharp cry cutting through the calm like a knife.

With a mouthful of Gobbers, Rose slurred, "Mah…woo are noyzeey."

The hawk, with a sudden rustle of wings, landed with a heavy thud, hopping onto the table beside her.

"Screeeech!"

Her heart skipped a beat as she noticed the frayed leather string still dangling from his leg, the scars marring his face and chest—a testament to the dangers he had endured. Rose gasped and reached out, her voice trembling with relief, "Scar-face! I'm so glad you're okay. I thought I'd never see you again!"

Overcome with joy, she pulled the hawk close, hugging him tightly, her fingers gently stroking his ruffled feathers. He rested his head on her lap, his body still and calm, as if he, too, found comfort in seeing her.

"Thank you for trying to save me from Silvia," she whispered, her voice heavy with emotion. "You were so fearless!"

The hawk let out a soft screech, as though responding to her gratitude.

For three blissful days, the hawk and Rose adventured together—treasure hunting through the misty woods, playing games that made them both laugh until their bellies ached, napping beneath the soft blue sky in fields of lavender, and gorging themselves on sweet treats. Every moment was an unexpected joy. Rose had never met a hawk so clever; he'd gather firewood with uncanny precision, his sharp talons expertly plucking the branches and stacking them into neat piles.

"Strange," she murmured one evening, watching him with a furrowed brow, "Where are you from, super bird?"

It was the last day of Rose's time alone, her sisters still away at the spring fair, and she hoped her new friend would stay. Having a bird to share her solitude was a welcome change. She wrapped herself and the hawk in the safety of her magic cloak and they fell asleep beneath the shade of a towering oak tree, its leaves whispering in the breeze. As Rose awoke, a strange warmth filled her chest. She gazed up at the sky, as though seeing it for the first time. In that moment, she realized it was the first time she had ever truly felt happy—truly at peace—even if it was just with a bird.

But the serenity was short-lived. Scar-face suddenly jerked awake, his sharp eyes scanning the skies. Without warning, he soared high above the treetops, his wings slicing through the air with graceful power. Time passed, and just as quickly, he returned, landing softly on her gown sleeve. With a slight bow, he presented a delicate pink daisy, its soft petals trembling in the cool air.

Rose's heart swelled. "How sweet! Thank you, Scar-face," she giggled, her hands brushing his feathers in appreciation.

The day was slipping away, and Rose knew it was time to head home before the sun fell below the horizon. She wrapped herself in her cloak and began her walk, the hawk trailing behind her in silence.

The sky above was a mix of gold and purple as Scarface flew high, casting a silhouette against the setting sun. The world felt still—peaceful, even—until a distant voice broke the quiet.

"Beeeerwiiiick!"

Rose's heart pounded in her chest as she quickened her pace. "I have my emergency elf dust for protection," Rose muttered to herself, clutching the small vial tightly on her necklace. Her cloak shimmered invisibly around her, but she held the vial tight, prepared for anything.

Suddenly, as the shrill voice shattered the calm, her cloak caught on a low-hanging branch, tugging free and revealing her to anyone within sight. A few fairies, hidden in the underbrush, squealed with delight. They popped out of their hiding spots, giggling as they scribbled in their journals, before darting away. Odd flowers—large, bow-shaped blooms—swirled in the breeze, their curious petals briefly swirling around to look at her before returning to their original positions.

"Berwick," the woman's voice called, "is that you?"

Rose froze, ducking behind the tree to hide, her breath shallow. Through the leaves, she spotted the woman—Belladonna, the lotions and potions lady from the fair.

"I see you, Berwick!" Belladonna shouted, pounding her staff on the ground as though casting a spell. In an instant, Scar-face shot down from the treetops, landing neatly on the staff's handle.

Rose, barely breathing, pressed herself against the trunk of the tree, hidden from view. A herd of pixiaries, those tiny glowing creatures, caught sight of her from behind the tree and instantly gathered around her. Their luminous bodies—shifting between magenta, lavender, and pale white—danced in the air like floating stars. Rose held her finger to her lips, motioning for them to stay still and keep quiet, praying they wouldn't reveal her hiding spot.

Minutes passed, though it felt like hours, before Belladonna and Berwick stepped through a gap between the bushes, disappearing into the shadows of Everwood.

With a heavy heart, Rose began to walk home, the weight of betrayal pressing down on her chest. The pixiaries, sensing her shift in mood, hovered around her, trying to help her find her way home.

"Okay then," Rose muttered bitterly, feeling the sting of Berwick's deception. "After all that time… he was just a spy?"

The pixiaries, determined to cheer her up, flitted around her, lighting her path through the growing darkness. As the sun sank lower, Rose knew she couldn't wander alone in the dark woods. The tiny glowing lights hovered around her like fireflies, guiding her to safety.

Finally, they reached the secret entrance to her hidden home. Rose pushed on a particular branch, and with a swirl of leaves, the gardenia bushes parted to reveal a swirling portal. The pixiaries darted in behind her, their lights flickering like tiny stars before the entrance closed with a quiet sigh, sealing her away from the world outside. Rose walked through the shallows toward her treehouse, the sunset's warm tangerine glow painting the sky. When she reached the oak tree, she gazed at the sky one last time, taking in the fading colors, before entering her home.

Up in her cozy treehouse, Rose slumped onto her bed, exhausted. She crawled beneath the covers, her heart—broken. As the soft hum of crickets filled the air, she couldn't stop the swirl of thoughts racing through her mind. *How quickly things change.*

The thought of never seeing her bird friend again tightened in her chest, and her eyes welled with tears. "No… no… no more, Berwick," she whispered into the night, her voice breaking.

Rose played with one of Berwick's feathers that was floating until her eyelids grew heavy, and she drifted to sleep. Outside, the pixiaries hovered, watching over Rose's treehouse as their lonely friend slept.

Chapter Thirteen

Crazy 8's

The Fairy Tale Times: The Phantom Nymph is on the Prowl - Lazu Foggytwig reports: "I was dusting off the tops of tulips outside my house when I heard a scream. Or maybe it was laughing. Either way, I rushed to see what was happening. I saw no one on a typically crowded Bellefont Beach. However, I did see several fins gliding through the water. It was the Beast! I'm sure of it! Continue on page 2.

When Captain Jonas "Razor-Face" Cutter read in the paper that the nymph was spotted, he arrived at the port of Bellefont on his ship, The Angel of Doom that afternoon. Undoubtedly, he wanted to be first to capture the beast nymph for the greatest bounty ever, yet still enjoy a bit of the Spring Fair.

However, while townspeople were gawking at the arrival of Cutter's ship, no one noticed a boy and a monkey sneaking off like two stowaways. Wearing a raggedy tricorn hat like a former pirate captain gone rogue, the stow-

away boy climbed down the vessel's side with his monkey pal. The two cheats ducked behind large barrels before slipping into The Salty Parrot. Inside the tavern the air buzzed with chaos as a band called Tangle and the Shiny Flies thrashed on guitars and pounded drums, screaming "The Devil Made Me Do It" at a volume that could drown out a cannon blast. Pirates slurred along in unison.The ruckus came to abrupt holt when Captain Wilhelm walked in. Trailed by his entourage, Sid, Dean, and Silvia, Wolfgang's piercing gaze swept the room. Brimming with irritation, he walked up to Tangle and shot several holes into the floorboards right in front of the snarly-looking singer. Pirates scattered like rats on a sinking ship, some dove under tables, some bolted for the door, and one unfortunante soul, frozen in terror, left a growing puddle on the floor.

"Keep it down!" Wolfgang growled, glaring around the room, ready to shoot the next noisy pirate.

"Yes, Sir!" Tangle squeaked.

After that, the band decided to take a break— indefinitely. Heartless and nasty, Captain Wilhelm returned his pistol to the holster strap across his chest and approached a table in the corner.

Gordy 'Golden Boy' Machado, Captain Cutter, and the stowaway boy with his pet monkey were seated at a table with a deck of cards in the middle, looking like a game was about to start.

"Machado, you ready for some crazy 8's?" Machado, a devious pirate captain, had just arrived on his ship, The Golden Jewel, that afternoon. As he clinked coins together in his pocket, Gordy revealed his gold-toothed smile.

"I'm ready to play, Wilhelm," he nodded. "Yes, Sir, I am ready to play. Yes, Sir, I'm gonna take all your gold and then find that nymph beast— before you, of course!" Wolfgang gave Gordy a greasy grin. "You? Ha! You're kidding me! I bet you don't even know what she looks like! But we'll soon see what you're made of, Machado. Yes, indeed, we'll soon see." Wolfgang walked around the table and stood next to a handsome scar-faced pirate with devilish blue eyes, Captain Razor-Face Cutter. Razor-face had a gift for sliding extra cards out of his sleeves like a magician.

"And Cutter?" Captain Wilhelm said with a cackle. "I'll enjoy taking your gold."

"I don't think so, Wolfgang," the blue-eyed pirate winked, "I believe I'll be taking yours first—big man!"

Next to Cutter was the stowaway boy. He was barefoot with a red sash around his waist and pants ripped to his knees. Next to him was his monkey pal, wearing a skull-and-crossbones bandanna with a cigar stub hanging from his mouth.

"And who are you two vagabonds?" Captain Wilhelm snickered.

The boy's blonde hair was so dirty it was brown. With big amber eyes, he looked up at Wolfgang fearlessly.

"I'm Ozzy, Sir, and this is Smokey." The rascal monkey made squeaky noises and hugged his buddy.

"Isn't that—McSly's pet?"

"Yup," the boy replied, "But he was not happy with how McSly treated him. And neither was I so— here we are. Funny how that is."

Captain Wilhelm wrinkled his nose, "Good god—you stink!"

Unaffected by the captain's meanness, Ozzy said, "We've been at sea for a while— what do you expect us to smell like?" Shrieking, Smokey spun in circles before Ozzy calmed him down.

"What makes you think I want to waste my time playing cards with you two stinky vagabonds who have nothing to wager," Wolfgang snapped.

"Oh —Sir, I have something everybody wants." Ozzy reached into his pocket and pulled out a piece of burnt parchment.

Wolfgang's mouth hung open. "Is that… the —map to the Phantom Nymph's Lair?" Wolfgang mumbled with unbelieving eyes.

"A corner of the map." The boy replied.

Captain Wilhelm laughed. "But why would I want it if The Phantom Nymph is dead? You imbecile!"

"No--she's not!" the boy gave a sneer, "She's been reported seen in Everwood."

Machado confirmed, "He's right! Don't you read *The Fairy Tale Times*, Wolfgang!"

Ozzy added, "This is my proof that I have it. Yes, indeed I do, but I hid it."

"Inconceivable!"Wolfgang scowled. Smokey screeched with excitement. Ozzy winked, then nodded like he knew he had what everybody wanted—the map to the phantom nymph's lair.

At first, Captain Wilhelm was surprised. As his mouth morphed into a snarl, he thought about the fact that his son's murderer was walking around free. His face turned flush with rage. *I want to tear the nymph beast to pieces first, then I'll kill the stinky boy— just for having something I want!* After his temper subsided and Wolfgang could speak again, he grumbled,

"You…you have the map, you say?" The wicked pirate captain looked annoyed by the boy's luck. "How could a stinky little boy like you have such a thing?"

"I signed up to be a pirate on The Revenge…and well." Ozzy stated, "then, when we were on our recent journey to kill the phantom nymph beast in the Atlantic, I happened to be in the captain's quarters. For one reason or another, I stumbled upon the burnt map, among other things." Ozzy winked, rustling some coins in his pocket, indicating he had taken some gold from Captain McSly. "The map is safely hidden until you want to give me some gold, or I thought playing cards would be fun."

"Yes, Sir, but I have a requirement."

"What? You…you cheat of a stinky boy!"

"Yes, Sir, I want you to do the 'salty dog' swear with me first."

Wolfgang's expression made it obvious he didn't know what a Salty Dog Swear was. But everyone on the island knew it was an enchanted bond that protected the initiator from death by pirates.

Ozzy added, "Any pirate with the biggest pistols in the room is dangerous, so I want to protect myself. So if you don't do it, I won't play cards…Easy as that!"

Wolfgang wanted the burnt map to the nymph's lair so bad, so crazy bad, so stinkin' bad, so over the top bad, that he was willing to do a 'salty dog' swear, even though he didn't know what it was. Behind Captain Wilhelm, Silvia leaned in and whispered urgently, "Captain, this isn't like a pinky swear… it's much worse. It's an enchanted bond, Sir."

Sid and Dean exchanged uneasy glances, their brows furrowed with concern. Should they warn the captain? They debated, but in the end, they decided silence was safer.

Wolfgang turned his gaze to Silvia, locking eyes with a fierce intensity. His voice, though barely a whisper, carried the weight of vengeance. "I don't care."

Captain Wilhelm straightened, his clenched jaw. "I'll do the 'Salty Dog' swear, stinky boy. I ain't afraid of some child's play!" With that, Ozzy stood up, moving to stand beside Wolfgang. They locked pinkies, and an eerie energy swirled in the air, as if the very earth knew what was happening.

"Do you swear, by the universe itself, that you will never harm or kill me or Smokey, or else you will be cast down to the bad place, where pain and agony await you for all eternity?" Ozzy's voice was steady, his eyes sharp as daggers.

With hate in his soul and defiance in his heart, Wolfgang sneered, "Yes—I swear!"

The tavern fell dead silent. Several pirates with mouths gaped, tumbled off their stools. A woman shrieked in horror as though she had seen a man's soul ripped from his body. Whispers swept through the room. "I can't believe he did it…"

Wolfgang smirked, oblivious to what had just transpired. "Let's get this game started, shall we?" He snapped, reaching for the deck of cards.

The table was piled high with gold coins from Machado, Cutter, and Wolfgang, with Ozzy's scorched map scrape resting precariously beneath a heavy stack of coins. The stakes had never been higher.

Wolfgang dealt five cards to each player, the shuffle of the deck sharp and fast. He slapped the top card face up—a five of spades—and placed it next to the deck. "The objective of Crazy Eights," Wolfgang grinned maliciously, "is simple: you win by being the first to discard all your cards. Just match the suit or number, or you'll be forced to pick up a card. And if you get an eight? Well, then you can pick any suit you want, you cheating fools."

Laughter erupted around the table as the pirates exchanged jabs. "But Cutter!" Wolfgang bellowed, raising his voice above the din. "You're to my left. Go on, you first!"

Cutter growled and slammed a two of spades down. Machado followed with a king of spades, then Ozzy slapped down a king of hearts, and Wolfgang followed with a five of hearts. Machado threw a three of hearts next, and Ozzy played a Crazy Eight! The game was heating up quickly, and Wolfgang, eyes glinting with anticipation, was down to just one card. He could practically taste victory, but tension tightened his chest.

When it came time for Cutter to play, he slapped down a two of diamonds, leaving him with only one card. Ozzy took his turn next, and with a deep, deliberate breath, placed a king of diamonds. The room was electric with excitement, every pirate watching with bated breath.

Then came Wolfgang's turn. Sweat beaded on his forehead, his hands trembling. With no diamond and no king to play, he was forced to pick up a card. And then another.

His frustration boiled over. He could feel the victory slipping from his grasp.

Suddenly, in a blind rage, he jumped to his feet, pulling a pistol from his holster before anyone could react. “Boom! Boom! Boom!” The deafening gunshots rang through the air, and the tavern fell into stunned silence. Captain Cutter and Captain Machado lay dead on the floor, their lifeless bodies sprawled across the floorboards.

“I win,” Wolfgang snarled, a twisted grin spreading across his face.

Pirates scattered in all directions, some bolting for the door, others hiding under tables. But no one dared to speak. The room remained paralyzed in fear, the air tense.

Wolfgang, clutching the sack of gold coins, strode toward the back door. “Come with me, you stinky little cheat!” he barked, dragging Ozzy by the collar.

Sid, Dean, Silvia, and Smokey trailed behind, watching as Wolfgang pushed through the door. Several cats bolted into the alley, startled by the chaos. Captain Wilhelm threw Ozzy to the ground.

“Tell me where the map is now,” Wolfgang spat, his eyes burning with fury, “or I'll do you in.”

Ozzy didn’t flinch. He looked up at the deranged captain, unfazed by Wolfgang and his threat. "I will, Sir," Ozzy said coolly. "But unfortunately for you, the ‘Salty Dog’ swear protects me.”

Wolfgang's finger twitched on the trigger of his pistol, but something was holding him back. He could feel it—the magic, the bond. His mind raced as he realized the vow had power over him. He couldn't kill the boy. He couldn't even harm him.

Ozzy slid out from under Wolfgang's legs with a casual grace, brushing the dirt off his clothes. Smokey, ever the troublemaker, let out a triumphant whoop, leaping into the air and performing a series of backflips.

"You good-for-nothing punk!" Wolfgang snarled, aiming his pistol at Ozzy once more. "I'll kill you for this!"

Ozzy just smiled, his confidence unwavering. "If you break the 'Salty Dog' vow," he said with a smirk, "not only will you be cast into a dark, eternal darkness, but it'll be the most excruciating, painful experience of your life. Me and Smokey? We're safe. The universe won't let you touch us. But you? If you even try, you'll die. And you know why? Because you still need us—if you ever want to avenge your son. Don't you need the map?"

Smokey wiggled his hips obnoxiously, taunting Wolfgang to pull the trigger.

The captain's hands trembled as he holstered his pistol, his face contorted with rage and frustration. He stared at Ozzy and Smokey, his need for revenge still burning inside, but deep down, he knew—he needed them both

Captain Wilhelm snarled in a low, husky tone, "I need the map—now, stinky boy." Gritting his teeth, he added, "Where is it?"

Ozzy answered confidently, "Give me the bag of gold, and you'll have your map."

Wolfgang's eyes rolled again at the thought of being bossed around by the stinky pirate boy and his insufferable monkey pet. Finally containing his anger, Wolfgang answered, "Show me the map and the bag of gold will be yours."

"Deal," Ozzy said, "I'll be right back."

After Ozzy and Smokey took off to retrieve the hidden map, Wolfgang whispered to his entourage, "When he returns—kill him! Nothing in that 'salty dog swear' should stop the three of you from getting rid of him and his evil monkey!"

"Yes, Sir Captain," Sid said.

Not far from the back alley of The Salty Parrot Tavern was a grocery store called Frannie's Place. Ozzie and Smokey casually walked towards the side of the store, where they stopped at a spot on the sidewalk. With Smokey on the lookout, Ozzie lifted two loose bricks in a particular spot, slid out a rolled-up piece of burnt parchment, and then quickly hid the map in his sash belt. As Ozzy replaced the bricks, he noticed a gremlin unloading a Krusty Puff's wagon, but the worker didn't look interested in anything but doing his job. The pirate boy and monkey felt successful on their map recovery mission and raced back to the alley where Wolfgang was waiting.

But unknown to Ozzie, Wolfgang had already returned to his ship.

Dean, Sid, and Silvia were waiting for them. They had their orders: retrieve the map, kill the stinky boy and obnoxious monkey, and return the gold coins to Wolfgang.

As Ozzy approached the meeting spot, he stood near some barrels in case the deal went sideways, yelling, "One of you, come get the map!"

Ozzie and Smokey had a plan.

As the innocent wanna-be-pirate Dean made his way towards Ozzy with the bag of gold coins, the brilliant but stinky boy thought of some added protection—Dean.

Ozzy knew Silvia Obsidian would try to do him in. He wasn't stupid, so the minute Dean came close, Ozzy twisted Dean's arm and suddenly made the not-so-bright pirate— his hostage, or human shield, whichever worked better. In the distance, Sid and Silvia were waiting for Dean to distract the stinky boy so they could zap him with Silvia's magic.

"Dean, he's such an idiot! The blasted stinky boy has him as a hostage now. I shouldn't have sent Dean-o to do the dirty work." Slapping his hands together angrily. "What should we do now, Silvia?"

The pirate fairy smiled at Sid. "I'll do the stinky pirate boy in—watch this!"

Chapter Thirteen

A bolt of lightning launched from Silvia's hand directly towards Ozzy. But Smokey warned Ozzie, and the boy dodged it. The bolt sizzled one side of Dean's hair instead. The fairy threw another bolt of lightning, trying to flombey Ozzy and Smokey, but the tag team was more clever and dodged Silvia's magic again. The lightning bolt missed again. Instead, it hit some crates from Phaedon's Fancy Dancy Delights, making a massive cream cake explosion, splattering gooey, sugary cake in all directions after impact. Phaedon came out the back door of his shop, outraged. Thinking quickly, Ozzy tied Dean's hands and stuffed the burnt map into his mouth.

Using Dean as their shield, Ozzy and Smokey shoved him straight at their enemy, knocking them down like bowling pins.

"Special delivery!" Ozzy shouted.

Grabbing his monkey pal, the two of them quickly fled the scene and into the depths of Everwood with their bag of gold.

Later that day, Captain Shu'gar was dining with Princess Lana Pineblossom from Devonshire, utterly bored, when an urgent interruption shattered the dull conversation. He was more engaged with his little pug, Krusty, the symbol of his cerael success. Krusty's wrinkled face, marked with countless scars from his adventures, often twists into a sly, knowing grin, as if he knows more about the dangers of the high seas than anyone dares to admit.

"Sounds...thrilling, Lana!" Captain Shu'gar muttered, flashing a fake smile.

Unquestionably handsome with thick, burnt umber hair, a strong brow, and piercing baby blue eyes that drew women to him like moths to a flame, Captain Samson Winkfield Shu'gar was a man of many qualities. However, kindness was not one of them. Rudeness, on the other hand, he had mastered to an art.

"Excuse me, Sir," came the soft whisper of Bulldog, Shu'gar's elf man-servant. "I have important news."

Bulldog, taller than most elves and a rare combination of magical power and muscular build, was as formidable as he was loyal—a perfect protector for the captain. As Lana rambled on about some trivial matter, Shu'gar interrupted her without hesitation, just as she was about to tear up.

"Excuse me—" he cut in, uninterested.

Lana blinked, stifling a sniffle, then nodded in resignation. "Of course."

Shu'gar leaned in toward Bulldog, his impatience palpable.

"One of our gremlins spotted a young pirate and a monkey digging up a map," Bulldog reported, his voice low and urgent. "He thought they looked... suspicious."

Shu'gar's seemed interested.

Bulldog continued, "It was in *The Fairy Tale Times* today. A card game at the Salty Parrot ended with two pirates dead. Apparently, Captain Wolfgang Wilhelm, a notorious sore loser, won the map to the phantom nymph's lair—by force, of course. But the stinky stowaway reports that Captain McSly did not slay the beast... she has been spotted in Everwood. You still have a chance to cross paths with her again."

Why wouldn't the Phantom Nymph sighting be in the news? McSly didn't kill the beast? Shu'gar's heart skipped a beat. The Phantom Nymph. The map. It was his.

"Bulldog," Captain Shu'gar barked, his voice suddenly commanding. "Send Torch and Basher to find Wolfgang and his crew—immediately. They have the map, and I want the phantom nymph... before anyone else does!"

He lowered his voice, turning to Princess Pineblossom with a greasy, insincere smile. "Pardon my sudden departure, Princess. But you understand... matters of *great* importance."

Chapter Fourteen

Our Neighbor is a Sorceress

After several hours, they finally arrived at the secret entrance to the shallows. As Mugsy pressed a particular tree branch down like a lever, a mysterious energy suddenly appeared. It intertwined between two gardenia bushes before transforming the barrier of the brush into a magnificent doorway. After the wheeler carriage, pulled by two glossy chestnut horses, trotted through the shimmering portal with a soft creak of the wooden wheels, the secret opening magically transformed back into the fence of gardenia bushes, as if nothing were there. However, hidden in the dense shadows of Everwood, someone was watching them. Their eyes glittered with silent curiosity, studying the magical entrance and quietly taking note of every detail.

Finally arriving home, the sisters were talking nonstop, unaware of where they were. When Mugsy opened the carriage door, belting out, "Surprise! You're home!" all the sisters jumped with fright.

"He's not a very good groomsman—scaring us half to death," Reeva mumbled to Chloe.

"He's a mouse, Reeva dear. He loves frightening you more than helping!"

High up in her treehouse, Rose was happily working on a painting of something large and blue. Remnants of smooshed and torn irises, pansies, and bluebells were stuck, stained, and smeared on a sheet of white cloth on the floor. When she heard the bumbling carriage and horses' hooves, she quickly thought of excuses to avoid eating supper with her sisters. She wanted to avoid annoying questions that would make her cry over being dumped by a bird. While the sisters were unpacking their goods from the carriage, Rose found a hat to put on. She pulled it over her swollen eyes and shouted down from her treehouse window, "Welcome home!" She waved gleefully, which was not normal, "I hope you all had a great time! Great to see you! I can't wait to hear all about it!"

Zoe waved back reluctantly but whispered to her sisters, "Why is Rose wearing an ugly hat and acting so happy? It's *so* not like her."

"Be quiet, Zoe! Just be nice!" Chloe said, then threw her hand up, shouting, "We love you, Rosey!"

Reeva added, "We can't wait to tell you about our trip. And are you joining us for dinner? Or staying up there forever? I'm warning you. Zoe is cooking supper tonight!"

All the sisters laughed. But Rose, still standing at the window, felt her emotions starting to stir inside. But as tears began to fall, Rose could not control her feelings and

quickly announced, "I'm sorry. I'm not feeling very well, so I won't be joining you for supper." She blew a kiss and then dissapeared from view.

"Oh dear," Chloe remarked with a confused look. "I wonder what's wrong with her? She's acting strange."

Zoe added, "Rosey! You'll miss my amazing supper if you don't feel better soon."

"Be quiet, Zoe. No one cares about your food." Reeva snapped, looking up at Rose's empty window, wondering what was wrong.

The raven-haired nymph had been reading a cookbook by the famous elf chef, Fanny Fungus, called *Mushroom Madness*, on the carriage ride back. So, as soon as they arrived home, she whipped up a fungus feast of Dilly Dobbers stuffed with Shrimpeez and Blubedoo Patties with the swish of her hand.

The sisters were laughing about a funny story at the fair when Rose emerged from her treehouse and joined them at the table for dinner. Still wearing her hat to hide her teary eyes, Rose gave Chloe a phony smile before sitting across from her at the table.

"Nice of you to join us, Rosey," Chloe said. Please help yourself by eating some of Zoe's remarkable fungus foods. Hopefully, you won't gag at the smell of it like I do. It's delicious if you like food that resembles a regurgitated mystery." Chloe opened her mouth full of chewed mushrooms, which made Rose laugh.

“Thank you for the unnecessary commentary,” Zoe barked.

The sisters giggled even more.

“Rose’s fingers are purply blue! She must be sick!” Reeva teased.

“Oh no…something worse than Zoe’s fungus food. Rose’s art!” Chloe teased.

“Ha-ha-ha-ha,” Rose fake laughed.

“We hope you’re not sick from hanging out with Chloe too long.” Reeva commented, making a sympathetic face, “I would feel sick, too.”

Rose laughed. “Really, I’m fine.”

Zoe twirled her hair around her finger like it made her think more clearly, then abruptly sat up straight like an idea just came to her.“Can we create havoc on the creature that hurt you? If you tell us who it is, we could perform the *Rashipoo* spell,” Zoe joked, hoping to get a smile from her sad sister. We can teach whoever hurt you a lesson with an extremely itchy rash on their face, or bottom, or wherever, really.”

“Thank you, but no.” Rose held her hand up,“I’m thankful you want to help, but I'm okay.”

Zoe and Reeva finished their Bluebedoo Patties and returned to doing their needlework. Reeva hadn’t finished anything and was sneaking her food under the table and feeding the squirrels instead. She whispered to Rose,

"Are you upset about having fungus food for dinner? I can relate. The nerve of our sister trying to serve us fungus!"

"The nerve!" Rose lied, not wanting to tell Reeva that she loved mushrooms.

The chestnut-haired nymph snapped her fingers. In an instant, a bowl of banana cream pudding appeared. "Why eat supper," Reeva said, licking her lips, "when I can go straight to dessert—hmm!" She ate quietly at the end of the table with a smile.

Chloe teased Rose obnoxiously, "We hope you didn't scare too many people while we were away."

Rose scowled at Chloe. A wicked thought crossed Rose's mind, and without thinking, she grabbed the bowl of banana cream and plopped it squarely on Chloe's head without thinking.

"Oh dear," Rose mumbled snidely feeling satisfied. "You look like an ice cream sundae. You must have a curse!"

Laughter rang out from everyone, except for Chloe, of course. She stood frozen, eyes wide with shock, before wiping the banana cream from her hair, her cheeks burning with anger.

Meanwhile, Zoe and Reeva chattered happily, recounting their adventurous day at the fair to Rose. Chloe, still covered with banana cream, was left to wash herself off as the sisters exchanged stories. The sky outside had deepened into shades of orange and violet, the last rays of the sun sinking beyond the horizon. A small fire crackled softly, the embers glowing like tiny stars. The scent of pine lingered on the cool evening air, mixing with the warmth of the fire and the distant song of crickets.

Reeva stretched and yawned. "Can we talk more tomorrow?"

As they began to pack up, Rose offered to clean, knowing her sisters were likely tired after their long day. With a few grateful hugs, they disappeared into their treehouses, leaving Rose alone to clean up.

"Excuse me," came a soft voice from the shadows.

Startled, Rose grabbed a cloak from the table and slipped behind a nearby oak tree, her heart pounding in her chest. Rose peered cautiously from behind the trunk as a figure approached through the soft twilight.

How could anyone have entered the shallows without my noticing? Rose wondered. Her mind raced as the silhouette of the stranger drew nearer.

"How could this person enter the shallows?" She whispered.

As the stranger approached, they slowly let their cloak fall back. Rose recognized the woman. It was the woman from the Spring Fair.

"I'm sorry to scare you," she said sweetly. The other day, I was out for a walk and saw you carrying a basket as if you were collecting something. I called out, but you didn't hear me." Belladonna lied, "when I saw you walk between two gardenia bushes, I thought it was the door to your house, so I entered tonight, hoping to introduce myself. I'm your new neighbor, Belladonna Barbosa."

Rose stayed hidden in the shadows. "Nice to meet you, my lady."

Her mind buzzed with questions. *How could she have seen me while I was wearing an invisible cloak? She seems so kind... and too beautiful to be of any harm.*

"How are you, Miss?" Belladonna asked, her voice sounding kind.

From the shadows of the oak tree, Rose replied. "I'm fine, my lady."

Just as Rose was about to step out from her hiding place, her hawk friend Berwick suddenly swooped down from the sky and landed gracefully by Belladonna's feet.

"This is Berwick," Belladonna said.

The hawk immediately took flight again and perched on Belladonna's arm. "He's quite handsome," Rose added trying not to sound jealous.

Belladonna smiled warmly, though something flickered in her eyes. "Thank you, dear. He's rather fond of me."

A slow breeze stirred the air around them, as if carrying the weight of unseen magic. Belladonna adjusted her cloak around her shoulders.

"I overheard something about a curse," Belladonna said, her voice a touch softer now. "I wanted to offer my assistance. I'm a sorceress, after all."

Rose blinked, her heart skipping a beat. "A sorceress, my lady?" she squeaked, her voice high-pitched with shock.

Belladonna's smile widened, her eyes gleaming with a quiet satisfaction. "Indeed, I am."

Rose's thoughts spun like a whirlwind. *This explains everything! She's a sorceress, surely she can help me! Maybe that hawk led me to her.*

Rose finally decided to step out of the shadows.

After a moment of hesitation, her cloak fell back, revealing her striking platinum hair and the intricate gold markings on her brow that glinted faintly in the dim light. "I'm Rose, my lady. I live here with my sisters," she said, offering a gentle smile.

Belladonna's eye twitched slightly. Her lips revealed a slight sneer. "Nice to meet you, my dear."

Rose studied the sorceress carefully, her suspicion growing. After the ordeal with Natts and the two pirate imposters, she couldn't help but inspect this new visitor closely. *She doesn't look like a pirate.* Rose thought, scrutinizing Belladonna's flawless skin and hairless chin.

Belladonna, oblivious to Rose's thoughts, stroked Berwick's feathers lovingly, her fingers slow. Rose had no idea that Belladonna, being a sorceress, could hear every word that passed through her mind.

Mission accomplished, Belladonna thought with quiet satisfaction. *The innocent nymph trusts me.*

A sudden gust of wind, heavy with the scent of earth and magic, swept through the clearing.

"Are you…" Belladonna paused, eyes narrowing slightly, "the phantom nymph?" she asked.

Rose stiffened, her breath catching in her throat. "Those are the rumors. I'm afraid."

Feeling the weight of the curse, Rose lowered her head. "But I don't have any magical powers, my lady," she said, "I feel I've been cursed."

Belladonna's smile spread wider, her eyes gleaming with a dark satisfaction. *Perfect,* she thought. *This is everything I wanted.*

"I see," Belladonna said with fake concern. "How can I help, my dear?"

Rose's eyes began to well with tears. She gathered her emotions and asked, "Are you a powerful enough sorceress to break this curse and return my magical abilities?"

Belladonna pretended to act concerned as the nymph wiped a tear from her eye. With a cunning smile, the sorceress replied, "Yes….Yes, I can indeed."

Rose was speechless. She clasped her hands together as if a wish had just come true and shouted, "Thank you, my lady!"

"Well then," the sorceress said, "spell removals are twenty duros." Belladonna pulled her cloak over her head."Please come to my home tomorrow. I have no previous engagements."

At that moment, the nymph's gleam of hope left her eyes. "But I… I don't have any duros, my lady," she admitted, her voice barely a whisper.

Belladonna said nothing, her eyes calculating as they locked onto Rose.

"I… I have things I could trade," Rose stammered, her hands trembling. "Please, let me show you."

Still, Belladonna remained silent, her expression unreadable. For a long moment, she seemed to relish Rose's discomfort. "I can cook and clean," Rose said desperately, her voice cracking. "My sisters can vouch for the quality of my cleaning. Please, I will honor my debt. I swear, I won't disappoint you."

After what felt like an eternity, Belladonna finally spoke, her tone soft yet firm. "I'll evaluate your trade when you arrive."

Rose's face brightened with relief. "Thank you, my lady! Thank you!"

Belladonna's eyes glittered with something darker. "If your items are unacceptable," she warned, "two full moons of work will be the price."

Rose's face fell, but she nodded solemnly. "Yes, my lady."

Belladonna tilted her head, as though enjoying Rose's sadness. "You can find me by going twenty paces down Blackwood, then ten down Cedarwood. My house is behind the purple irises, with an orange door."

Rose smiled. "Oh, Thank you, my lady! I will see you tomorrow then!"

"Yes…see you tomorrow."

The next morning, Rose joined her sisters at their favorite breakfast table by the water. The table had fresh bread, powdered cream puffs, and sweet grape juice, all set on top of a crisp white linens. A vase overflowing with lilies stood at the center, their fragrance mingled with the fresh morning air.

"Nice of you to join us," Chloe teased, eyeing Rose with a sly grin. "My favorite phantom."

Ignoring Chloe's jibe, Rose sat down at the table next to her, poured some juice into a cup, and observed Chloe playing with a necklace she had bought at the fair. Reeva was sitting across from them, spreading jam on a piece of bread. Before stuffing her mouth, she announced,

"Zoe is 252 years old today! Happy Birthday, dear sister!"

Zoe was sitting at the table, too, drinking tea and reading the paper quietly. She lifted her head from reading and laughed. " I don't feel a day over 140!"

The sisters laughed.

As far as aging— nymphs did not. They were fortunate to have that quality. Although nymphs were immortal— they could die, and unfortunately, some have met an untimely death.

"I think you still qualify as the oldest nymph on the Isle, Zoe," Chloe noted.

"Ha!" Zoe looked insulted. "And you qualify as…the least attractive Chloe?"

"I think Rose has me beat!"

But Rose ignored Chloe, as usual, and announced, "You still look like a teenager, Zoe….Happy Birthday!"

"She does, doesn't she?" Reeva winked and lifted her teacup. "Let's celebrate with cake tonight."

After a few minutes, the conversation ended, and the sisters returned to eating. Rose thought, "I don't really care what my sisters think, so I will share my news with them."

"I have an announcement to make."

And as usual, Chloe teased, "Dear God of the Trident, your daughter has something to say!"

Rose ignored her obnoxious sister and continued, " As I was saying, we have a new neighbor."

"We do?" Zoe said excitedly. "should we invite them over for tea?"

"Not yet," Rose said, "she's a sorceress."

"A sorceress?" Zoe remarked, "I know what you are thinking, dear sister, and it's a bad idea. We've been through this before."

"She's a sorceress who claims to have the power to break my curse," Rose growled. "It's not a bad idea to me."

"We've been through these six unlucky times already," Reeva noted. "We will not contribute to what we know will be a failure. I just want to say, don't get your hopes up."

"I never asked you for anything!" Rose said, sipping her juice and wishing she hadn't mentioned anything to her sisters.

Reeva looked up from spreading more jam on the bread, sighed heavily, and added, " Please don't go. We've been through this before."

A gentle breeze blew leaves across the table, distracting everyone's mind away from the conversation. Chloe returned to admiring her new necklace. Reeva continued eating her jam on bread, and Zoe sat back and returned to reading and sipping her tea.

Rose drank her juice, ignoring her sisters, thinking excitedly, "I wonder how early I could arrive at Belladonna's house?"

Chapter Fifteen

A Spell Broke Instead

The next morning, Rose woke up early, too eager to "sleep in" as she usually would. Her mind raced with possibilities."A hundred Coco Loco cookies…a bigger treehouse...a fancy jacket…or maybe a whole wardrobe full of fancy dresses...several pounds of gold…and… and maybe some more gold." She couldn't decide what to create first with her new powers."Definitely more Coco Loco cookies," she whispered, grinning to herself.

As she tied her ivy and daisy headband, a dragonfly fluttered in through the window. It shimmered for a moment before transforming into a ball of light, which expanded into her elf friend, Natts.

"And where are you off to?" he asked, raising an eyebrow.

Rose was inspecting her reflection in the mirror as though something was wrong with her face. "Hello, Natts! I'm meeting my new neighbor, who just so happens to be a sorceress." His mouth dropped open in disbelief. The

nymph beamed, her eyes twinkling with excitement. “Soon, I’ll be as powerful as my sisters!”

“I don’t believe it!” Natts gasped, then leapt onto her bed, bouncing up and down as if celebrating her good fortune.

“I know it sounds unbelievable,” Rose said, her voice bubbling with joy. “But I met this sorceress yesterday, and she confirmed it—she can definitely break my curse!”

As she spoke, she absentmindedly began to dismantle some of the treasures she’d gathered, pulling them off the walls one by one.

“Well…” Natts started, his face pulling into a thoughtful frown. “I hope she’ll accept your treasures as payment.”

“I hope she will! This is all so exciting!” Rose exclaimed, practically glowing. “But did you check for facial hair? She could be a pirate in disguise, you know!”

Rose laughed. “I promise, I checked. No facial hair. No pirate disguise. She’s definitely not a pirate.”

“Well, that's a relief. So, what’s this sorceress's name?” Natts asked, eager to know more.

Rose pulled out a cream-colored cloth sack from under the bed and began filling it with the treasures she’d collected.

“Belladonna Barbosa.”

Natts paused, his brow furrowing in thought. Then, with a shrug, he blurted, "I've never heard of her. But that doesn't mean anything. I'm sure she's brilliant."

He tried to hide the worry creeping into his voice, but his enthusiasm still showed through. "I'm so excited for you! Finally, your curse will be a thing of the past!"

Rose stood, her sack brimming with her found treasures, ready to leave. "I'll tell you all about it when I get back," she said, a smile tugging at her lips.

"Without a doubt," Natts winked.

Rose grabbed her magic cloak from the chair, slung it over her shoulders, and skipped down the spiral staircase excitedly.

Standing at the edge of the shallows, she quickly ran through her plan. "Twenty paces down Blackwood, ten down Cedarwood, where the irises are blooming." She adjusted the cloak around her shoulders, pulling the hood up. "Shouldn't be too hard."

Fifteen steps into Blackwood, she heard a rustling in the bushes. Lemon-colored hair stuck out from behind a lavender bush like a beacon.

"Natts! I see you!" Rose called.

The elf popped up from his hiding place. "Is my elf dust too sparkly?" he asked, raising an eyebrow.

Rose momentarily pulled off her cloak, grinning at him. "How do you always spot me under my invisibility cloak?"

Natts crossed his arms, smirking. “You’re never fully covered, you know.”

“Guess I’ll have to be more careful,” she said, her hand resting briefly on his shoulder.

“Better,” he replied with a wink.

Rose shrugged her cloak back into place, and they continued together. She counted another five paces down Blackwood, then ten down Cedarwood, until they reached the irises, their delicate petals glowing in the morning light.

“This must be it,” Rose murmured. She looked at Natts. “Wait out here. I won’t be long.”

“Right-o, my lady,” he replied.

Rose stepped up to the small cottage tucked off the road, its orange door adorned with cheerful flower carvings. She hesitated. "It looks… welcoming. I think," she muttered, nerves tightening in her chest.

“Everything will be fine,” Natts called from the bushes, his voice sounding reassuring.

“Okay,” she whispered, trying to steady her nerves.

She approached the door, and Natts disappeared into the brush. She knocked, waiting a moment. When no one answered, she looked over her shoulder for Natts. He peeked up from behind a cluster of lilies and gave her an encouraging wave to push forward. Rose uncovered herself from her cloak, suddenly materializing. *I better hide this.* She placed her invisibility cloak near a bush in front of the cottage. *When I'm done, I won't need you anymore, anyway.* Rose let out a sigh and walked forward. The door was slightly ajar, so she nudged it open.

"Hello? Is anyone home?"

Inside, Belladonna stood in the corner, straightening a cluttered table. Crates, baskets, and bowls were strewn about in chaotic fashion.

"Rooooose!" Belladonna's voice rang out.

"Hello, my lady," Rose greeted timidly. "I hope I'm not too early?"

"Not at all, my dear. Please, come in!" Belladonna gestured warmly. "Forgive the mess—it's from the Spring Fair. I haven't had time to tidy."

As Rose stepped inside, her hawk friend swooped across the room, landing on a large grandfather clock. He perched there, eyes glinting as though urging her to take notice of him. Rose followed his movements, smiling softly as he repositioned himself, clearly wanting her attention.

"Please, take a seat!" Belladonna pointed at the large oak table in the center of the room. A porcelain teapot, wooden bowls, and several teacups were stacked on top.

Although Belladonna's cottage seemed packed with stuff, the nymph saw nothing that resembled a chair. The table looked like it wasn't used for anything but cluttering to Rose.

"I don't see a chair, but I suppose I could drag a crate over to sit on. Would that be appropriate, my lady?"

"Oh dear," the sorceress exclaimed, "nothing to sit on? I've just moved in, so I'm a bit disorganized. My apologies." She chuckled awkwardly, then gestured toward a tree stump in the corner that she was using for chopping herbs. With a wave of her hand, the stump instantly transformed into a beautifully carved chair. It floated across the room and landed in front of Rose. *I've definitely come to the right place.*

"There, that's better," the sorceress said, her smile sly.

Rose reached into her sack and held out a small bundle of treasures. "Here's my payment, if you'll accept it, of course."

Belladonna gave a gracious bow before taking the sack. "Please excuse me a moment, my dear. I'd like to inspect your treasures."

"Of course," Rose said, settling into the chair.

Belladonna retreated into her bedroom, the sack of treasures in hand. Upon entering, she was greeted by the sight of a furry black creature sprawled lazily across her bed.

"Wake up, you lazy cat!" she hissed.

Juniper suddenly uncoiled then stretched, before sitting next to the sack. As she licked her paws like she owned the room, Juniper asked in a snarky tone, "What have we here, Master?"

"These treasures are from my neighbor Rose," Belladonna replied, giggling. "By the way, she's cursed."

Chapter Fifteen

Belladonna's magic allowed her to hear Juniper's thoughts.

A gold button rolled out of the sack, landing on the bed. Juniper poked it with a paw, confused, then realized it wasn't a coin."A muddy button? This is what you accept as payment?" Juniper scoffed.

Belladonna pulled out a top hat that had clearly been gnawed on by mice.

"Eww, really?" Juniper grimaced, "what's next moldy cheese with mouse droppings? This sack looks like it fell off the garbage cart last Friday—"

"Enough!" Belladonna snapped. "It doesn't matter. The girl is a nymph, with centuries of life force."

The cat slinked back, fearful she'd said too much. Belladonna's temper was notorious.

"I'll take your life force, too, if you don't hush!" Belladonna threatened, her voice venomous.

The sorceress took a deep breath to regain control, her focus shifting to the bookshelf beside her bed. She spotted the book she was looking for: *Remedies for Curses* by Sylvie Runetoe.

"That's the one," she murmured. Pulling it from the shelf, she slipped a blank piece of parchment between its pages, and with a flick of her fingers, the parchment filled with a remedy—a perfect solution for her plan.

"I'm ready, little one," Belladonna said, scratching Juniper under the chin. The cat purred, her lavender eyes glistening as she tried to win back Belladonna's favor.

"You'll do nothing but look cute, Juni, okay?" Belladonna said, her voice firm. Juniper, looking terrified, nodded and sat still.

Belladonna returned to the living room, the book of remedies in hand. She placed it carefully on the table, then waved her arms, muttering an incantation. A stack of wooden crates transformed into a new chair, which Belladonna immediately sank into with a relieved sigh.

"Well, that's better," she said, flashing Rose a smile. "Apologies for the wait, my dear. I accept your treasures."

Rose smiled and nodded, "I'm glad you like them."

Belladonna's smile turned tight, her eyes glinting with malice. "Oh, I do," she purred, though her grin faltered as she forced the words out. With a wave of her hand, the porcelain teapot floated up, poured Rose a fresh cup of tea, then gently returned to the table. In a second wave of magic, pink-and-white cupcakes appeared, arranged elegantly on a platter.

"Now then," Belladonna said, "I'd like to perform a tea leaf reading to uncover the specifics of your curse. We must know everything to avoid any… accidents."

Rose, eager for answers, nodded. "Thank you. I understand."

Belladonna gestured to the teacup. "You must drink it all, and then I'll take a look at your cup."

Rose, anxious for a remedy, drank her tea in one swift gulp.

"Good…good," Belladonna mumbled under her breath, eyes narrowing. With another flick of her wrist, Rose's empty teacup floated across the table into Belladonna's waiting hand. The sorceress studied the remnants inside, her fingers tapping her chin as she pretended to contemplate.

"Ah, yes. It's clear what your curse is," Belladonna said with a cunning smile.

"What is it, my lady?" Rose asked, leaning forward.

Belladonna pulled the book back out, pretending to flip through it in search of the answer. "Here it is…*The Curse of the Beast*. It's all here: white hair, cobalt blue eyes, and an inability to perform magic. It matches perfectly."

She slid the book over to Rose, letting her see the passage about the curse.

"Now, just sit back, drink your tea, and relax while I gather the ingredients for your cure," Belladonna said, her voice coated with sweetness.

With another wave, she refilled Rose's cup and raced around the room, collecting bottles of strange ingredients. Belladonna bit her lip, stifling her evil cackle. She added each ingredient to a bowl, each one carefully measured.

"How did you manage all this time without magic?" Belladonna asked with a pretend look of concern. "What if pirates had found you?"

Rose hesitated, then answered vaguely, "Oh…I have my ways."

Belladonna gave a sly smile. *How long will your ways last, dear Rose?*

The nymph's eyes scanned the room, taking in the scene with a mix of curiosity and unease. Shelves lined the walls, stacked with bottles of brightly colored liquids that glowed in the dim light, their contents shimmering like liquid jewels. Bundles of dried herbs hung from hooks, their leaves curling and shriveled, filling the air with a pungent, earthy scent. Crates from the spring fair were stacked haphazardly in the corner, a forgotten relic of the past season. The room smelled pleasant, yet strange, as though the scents of both life and decay were interwoven.

Rose's gaze drifted to Berwick, who was curled up on the grandfather clock, his tiny wings twitching as he slept. The clock's brass pendulum ticked quietly, but its steady rhythm did nothing to calm her nerves.

"I wonder why he's so tired," Rose whispered aloud, more to herself than anyone.

Without warning, Belladonna spun around, and in a blink of an eye, she was standing behind Rose, her presence sudden and unsettling. Her long, dark cloak swirled around her like a living shadow. The sorceress's voice, smooth and hypnotic, whispered in Rose's ear.

"Berwick always takes a nap around this time."

Rose's eyes widened in shock. She hadn't said anything aloud, yet the sorceress had heard her thoughts as clearly as if she'd spoken them. Before she could respond, Belladonna was back at her table, swirling a wooden spoon in a large, cracked bowl, her motions deliberate and precise as she mixed the ingredients with an almost feverish intensity.

"I'm ready!" Belladonna announced, her voice ringing like a sweet melody in the otherwise quiet room. The sorceress lifted the bowl, its contents glowing faintly, and placed it on a pedestal in the center of the room, a small but powerful focal point. She pointed at the space directly across from her, her fingers long and graceful.

"Stand here," she commanded, her voice smooth yet insistent.

Rose stood up quickly, her feet moving before her mind had fully caught up with what was happening. She crossed the room, feeling nervous yet excited. Her heart beat faster in her chest.

"Just relax," Belladonna murmured, her tone oddly comforting, "I'll say a few words, and it will be over before you know it."

Rose nodded, but a tight knot of nervous anticipation formed in her stomach. "Okay. I can't wait for this spell to work—"

"Please," Belladonna interrupted, her voice suddenly sharp and commanding. "Just focus on wanting magical powers, my dear."

The air in the room grew heavier, the light dimming as though the very space around them was holding its breath. Rose felt a strange, almost electric energy building. The spell removal was taking longer than she had expected.

"Now be still," Belladonna instructed, her voice low and commanding. "Close your eyes. Remain silent, or the spell won't work."

Rose complied, her body stiff and trembling. Belladonna's voice began chanting in a language that Rose could not understand—words that felt ancient, filled with power.

"Boo, da baba chi. Boo, da baba chi."

A thick green smoke began to rise from the bowl, swirling upward in tight spirals, casting an eerie glow that danced across the walls. It filled the room with a strange metallic scent, making the hairs on the back of Rose's neck stand on end. Belladonna's voice grew louder, more insistent."Bip a dee, Bip a dee, Daaaa Daaaa Daaaa!"

In a heartbeat, Rose felt herself rising from the floor. Her feet lifted an inch, then several, as though some invisible force was pulling her upward. Her dress and hair began to float around her, drifting like water in slow motion.

The green smoke wrapped itself around her legs, then her arms, tightening around her like a constricting serpent. Rose felt a surge of panic, her body unable to move, trapped in the grip of magic that felt both cold and suffocating. The legendary phantom nymph—once free and light as air—was now a prisoner in a web of green smoke.

"Another sweet, innocent victim," Belladonna murmured with an almost gleeful sigh, rubbing her hands together as though savoring a treat.

"What's happening? I can't move!" Rose gasped, her voice full of fear.

Berwick, still perched on the grandfather clock, began to flap his wings frantically. Belladonna's laugh, cruel and mocking, echoed around the room, the sound so jarring that the flames of the nearby candles flickered and extinguished in fright. Mice squealed in the corners and scurried into their holes. The spiders leapt from their webs and scuttled into cracks and crevices. Juniper, still asleep on an overstuffed chair, let out a blood-curdling scream, diving beneath the cushions in terror.

"You are so naive, nymph girl," Belladonna sneered, her eyes glinting with malice. "It was far too easy to lure you here to my cottage."

Desperation surged within Rose, her heart racing. With every ounce of her will, she reached out with her mind, sending a frantic message to her sisters. *Chloe please help me!*

"You'll never get away with this," Rose shouted, in desperation. "My sisters—"

Belladonna's wicked grin widened as she leaned in closer to Rose, her voice venomous. "Your sisters are next!" she hissed. "Once I drain your precious life force, I'll do the same to them."

Belladonna extended her arms, her fingers curled, muttering, "Zeee deee bah… Zeee deee bah!" Her chanting voice rising in power.

A thick, violet smoke began to seep from the bowl, slowly curled into the air like smoke from a dark fire. The room seemed to hold its breath as the mist inched closer to Rose's face. She struggled, but the invisible forces held her in place, her limbs stiff, unable to break free.

"Please help me—someone!" Rose's voice trembled, her desperation cutting through the thick air.

From his perch in the shadows, Berwick's golden eyes sharpened. With a sudden burst of motion, he leapt into the air, his wings unfurling. He darted toward Rose, hovering protectively before her as the violet smoke twisted and clawed toward her. Berwick flapped his wings with fierce intensity, the powerful gusts forcing the sinister mist back toward its source.

Belladonna's crimson-painted lips twisted in rage. "What are you doing, you crazy bird?!" she screeched, her voice cracking like a whip.

The hawk ignored her, his feathers ruffling as he flapped harder. The violet smoke coiled and lashed like a living thing, resisting his efforts, but Berwick pressed on, forcing the magical fumes toward the sorceress's face.

"I command you to stop!" Belladonna roared, her emerald eyes blazing with fury. The smoke now swirled mere inches from her mouth.

"You'll regret this, you stupid bird!" Belladonna's voice dropped to a venomous hiss. With a sharp, twisting gesture of her fingers, she unleashed a spell.

The room erupted into chaos. Teacups, plates, and bottles sprang to life, their glossy surfaces catching the dim light as they shot through the air like missiles. The porcelain and glass hurtled toward Berwick, who darted and twisted. A saucer grazed his wing, a bottle shattered near his talons, but the hawk pressed on, unflinching.

Then, with a resounding crack, a heavy teapot struck him squarely in the chest. Berwick let out a strangled cry of pain as he spiraled to the floor, landing in a heap of feathers. His body lay still for a moment, wings lying awkwardly across the wooden planks.

From the corner of the room, a creaking floorboard signaled Natts's approach. Peering into the chaos, Natts's eyes widened at the sight of flying dishes and swirling smoke. Without hesitation, he flung the door open and stormed inside.

Berwick stirred weakly, his talons scraping against the floor as he tried to rise.

Belladonna sneered, her voice raspy, "you should've stayed down, little bird. Now, you'll join your nymph girlfriend in the afterlife!"

But before she could raise her hands again, Berwick launched himself skyward with a sudden burst of strength. With talons outstretched, he dove straight for her face.

"What are you—! My eyes! My eyes!" Belladonna screamed, staggering backward as Berwick's sharp claws raked across her cheeks. The violet smoke swirled chaotically around her now. As she gasped for breath, Berwick flapped his wings forcing the enchanted mist directly into Belladonna's mouth.

Natts, grabbing a nearby broom, began fanning the smoke toward Belladonna, too. The sorceress's body stiffened as the spell invaded her, a violet glow enveloping her from head to toe. Her screams were swallowed by the shimmering light, which pulsed brighter and brighter until, with a sudden, violent surge, the violet spell vanished into the air.

The emerald smoke holding Rose aloft dissolved instantly, dropping her unconscious body to the floor. The spell's embers flickered briefly in the bowl on the pedestal, before snuffing out entirely and leaving the room eerily silent.

Chapter Fifteen

Rain began to patter against the windows, a slow and quiet rhythm.

Natts lit a candle, the warm glow casting dancing shadows over the room. He turned toward Berwick, who now lay motionless. The hawk's body began to glow faintly, his feathers shimmering and falling away like ash caught in a breeze. Where the bird had lain now stood a boy, his dark curls spilling over his ears. He looked youthful, about twelve years of age. Scars etched across his cheeks and forehead told a story of battles fought.

In a rush, the boy knelt by Rose's side.

"Rose," the boy whispered again, his voice cracking. His hand trembled as he stroked her hair. For a moment, the only sound was the steady tapping of raindrops against the windows. Then, Rose's eyes fluttered open.

"Rose!" Natts yelped, his face lighting up with relief.

The boy hugged Natts, both of them laughing through tears. "We thought you were gone!" he said, his voice trembling with emotion.

Rose's gaze lingered on the boy, her fingers brushing against the scars on his cheek. "I know you," she murmured, her voice soft and full of wonder. "Berwick?"

The scarfaced boy laughed. "I'm glad to be human again, but my name is James LeMer."

Rose's eyes filled with tears, still in disbelief at what happened. Tears filled Rose's eyes as she reached out, pulling both James and Natts into a heartfelt embrace.

"And Belladonna?" Rose wondered.

There was the sudden sound of a squeaky hinge, like a door was slowly opening.

"Shhhh," Natts reached out and stopped everyone from talking. "Did you hear that? There's someone here!"

A black cat slinked across the room, ignoring Natts, James, and Rose.

"It's Juni," James whispered.

"Shhhh," Natts silenced him quickly.

Juni slinked over and sniffed the ashes of Belladonna's remains, then leaped onto the window ledge, exiting the cottage in a flash.

"That was lucky," Natts commented, "you changed into you, so who knows what that cat might be."

"You're right," James noted. "I'm thankful—Belladonna is toast!" James shouted.

Lying on the floor, not far from Rose, was Belladonna. The sorceress lay crumpled on the floor, her once youthful form now a pile of withered ash. Belladonna's reign of terror was over.

"She's dead. Don't worry about her anymore," Natts said,

"Thank you for helping, Natts," James added.

"Of course," Natts said with a bow.

"The old hag had me under a spell as a bird for a year!"

Natts rubbed his chin, adding, "Sorceress dies…spell broken … bird becomes a boy. It all makes sense now!"

Chapter Fifteen

James picked dried flower remains stuck in Rose's hair, then helped her up from the floor. Rose gave James and Natts a heartfelt embrace.

"Now that you're okay," Natts said, eager to share information with her. "I have something here you should read."

The elf handed Rose *The Fairy Tale Times*, showing her an article.

> "Twig Flickerthorn reports in *The Fairy Tale Times*: A Special Report: A map of the Phantom's Lair was won by Wilhelm's pirates after an explosion behind Phaedon's Fancy Dancy Delights. And Foghorn Shmee reports, "The Phantom Nymph has been spotted in Elflin. McSly's has not done the Nymph Beast in!" More on page 8.

Rose paced the floor, biting her nails.

"What can I do to help?" James asked Natts.

"Silvia Obsidian is notoriously wicked."

"Natts!" She cut him off, "We need to do something before my family is in the obituary!"

"Right." The elf scratched his head, thinking of a plan.

James flexed his arms and squatted, feeling his human form again. "Whatever plan you think of Natts, I'm in!"

"I've got it!" Natts blurted out, "We'll make Booby traps!"

"Booby traps?" Rose questioned the idea.

"I like it!" James said. "When do we start?"

Natts rubbed his hands together like some ideas were already brewing in his head.

Chapter Sixteen

The Booby Traps

Athough the captain's quarters on the Devil's Dagger was swanky, the smell of salty sea water and stale tobacco was soaked into the walls, the tables, the floor, and even the chairs. Candelabras dripped with wax, as gold-leaf carvings gleamed in their flickering light. But beneath the surface, the cabin felt as treacherous as its captain. Every groan of the wooden floor sounded like a warning—tread lightly.

"Ahh—success! I knew my Silvia wouldn't disappoint me," Wolfgang praised his fairy assistant. She looked pretty but mischievous in her dark tricorn hat and embellished black jacket. Sid and Dean were next to her. They all had bits of cream pie still on them. "Did you dispose of the stinky boy and his odious monkey?"

Waving the rolled-up map, Sid announced, "We got the map, Captain," Dean gave his buddy a wink of reassurance that everything would be fine.

"Captain Wilhelm," Dean added, " here… over here—we got it...we got it!" Sid quickly unraveled the sticky, burnt, and mutilated parchment onto the captain's desk, hoping to distract Wolfgang's mind about the stinky boy and the obnoxious monkey question.

Wolfgang inspected the new map excitedly, but within seconds, his face morphed into a snarl. "This map is a disaster!" Scratching the scruff on his chin in deep thought, he cackled in a slimy kind of way, "Silvia! I need you to resurrect this piece of garbage of a map." The two boys jumped back nervously, observing the pirate fairy. They wondered if she was powerful enough to fix it.

She gave the boys a smirk and winked at Wolfgang, confirming confidently. "Yes, sir.... No problem."

"My dear Silvia, please show these sea rovers how it's done!" But suddenly, Wolfgang's face morphed into an evil glare towards Silvia, Sid, then Dean. He made a gesture with his hand, indicating that she and the boy's lives were in jeopardy, *if* they didn't improve the map. Wolfgang adjusted his jacket with a greasy smile, "And when I return, it better be rectified." The captain growled before leaving the three of them to complete the map resurrection mission, slamming the door behind him. Silvia rolled her eyes, her sharp gaze flicking towards the captain before muttering,

"Fixing his mess again. That's all I ever do." The fairy pushed her onyx hair behind her ears and shook her arms like she was trying to relax. After cracking her knuckles, she whispered a spell. As the glowing map shifted and re-

formed, her tricorn hat cast a shadow over her face, hiding a faint smirk. Within seconds, a light flashed over the dilapidated map. Sid, Dean, and Silvia leaned forward and inspected the results.

"I think it looks like—"

The pirate fairy looked like she wanted to strangle Dean.

"Put a lid on it, Dean, before she zaps us into oblivion," Sid whispered.

She held her hands out again, waving them across the map. A string of electric light swirled on top, transforming the map's surface.

"Now it looks like—"

Quickly covering Dean's mouth with his hand, Sid smiled. "Ahhhhh! I think you got it this time."

When Wolfgang returned, Silva, Sid, and Dean felt like the problem was solved and were eating cakes to celebrate their map recovery mission. The captain could sense that the project was successful.

"*And*?" Wolfgang snarled as he entered the cabin, followed by a burly pirate, "How is the map?"

"I repaired it, Sir," Silvia assured.

Mongo stood calmly next to the captain, waiting for orders. The captain hovered over the new and improved parchment, judging its clarity.

"I suppose it will do," Wolfgang grumbled. He stood up and pointed at Mongo, barking out a plan, "The crew must stay here on the Devil's dagger. I will send these idiots into Everwood to find the entrance first. Silvia will get me when they are close. That will be all Mongo."

In the center of the cabin, on a large table, candelabras with white candles, cups of fruit juice, and trays of cakes were elegantly displayed. The two boys were stuffing their mouths full and studying the new and improved burnt map in detail, looking for the ideal path to find the 'secret entrance.' Dramatic shadows from lit candles danced on the walls like monsters as Wolfgang paced the floor, looking ready to have a temper tantrum. Just then, his face contorted before he barked,

"Did you figure out where you're going yet, you imbeciles?"

"We'll find the nymph for ya, Captain, don't worry. We'll slice her in two!" Sid gestured a slicing motion with his arm.

"Silence!" Wolfgang grabbed Sid by his collar and pulled him so close their noses touched. Sid could smell Wolfgang's stinky breath and grimaced. "Just tell me when you find the secret entrance, you idiot," He commanded with bulging eyes.

Sid gulped, hoping the captain didn't lose his temper and accidentally 'do him in.'

"I want the nymph alive! Do you hear me!" The captain pulled out a small knife from his boot and stabbed the tabletop. The dagger sank into the wood like butter. "Now take the map and find the entrance—Now!"

"Yes, Captain!" Sid answered. His whole body shook as he rolled up the map like his life depended on it, then waved to Dean and Silvia to follow.

"Silvia!"

"Yes, Captain!"

"Come get me when you find the entrance!"

"Yes, sir," Silvia said, before they all vanished out the door.

When they started their quest for the phantom nymph, it was nightfall. Although it was a half moon, Silvia cast a spell and created a sparkling light torch to guide them.

"It's safer than fire and just as effective."

Neither Sid nor Dean questioned her.

As Silvia held the oversized torch, they followed the map in detail, walking for several hours. When Dean stepped on a branch, the sound of the snapping wood woke bats. Hundreds scattered out of some trees. Dean shrieked, but Sid put his hand across his mouth him, before he could make another sound.

"Be quiet, you idiot! We don't want anyone to hear us!"

Thankfully, Silvia, Dean, and Sid were all dressed in camouflage costumes made of leaves, flowers, and small branches. When they sat together, they looked like a large bush.

"Now where...? What's the map say?" Dean whispered. "I can't see anything without Silvia's magic torch."

"Just relax!" Sid grunted, "Silvia… come closer!"

The map was now being held by all three of them in a huddle. The secretly sabotaged map Rose had redrawn was destined to make the scoundrel pirates fail unless fate was on their side.

"This is the way," Sid pointed at a spot on the map, slapping Dean on the head just because he could.

"I say we split up and look for this broken tree with the slashes on our own," Dean suggested, not wanting to be slapped again.

"I agree," Silvia nodded angrily. The fairy created two more magic torches. She handed one to Sid and the other to Dean.

"Here, this will help."

With hats and cloaks made of weeds, the two pirates and a fairy pushed through the ferns with their magic torches.

But little did the pirates know. They were being watched.

High above in the trees, Natts, James, and Rose had set the booby traps and were waiting for pirates to invade.

Like the sweet sound of a bird, Natts finally made the call to James and Rose, who were waiting in the distance for his signal before making their move in the booby trap plan. The sweet melody echoed through Everwood. After a few minutes of silence, Natts heard a sweet melody back, just like the one he had made.

"Did you hear that?" Sid heard the melodic bird call signal.

"What?" Dean asked, who was only several yards away.

"That sound," Sid said suspiciously, "It was…too pretty and sweet."

"Forget about it," Dean said, continuing to investigate the brush. I see something! I found the broken tree with the markings."

"Really," Sid walked over to confirm.

There it was. Dean found the broken tree with three immense grooves in it. They looked like someone put them there for a reason, and they did. Natts looked down from the trees, happy that the first booby trap was going as planned.

"You found it! Okay then…we're close."

Sid whistled for Silvia to join them.

The elf suddenly felt something on his face, like he'd walked into a spider web. It was a long platinum hair dangling from a branch over his head, glimmering in the moonlight.

"Look what I found," After plucking it from the branch, he held the white sparkling hair out for Sid and Dean to see. "It was hanging on a branch like the nymph had just been there," Silvia said with excitement like they could possibly find her too.

"Wow," Dean said softly, impressed by Silvia's find.

"She's a powerful beast. There is probably magic in that hair. Be careful," Dean remarked.

Natts whistled a sweet melody again twice, signaling that the booby trap was underway. Sid, Dean, and Silvia were convinced now that they were close to the entrance, if not possibly the nymph beast herself. The three pirates continued studying the map with their sparkling magic torches.

"Okay now," Sid rubbed his itchy nose with his dirty hand, wiping snot dribbling out his nostrils with his sleeve. "It says here that we walk five paces west of the broken tree with markings, then ten north."

Several bats flew out of a surrounding tree, making them all jump, "AH!" Sid fell to the ground. "That scared the bah-gee-beez out of me!"

"Come on now, let's go," Dean pulled Sid up, suddenly taking charge."We have no time to waste. It's almost morning."

The three walked five paces west of the broken tree with markings, then ten north.

"Here is a worn path. It's obviously the way to go," Dean pointed out.

There was a distinct path that looked like it had been walked down for years. Raspberry bushes were on both sides of its entrance.

"I agree," Sid confirmed. "Raspberries are the nymph's favorite. This has to be it." Sid punched Dean in the shoulder. "Silvia, its time to get the captain."

"Right," The fairy pirate agreed. With the flick of her wrist, a funnel of leaves and debris swirled into a funnel around her, and she was gone.

As the camouflaged scoundrels waited, they observed the beauty of the moonlight reflecting off dew-covered leaves like sparkling crystals. Everwood was still damp from the rain. The death of a powerful sorceress like Belladonna had affected the forest, bringing about a deluge like the cleansing of a dark force. Numerous small animals gathered to wonder at the pirate's funny disguises. But as Sid and Dean waited, they noticed something through the ferns. Peeking through the brush was the face of a small man.

"Who are you?" Sid asked.

"I'm a goblin hunter! Who are you?"

A man no bigger than a child, clad in shiny armor and with weapons strapped to his back, crawled out of the brush. He was holding a small dagger in defense.

"We are looking for a pond," Sid said. "Supposedly, it's not far from here."

"I see," the small man said, putting his dagger away. "I'm looking for goblins…nasty fellows." He adjusted the armor strapped to his back, then added, "I'm Gork. The King of Greenwood has commissioned me to rid the forest of goblins."

"Yes, nasty little things," Sid commented, "good luck with that."

"You're searching for a pond?" Gork asked.

"Yes," Sid confirmed. "The Shallows."

Gork made a funny face. "Well, I could swear on me mudders' grave that you be searching down dee wrong path for such thing. There is no pond in dees parts, I'm afraid."

"Really?"Dean commented, feeling stupid.

"I've lived here all my life— there be no pond!"

Sid and Dean looked at each other, confused. A high-pitched shriek echoed through the trees in the distance. The sound was terrifying. The goblin hunter pulled out his dagger again.

"This is goblin country, my friend— a known goblin hideout." Gork held up his dagger in the air, then said, "I'm off to get the goblins—Good luck finding your pond!" Taking off in a flash, Gork disappeared into the shadows.

After a few minutes passed, leaves and debris swirled into a funnel, and two silhouettes of figures appeared out of the middle of it.

"Captain, Sir," Dean bowed, "how are you, Cap?"

Impatient, childish, rude, and full of self-pity, a usual, was captain Wolfgang. "Where is the entrance, you blubbering idiot?" He barked. Silvia was by his side, arms crossed.

Sid wanted to be rewarded for something, so he said, "Look what I found, Captain!" He held out the platinum hair for Wolfgang to see.

"A white hair?" Wolfgang smiled but was more eager to find the entrance than be impressed by Sid's showing him the hair.

"Yes, Captain—a platinum hair!"

"Well then, Sid," Wolfgang said, drawing his pistol as if he was ready to shoot someone —just for being stupid. "If you are so smart, where do we go next, Smartypants? Where might we meet the owner of this hair?" Dean and Silvia sniggered joyfully, knowing Sid might be punished for being a know-it-all. "We are all following you!" Wolfgang said sarcastically.

Sid and Dean decided that Gork, the goblin hunter, was unaware of the secret pond and that they should stick to the plan of following the burnt map. After all, it was a hidden entrance, so naturally, he would never know of it.

"I'm sure this is it, Captain," Sid said, waving to everyone to follow.

Natts was sitting up in the tree, patiently watching. He had a smile on his face like he knew something they didn't.

"Are you sure?" The Captain asked again.

"This is it, Captain. I'm sure. This is it! This is it!" The markings on the tree, the platinum hair, and the raspberry bushes were enough evidence to prove to Sid that this was it. Sid puffed out his chest, a smug grin on his face. "This is it, Captain. I'm sure of it."

They trailed behind him down the narrow, overgrown path, the dense jungle closing in on all sides.

But then the earth gave way beneath their feet.

"Sid!" Dean shouted, his voice laced with panic. "We're sinking!"

"It's *quicksand*!" Sid screamed, thrashing wildly as the ground swallowed him. His once-confident demeanor dissolved into terror.

Silvia was already waist-deep, her magic torch hissing as it was extinguished in the muck. She clawed at the air, her eyes wide with fear.

Wolfgang snarled, grabbing at vines that snapped in his grasp. "Why do I *always* trust fools?" he bellowed, his voice shaking with rage and desperation.

High above, hidden among the trees, Natts watched the chaos unfold. A sinister grin spread across his face as he savored his victory. The trap had worked perfectly, and his enemies were helpless, sinking into their doom.

The jungle seemed to close in tighter, the echoes of their screams swallowed by the silence of the night.

The next morning at the Castle of Winkfield, Captain Shu'gar sat at the head of a long oak table in his lavish dining room. With one hand, he scratched behind Krusty's ears, and with the other, he was eating Krusty Puffs, his cereal that bore his beloved pug's likeness on its logo. Just as he was about to take in another mouthful, a sharp knock echoed through the room.

"Enter!" Shu'gar called, his voice deep.

The heavy door creaked open to reveal Bulldog, his loyal first mate. The burly man stepped in and bowed deeply, his polished boots gleaming from the sunlight streaming through the stained-glass windows.

"Ah, Bulldog," Shu'gar said, folding his newspaper. "What news do you bring me this fine morning?"

"Good morning, Captain," Bulldog said gruffly. "Basher and Torch have returned from Everwood. Their mission was a success, and they have...a surprise for you."

"A surprise, you say?" Shu'gar arched an intrigued brow, setting his spoon down with a clink. "I do love surprises. Send them in at once!"

Bulldog vanished as quickly as he'd appeared. Shu'gar leaned back in his chair, stroking his beard. *A surprise.* His mind raced with possibilities. "Perhaps they finally got their hands on Wolfgang's map," he muttered to himself, eyes gleaming. "Yes, the map! With it, I'll find my sweet Rose, and she and I will rule Winkfield Castle together."

He rubbed his hands together, a grin spreading across his face. "That would be a marvelous surprise indeed."

Before he could dream about it further, the door swung open again. Basher and Torch strode in, dragging someone between them.

"Captain!" Basher announced proudly. "Look what we found!"

Between them stood a slender figure draped in a long olive cloak. Strands of platinum hair spilled out from beneath the hood, shimmering in the light.

"Is it... really her?" Shu'gar whispered, his voice barely audible. He rose from his chair, his legs unsteady as his heart raced. Could it truly be Rose?

"It's the phantom, Captain!" Basher boomed. "We tracked Wolfgang's crew to Everwood, but then they vanished. When we searched the area, we found *her*—unconscious."

Torch held up a rope tied around the girl's wrists. "She matches the description from the *Fairy Tale Times*, Captain."

Shu'gar's breath hitched. "I can't believe it," he said, his voice trembling with delight. He bounded forward, hugging Basher and Torch with uncharacteristic enthusiasm.

The girl stood silent, her hooded face turned downward. Shu'gar stepped closer, unable to resist her aura of mystery. Her scent was intoxicating, floral and sweet. Every detail of her cloak whispered elegance. It was as though time had rewound to the moment he first saw her at The Salty Parrot Tavern.

"Untie her," Shu'gar commanded, his voice softer now. "And bring refreshments!"

Bulldog reappeared with a tray with bread, cheese, and fruit. He poured drinks into two goblets, glancing at Shu'gar for approval.

"Should I fetch the potion, Captain?" Bulldog murmured.

Shu'gar hesitated, his gaze locked on the girl. Then, reluctantly, he nodded. "Yes. We can't take any chances."

Bulldog slipped a vial of shimmering liquid from his pocket. He tipped a few drops into one of the goblets, then placed it before the cloaked girl.

"My dear, you must be thirsty," Shu'gar said, gesturing to the table. "Please, sit."

"May I sit next to you?" she asked, her voice soft and melodic.

Shu'gar's heart fluttered. "Of course, my dear. Anything for you."

He dismissed the others with a wave, leaving the two of them alone. As sunlight spilled across the table, the girl reached for a piece of bread, but an apple rolled from the platter and fell to the floor.

"Oh," she said sweetly, "could you get that for me?"

Shu'gar laughed. "You don't need to eat one from the floor. Have another."

"But it was so perfectly red," she insisted, her voice honeyed and persuasive.

With a chuckle, Shu'gar bent to retrieve the apple. When he returned, she thanked him, taking a delicate sip from her goblet. Shu'gar raised his own, drinking deeply as well.

The girl reached up and, with deliberate slowness, pushed back her hood.

Shu'gar's smile froze. His goblet slipped from his fingers, clattering onto the table.

It wasn't Rose.

The face staring back at him was grotesque—warty, wrinkled, and framed by platinum hair. Her yellowed teeth gleamed as she grinned wickedly.

"Pucker up, big boy!" the woman cackled.

"Ophelia Dred?" Shu'gar gasped.

Before he could react, his knees buckled. His heart fluttered—not with fear, but with uncontrollable affection. A dopey grin spread across his face as he stumbled toward her.

"Ophelia," he whispered dreamily, "you're...you're perfect."

Somehow, the potion had ended up in *his* goblet.

"Now, that's what I call a surprise!" Ophelia said, planting a kiss on Shu'gar's lips.

Krusty growled from his perch on the table.

When Bulldog returned, he saw the catastrophe and ordered Ophelia Dred to return to Everwood and never come back.

"But where did my cootchie-cootchie-coo sweetie-pie go?" Shu'gar asked like a love-struck fool.

"Captain, Sir," Bulldog said, "you've been booby-trapped!"

Chapter Seventeen

Tye Finds His Eye

The Fairy Tale Times: A Special Report: "Well-known Lord of the Krusty Puff Cereal empire Captain Shu'gar is smitten with a Hag." Luna Bellpepper of the Lavender Fields reports: It sounds unbelievable, but 600-year-old Ophelia Dred, a hideously wrinkled sorceress, has somehow captured Captain Shu'gar's undying love. They were witnessed smooching in the lavender fields by Luna at two minutes before noon. An unidentified source disclosed that Love Potion #9 was to blame." Continued on page 3.

The rhythmic patter of rain against the windowpane woke Rose abruptly. Blinking sleep from her eyes, she stared at the jagged cracks snaking through the ceiling, their web-like patterns illuminated faintly by the gray morning light. Despite everything, she felt fortunate.

"Belladonna's dead. Wolfgang and his crew, swallowed by quicksand. And McSly?" Rose thought with a smirk. "He thinks I perished at sea posing as a sea monster in disguise. I suppose the danger's over now."

Shifting under the heavy, patchwork quilt, she turned her gaze to the open bedroom door. Beyond it, Belladonna's cottage living room was bathed in the dim glow of a dying fire. James lay sprawled across a lumpy couch, his arms dangling over the edges as he snored like a hibernating bear. Across from him, Natts was curled into a tight ball in a rickety armchair, a pillow pressed firmly over his head. Neither seemed likely to wake even if the cottage itself crumbled around them.

"I'll do the same," Rose murmured, sinking back into the warm cocoon of blankets.

But just as her eyelids fluttered closed, a foul stench invaded her senses, yanking her back to wakefulness. She sat upright, choking on the putrid air.

Standing on her chest was a small, wiry figure with sickly green skin and glowing orange eyes, his sharp little nose looked like a bird's beak. The goblin's floppy, puppy-like ears twitched as he puffed on a stubby cigar, its smoke curling into spirals above her head. His boots, patched and worn, left smudges of dirt on the quilt as he squinted down at her, his eyes radiating confusion.

"You're not Belladonna!" he squeaked, his raspy voice like nails scraping stone.

Rose reacted instinctively, shoving the goblin off her chest. He tumbled to the floor in an undignified heap, his cigar flying from his mouth.

With surprising agility, the goblin scrambled back up, leaping onto the bed. This time, he leaned in so close that Rose could count the faint scars crisscrossing his crooked nose.

"Aren't you scared of me?" he demanded, his fiery orange eyes narrowing.

Rose tilted her head, unbothered. "No, not really."

The goblin gawked at her, throwing his tiny hands into the air in exasperation. "What?! I give up!" he exclaimed, stomping his feet on the mattress.

"What do you mean… you give up?" Rose asked, raising an eyebrow.

The goblin folded his arms, the stub of his cigar now tucked behind one pointed ear. "I give up trying to break this curse! I'll never scare anyone—not even you!"

"A curse, you say? That sounds… unfortunate."

The goblin scowled. "Tye and I came here hoping Belladonna could fix us, but of course, she's gone! Just our luck."

A second goblin was rifling through rows of dusty jars on a nearby shelf. This one was even smaller, with electric-green eyes, a gold hoop earring, and an eye patch that lent him a roguish air. The first goblin puffed up his chest dramatically. "Name's Bognok, but everyone calls me

Booger."He jabbed a thumb toward his companion. "That's Tye."

Tye turned briefly to wave, then resumed inspecting the jars, muttering under his breath.

"I'm Rose," she offered.

Booger sighed heavily. "You see, we've been cursed. Goblins are supposed to be mean—terrifying even—but we're not. We're…repulsively kind." He said the last words as if they burned his tongue.

"How dreadful," Rose said, trying to stifle a smile.

Booger's orange eyes gleamed with self-pity. "It gets worse. Belladonna swindled us. We gave her all our gold, and when that wasn't enough, we sold her our body parts!"

Rose blinked in disbelief. "Your…body parts?"

Booger lifted his hand. "Yep. I lost two fingers. Tye gave her his eye. And in return? She gave me cigars and this ridiculous eye patch for him. She said it would make us meaner, but no! We're still disgustingly sweet!"

Tye, overhearing, plucked a wilting bouquet of dried flowers from a vase. Shuffling shyly toward Rose, he presented them with both hands. "For the pretty lady," he mumbled, his green skin blushing pink.

Rose accepted the flowers, her smile widening. "Thank you, Tye. That's very sweet."

"Sweet! Exactly!" Booger groaned, throwing his hands up. "We're hopeless!"

Tye gasped suddenly, pointing at a jar labeled *Goblin Eyes*. Inside, pale white orbs floated in liquid, each dotted with an colorful iris's.

"There it is!" Tye cried, his finger trembling. "That's my eye!"

Booger squinted at the jar, then patted Tye's back. "Maybe when Belladonna comes back, she can put it in for you."

Rose hesitated before breaking the news. "Booger… Tye… Belladonna isn't coming back. She's dead."

Both goblins froze. Booger's face twisted in disbelief. "Dead?"

"Yes. My friends and I found her last night. It looked like natural causes."

The goblins erupted into chaos, stomping, shouting, and banging the walls. Rose darted to the door, shutting it gently to avoid waking James and Natts.

"Booger! Tye! Please, calm down! Look, you can take anything you want from this room. Just stop yelling!"

The goblins paused, their fury replaced with glee.

"Anything?" Booger asked, his wide grin revealing crooked, yellow teeth.

"Anything," Rose confirmed, sinking back onto the bed.

"What a morning," she muttered, shaking her head as the goblins cackled like mischievous children.

"Now, we'll never break this curse!" Booger mumbled. "We'll have to start all over again!"

"Yeah!" Tye banged the walls, chiming in, "All over again! The evil sorceress was a phony anyway!" Booger affirmed. And Tye chimed in, "She was never going to fix us."

"That's right," Booger threw his arms in the air in agreement.

"I can't believe we all fell for her lies," the nymph whispered. "We are such idiots."

As the two goblins rummaged through Belladonna's things like two kids in a candy store, Rose sat on the bed and stared at the jars of fermenting spiders, pig gizzards, mouse eyeballs, and bat wings floating in brightly colored liquids. They were displayed very deceivingly with the little bows on each bottle and jar, plus neatly lined up on shelves like decorations. However, something familiar caught Rose's eye. It was her sack, lying like a puddle of cream-colored cloth on the floor. Sliding off the bed, she picked it up excitedly. Feeling something inside, she immediately reached in to see what it was.

"My gold necklace!"

She held it out and noted it still had her emergency vile of sparkling elf dust and lucky gold button. "I guess you're still meant for me."

As she slipped it over her head, a strange warmth wrapped around her heart. Unsure about the feeling and what it meant, she knew that the gold necklace with its two lucky gems had some significance in her life.

"My good luck charms, I suppose."

The goblins had finished collecting their treasures.

"Thank you, Miss," Booger said, picking his nose again. Feeling foolish for not asking anything about the generous stranger, he asked, "What is your name again, Miss?"

"Rose," she said with a smile. The nymph couldn't believe they didn't question her.

Booger added, "That's a pretty name, my lady."

"I suppose they never read The Fairy Tale Times," She thought, as she observed the blushing cheeked goblin.

"Tye and I have what we want, Miss Rose." They both picked out various goodies from compartments around the room.

"I'm glad," the nymph said, smiling. "Where are you two going now?"

They whispered back and forth for a considerable amount of time before they decided.

"We're going home," Booger said, "Tye and I are tired of chasing sorceresses to break our evil curse."

The nymph could relate to this decision. She was feeling the same way.

"And where's home, my friends," she asked curiously. "That's a secret! We heard there was a goblin hunter in

Everwood. We're trying to stay on the down-low, if you know what I mean."

Booger gave Rose a cheeky smile before nudging Tye that it was time to go.

The two goblins climbed onto the window sill in Belladonna's room, their entry and exit point. They held up their bags of goodies and blew a kiss goodbye to the platinum-haired beauty, before jumping out the window and disappearing into Everwood.

After confirming that James and Natts were still unconscious, she crawled back under the warm and cozy quilt and closed her eyes. As she lay there listening to the rain and thinking of the two goblins, she was glad she wasn't alone with her curse problem.

"Maybe that's what I should do. They're right. I need to stop chasing sorcerers and embrace who I am." Rose thought for a moment." Stop hating myself for everything I'm not and start loving myself for everything —I am."

The nymph fell asleep again to the rhythmic tapping of rain. Eventually, after an hour or so of blissful sleep, she awoke again to banging in the other room. "James? Natts, is that you?" she mumbled. She got up and entered the living room, where Natts and James had been sleeping. A pot of tea, a cup, and a tart were on the dining table like they were meant for her. After pouring herself tea and devouring the pastry, she noticed James on the porch. Rain was pouring down off the roof as he chopped wood. Within seconds, the front door banged open, and he and Natts hurried in.

"Hey!" James smiled at the sight of her, then dumped the chopped wood he was carrying next to the fireplace.

"Good morning, pretty lady," Natts said sweetly, entering behind James with wood in his arms.

James tossed a log into the fire in the fireplace, causing sparks of ash to jump into the air.

"Are you cold?" he asked sweetly towards Rose.

"I am a little." She held up the cup of hot tea, warming her hands.

"Thank you for the pastry, Natts! I was starving."

He nodded and smiled, "Of course."

Scanning the titles of books on Belledonna's bookcase: How to Fly, Cauldron's Make Better Soups, Flower Magic is Where it's at, Magic Recipes Today, Rose said, "If only I looked at some of her books before I agreed to her sorcery."

James found some quilts in a closet.

Reentering the room with a large quilt, he wrapped it around Rose's shoulders as she read the book spines on the shelves."Well, it's too late now," he said, "she's ashes. You should be proud of yourself, Rose. You saved countless lives, not to mention— mine. I think you're a hero."

Rose looked over at James, making a funny face. "You're joking, right?"

"No, I mean it." James poured himself a cup of tea and then moved a chair close to Natts next to the fire. They both stared at Rose, mesmerized by her beauty. With messy hair, puffy eyes from lack of sleep, and an oversized quilt wrapped around her, she still looked like a deity, even though she was powerless.

"I'm not the hero!" Rose insisted, "Clearly, you and Natts are!"

"Oh no!" James shook his head. "I did nothing. But as a hawk, I fanned a little wind on the spell and scratched her eyeballs until she screamed in pain, but I don't regret my actions. I mean, hawks do that sort of thing, usually."

The elf agreed. "The wicked sorceress got what was coming to her."

James got up and slid a chair close to the fire for Rose to sit on.

"Here, sit down and get warm."

As she sank into the cushions and stared into the burning flame, Rose wondered, "Do you think I should be worried?"

"About what?" James asked.

"Do you think she had an evil boyfriend that would want revenge on me?"

"I seriously doubt it," James laughed.

Rose laughed, too. "I'm used to being blamed for everything. That's all."

"You've done nothing wrong. I'm the one who technically fanned the smoke in her face."

Natts added, "I fanned smoke at her too."

"See... Natts is a villain, just like me. I wouldn't worry."

Rose laughed. "Talking about funny. I should tell you that we had visitors this morning."

The flames of the fire sputtered and popped like it could tell there was an energy in the room. Natts held some magic dust in his hands, and, in seconds, he created some mud cakes, an elf's version of a chocolate cupcake.

"Early this morning, these two goblins showed up for an appointment with Belladonna."

"What?"James said, "Why didn't you wake us up? I'm glad you're alright!" James spouted out, worried about Rose.

"I'm fine! They had an appointment to get their evil curse of 'niceness' removed."

James and Natts started laughing at the ridiculousness of the curse.

But as Rose laughed too, a thread of light appeared, spiraling around Rose. James and Natts were too busy rolling on the ground laughing even to notice. After a few seconds, the light merged into her body like a charm or spell had taken place.

"Did you see that light thing spiraling around me?"

"What? What light thing?" James asked, scratching his butt, "I'm still trying to figure out how niceness could be horrid?"

Natts laughed in a high-pitched, squeaky voice that sounded frightening, then popped a piece of mud cake into his mouth.

"Whatever it was, it was only meant for you, Miss Nymph, because I didn't see anything," Natts mumbled with a wink.

The room seemed brighter to Rose. She wasn't sure if she was crazy, but everything looked, felt, and seemed different—but better. Natts got up and stood between the two of them, wrapping his arms around them both.

"I love you guys," he announced with a squeeze.

Rose answered back immediately, "I love you too, Natts!"

"Yeah, buddy," James added, "you're the master of booby traps!"

Rose was thinking about everything, feeling happy to be alive, feeling lucky to have met James and Natts, and how they wanted to protect her.

Rose added, "you know, this cottage is the perfect place for you to live."

"Yes…it is!"James smiled.

"I agree," Natts said, "but I better stay here too. You're too young to be on your own, and besides, you'll never survive without a magical being to protect you."

"I suppose you're right." James agreed.

"I need to go home," Rose mumbled quietly, staring at the flames in the fire and thinking about her sisters and how they knew nothing.

"Of course," James agreed.

"Let's go then!" Natts chimed in. Using a pinch of elf dust, he waved his hand and tossed the crystal dust over the embers, extinguishing them safely before they took off for the shallows.

When they arrived, the three sisters were eating breakfast at their favorite table by the pond. After Rose introduced Natts and James, they did their best to tell their stories to Chloe, Reeva, and Zoe.

Natts explained the Krusty Puff cereal taste test and map-burning drama on the Revenge, before turning the sister's attention to James.

He did his best to explain how he used to be a hawk named Berwick because he was under a spell by the evil Belladonna. He decided to follow Rose, who eventually helped him return to a mortal. Once he flapped Belladonna's spell right back at her, it led to her demise.

"I'm glad the phony fixer got what she deserved—an early death due to evil doings." Chloe noted, "It's time for great things to happen for our Rose. She deserves happiness!"

Rose returned from her treehouse wearing a fresh, elegant dress.

James rose from his seat and pulled out a chair for her at the table by the pond, like any gentleman would.

"Thank you," Rose said, her smile as radiant as the sunlight filtering through the trees.

“I like your dress,” James remarked.

“Thank you again. It was a gift from Chloe.”

“I’m shocked! Chloe did something thoughtful?” Zoe said, unbelieving.

“She gave me several dresses,” Rose commented, beaming.

“It does seem shocking, doesn’t it,” Chloe remarked, agreeing with Zoe in a snarky tone. “But it’s you that cares about our sister Rose, dear Zoe. I went shopping in your closet— Ha!”

Laughter erupted around the table—everyone except Zoe, of course. She crossed her arms and narrowed her eyes. "Now that you mention it, that dress *does* look familiar.”

Reeva, Zoe, and Chloe continued interviewing James and Natts, laughing aloud as they listened to their stories.

“I stole the chocolate pie, shimmied under the man’s legs, and took off like a jackrabbit!” James admitted.“The joke was ultimately on me, I suppose.”

“What do you mean?” Zoe asked.

"I ran with my friends into Everwood forest to hide, and I ended up getting zapped by the sorceress by accident. I thought I was doomed. I've been trying to figure a way out for..for—"

Chloe, always quick to defuse tension, waved her hand dramatically. "Little did you know," she chimed in with a sly smile, "that years later, a once-troubled orphan would be transformed into a hawk and then un-spelled by none other than an *exquisite nymph*!" She gestured toward her sister.

"Thank you, Rose," he said, his voice barely above a whisper, but sincere.

Rose's cheeks flushed pink, as she smiled shyly, brushing a loose strand of hair behind her ear. "I'm just glad I could help," she murmured.

As the moment passed, Zoe's mind began to churn. Her eyes sparkled with mischief as she leaned back in her chair, thinking of something for James and his new guardian, Natts, to worry about."As much as I'd like to be pleased for you in your new home, Belladonna was an evil sorceress. I have no doubt there are some dangerous things in that cottage. I'd be careful."

"Thank you, Zoe, for your ever-cheerful words of doom!" Chloe quipped, rolling her eyes.

The group burst into laughter, the tension lightened for a moment.

Rose chimed in, "Don't worry, Zoe. I'll be helping to clean out Belladonna's colorful collection of poisons tomorrow morning. If there's anything dangerous, Natts will take care of it." She turned toward Natts and James, offering a warm smile. "I'll see you both tomorrow."

Natts stepped forward, a sly smile on his lips. With a swift flick of his hand, the elf tossed a handful of shimmering elf dust into the air. It swirled and sparkled, catching the light before enveloping him and James in a magical glow.

"Until tomorrow," Natts said, his voice fading as the light grew brighter. In a blink, they vanished, leaving only the faint shimmer of dust floating down to the ground like tiny stars.

Rose watched the empty spot where they had stood, a thoughtful expression on her face. "They'll need more than elf dust if Belladonna's magic is in that cottage," she murmured.

Chloe gave an exaggerated shrug, linking arms with Zoe. "Oh, relax. They have Natts's magic, they'll be fine. Probably."

Zoe narrowed her eyes. "*Probably* isn't exactly comforting."

The sisters walked off, their chatter fading into the afternoon, leaving the sunlit pond once more.

Chapter Eighteen

Born with a Gift

Now that Belladonna was gone, the cottage was the perfect refuge for James. He was overjoyed to be human again, a feeling that still felt fresh and new, despite having spent a year in the magical haze of her twisted enchantment. The cottage was cozy now and far more welcoming, than the cold and imposing presents of Belladonna's lair. But at only thirteen, James still needed a guardian. Thankfully, Natts, his unpredictable but fiercely loyal caretaker, had stepped up to the task, agreeing to look after him until he graduated in five years.

Standing in front of an old, cracked mirror, James fought with his unruly, wavy hair, tugging at the strands that seemed to have a mind of their own. He squinted at his reflection, trying to tame the wild mess of curls. "I suppose I don't look too ridiculous," he muttered under his breath.

"Oh, yes, you do," Natts replied without missing a beat, his voice sparked with humor. He was busy piling every-

1000 PROPHECIES TO KEEP YOUR EYE ON
THE LOST WONDERS OF EPIC MAGIC
MADAME LENORA
SNAKE EYES

thing he'd found of Belladonna's—bottles, scrolls, and strange trinkets—into a large crate, his hands moving quickly.

James shot Natts a glare before entering the kitchen, where his hair still stuck out at odd angles. The soft glow of morning sunlight filtered through the windows, casting a warm, golden hue on the room's old wooden beams and the mismatched furniture. Despite the cottage's cluttered state, it had an undeniable charm.

"How does the new owner of Belladonna's like his eggs this morning?" Natts asked, looking up with a sly grin, placing a plate of scrambled eggs and crispy bacon in front of him.

"Uh… scrambled—like my hair," James joked, feeling a nervous yet excited.

"Good! Because I already made them that way." Natts nodded approvingly.

James glanced at the plate and then back up at Natts. "I'm impressed. You managed to make them edible instead of deliciously burnt."

"Thank you, Mr. Smarty-pants," Natts said, rolling his eyes with a smile before sitting down to eat his own plate.

The kitchen was small, with shelves lined with dusty jars, strange herbs, and bottles of various sizes. Despite the mess, there was an odd comfort in the clutter. The morning light softened the harshness of Belladonna's influence, revealing the remnants of her devious and beautiful collections hidden in every nook and cranny.

"I'm so glad I don't have to eat worms, follow the old hag around, or sleep on a bed of twigs anymore," James gripped between bites of eggs. Natts, who was already halfway through his own meal, looked up with a knowing grin. "And I'm happy no one's mean to me anymore—except you, of course."

"Remember that when you're upset with me," Natts replied.

"Hey, I'm good with it, my fearless leader," James answered, grinning back at him.

"We've got a lot to do today," Natts said, setting his fork down with a serious expression.

"If anyone can tackle this cleaning project, it's you!" James teased, eager to avoid the chores ahead.

"Exactly." Natts pointed his fork at James with playful seriousness. "But, unfortunately for you, I have powers you don't. And I'm the boss! So when we get back from town, you will help me clean up this place. You hear me, bird boy?"

"Anything you say, Boss!" James saluted dramatically, his grin widening as Natts pretended to look stern.

Natts paused, his thoughts shifting momentarily. "Are you ready for your interview this morning?" he asked, his voice now carrying a weight of concern.

"Yup," James answered, his voice a little too excited. "Can't wait to pound some nails!"

"Now, listen." Natts became more serious, leaning forward slightly. "This interview with my friend, Mr. Bates, is serious business. I want you to extend your arm and shake his hand when you meet him. Got it?"

"I will." James nodded, his expression earnest despite the flutter of excitement inside him. He finished his eggs but remained seated, watching as Natts cleared the table, his movements swift but efficient.

"I can't watch you every minute," Natts muttered as he stacked the plates and utensils, a frown tugging at his features as he glanced around the cluttered kitchen. "I have to keep you busy!" With a wave of his hand, Natts spoke a few words under his breath.

Within seconds, the elf's appearance changed. His sharp features softened, his usually pointed ears now round and ordinary, and his youthful face was covered by layer of stubble. He wore a sharply tailored jacket that looked just like the ones mortal men wore, but something about his new appearance seemed… off. Despite his best efforts to look like a mortal adult, he still looked far younger.

James stifled a laugh but couldn't help himself. Natts looked utterly ridiculous, his babyface with scruff barely making him appear old enough to be James' older brother. Natts, however, continued speaking with full confidence, unaware of how absurd he looked. "Besides making money, you'll stay out of trouble if you get the carpenter job with Tudor Bates."

"We have a lot to do today," Natts continued, "sign up for eighth grade, interview for a job, pick up your new ride, and clean this entire house. Chop chop—let's go!"

"I feel so lucky to have a new dad like you!" James teased.

"Very funny!" Natts snapped," I know when you're lying."

James smothered his laughter, watching as Natts turned to the mirror again, adjusting his jacket and studying his reflection. "How do I look?" Natts asked, as he examined his disguise. "Can I not pass as your father?"

James raised an eyebrow and gave him a deadpan look.

"A pirate would see right through you and know you're an elf," James said, the teasing tone barely held back.

Natts stared at himself in the mirror, muttering something under his breath. Before he could figure out what went wrong, there was a knock at the door.

"Who could be visiting this early?" Natts mused aloud, but when he saw Zoe through the window, he hurried to open the door. "Good morning, Zoe! Come in, come in!"

Zoe, dressed in a stunning onyx skirt, a chocolate-linen jacket embroidered with intricate patterns, and a tiny top hat with a lavender veil, stepped into the cottage with grace. "Good morning, Natts!" she said with a sweet smile.

"I know there's a lot to be done with the cleaning, so I wanted to help by escorting James into town."

The sisters knew Natts was limited in his magical abilities, so they had offered to lend a hand.

"Actually… thank you!" Natts replied gratefully, his mood shifting at her kind offer. He quickly gave Zoe her instructions, and she and James left, traveling by magic to Hillside School in Archmere.

As the morning sun streamed through the cottage's cracked windows, casting long shadows across the cluttered room, Natts got to work. His hands moved quickly as he sorted through the endless jars and bottles, still humming a carefree tune. But the clinking of bottles distracted him, and he didn't hear the knock on the door. As he sang, the elf sorted through strange items in the kitchen, his back to the entrance.

"Do bee doo bee doo! I don't care if you're bossy with some saucy—do be do!" Natts sang loudly, swaying slightly as he worked.

Suddenly, with a soft *pop*, Rose materialized beside him. Natts let out a startled shriek and grabbed his chest, his heart racing. Rose doubled over with laughter at his reaction. When he finally recovered, he couldn't help but laugh too.

"Okay… okay, you got me there, Miss Rose!" Natts said, wiping his brow.

Chuckling, Rose teased, "That's it for my magic tricks, my friend." She placed her invisibility cloak on a nearby chair. "Where should I start?"

"Well," Natts smirked, pointing dramatically toward a corner of the cottage. "After that diabolical entry, I shall make you suffer with the worst thing to clean until I forgive you."

Rose raised an eyebrow but followed his gaze. Piles of books such as—*Rotten to the Core Spells* by Rasputin Blackstone, *Rangletangle's Blackest Magic*, and *Cornelius Wafflestomper's Wicked Ways*—were stacked haphazardly on a table. Next to the books were glass vials filled with pink, crimson, and emerald-colored powders, and jars of thick black liquids that shimmered with a menacing glow. Each item looked deceptively elegant but held a sinister power.

"Oh, joy. Belladonna's mixing table," Rose said with a dramatic sigh, pulling gloves from her pocket. "Thank goodness I came prepared. I brought gloves to wear this time. I don't want to risk getting anything fatal on my fingers."

"Absolutely," Natts chimed in, his voice distant. A faint smell of leather and mold filled the air as Rose moved a stack of spellbooks into a crate. Natts, still seated at the table in the kitchen area, was oddly babbling to no one in particular.

Rose caught fragments of his muttering: “I swear, I… ha ha… I can’t, no. Why not?”

She paused, distracted by his behavior. “Natts!”

“Yes, Miss Rose?” He whipped around, his face a picture of surprise.

“Did you say something, or am I hearing things?” Rose asked, genuinely puzzled.

Natts immediately straightened up, as if caught in the act of something secret. “What do you mean?” he replied, looking more flustered by the second.

“Either you’re talking to yourself, chatting with some invisible creature, or… well, going mad. I swear I hear you talking to someone in the corner.” She snapped, waiting for a rational answer.

“Everything’s fine!” Natts said quickly, but his voice lacked conviction. He avoided her gaze.

Rose raised an eyebrow but decided to let it go. “Okay then...is James around?”

“Nope.” Natts muttered, his tone oddly defensive. “He’s in town with Zoe. She showed up this morning, offered to take him to his job interview and sign him up for school.”

“Zoe told me she’d offer to help.”

The elf threw a bottle into the crate, where it shattered with a terrifying crash. He chuckled darkly, watching the glass shards scatter. “Ahh, that's satisfying,” he murmured, his gaze distant.

Rose, feeling a hint of concern for him, asked, "Are you feeling okay? Anything bothering you? You look like you might hurl."

Natts laughed, brushing off her concern. "What are you talking about, Miss Rose? I'm fine! Same old Natts. Geez." He popped up from his seat and headed to the kitchen, filling a glass from the pitcher. As he returned, he held it out to her. "Want some?"

She flinched, wary of some trick. Natts' face fell, looking offended. "That's it!"

When Rose realized he meant no harm, she mumbled, "I'm sorry. Are you offering me water?"

With a sarcastic glare, Natts snapped, "Duh! What else would I offer you? A glass of poison?" He muttered a few choice words under his breath before shoving the glass into her chest. "Here. Drink it."

"Thanks, I think," Rose replied, trying to make light of it.

A slight smile flickered across Natts' face. "So, I met a cute fairy the other day. I think I'm in love."

Rose's eyes widened. "Ah, that explains your strange behavior. You're in love!"

Natts shrugged, a little sheepish. "Yeah… I guess I am."

Rose smiled warmly, feeling genuinely happy for him. "I hope she's the one. You deserve happiness, my friend."

He met her gaze, his expression softening. "Thanks, Miss Rose. I hope so too. I've got this funny feeling inside."

Rose nodded, "I'm glad for you." As Natts continued gathering bottles, she added, "I'm sorry I thought you were going to throw water at me earlier."

Natts winked, grinning. "One never knows what's going on in an elf's mind."

As he lifted the crate to leave, Rose noticed a strange tattoo on his chest—a devilish design sprawled over his heart. "That looks unusual. Is that new?" she asked, pointing at it.

Natts scowled, clearly irritated. "Maybe. Who are you, my mother?"

After he exited, Rose sat back, stunned by the sudden mood shift. "Strange," she thought, stepping out of the room. "But love does strange things to people."

Outside, Natts dumped the crate's contents onto the burn pile. Rose saw James returning on his new horse, a wide grin on his face. Natts got up and stood at the doorway, waving to James. "How do you like your new ride?"

He waved back, still some distance away. "His name is Ajax! I love him!"

"I like the name," Natts called back, nodding. "It suits him."

Chapter Eighteen

James tethered the horse to a nearby fence. Natts went outside, joining him. "How'd the interview go with Tudor Bates?"

"I start apprenticing with him next week." James grinned.

Natts smiled knowingly. "Bates will keep you busy. Now, what about Zoe—did she get you signed up for school?"

James stifled a laugh. "I guess it went fine," he said, his tone light. "But I feel sorry for the woman who was helping me."

Natts raised an eyebrow. "Oh? What happened?"

"Zoe wasn't too happy with the way the woman treated me. She said the lady was bullying me." James' grin widened. "So Zoe decided to 'help.' She restyled the woman's outfit without her knowing."

"Touché to Zoe," Natts said with a laugh.

James chuckled. "The whole room was laughing. The poor lady was clueless."

"That's what bullies get when they mess with a nymph vixen."

James agreed. "You got that right."

Meanwhile, inside the cottage, Rose was having her own fun smashing bottles. She grinned as she threw another one into the crate.

"Hello!" James called out to her through the doorway.

"Hi!" Rose replied, tossing another bottle into the crate. "I'm glad you're back safely."

Rose threw a bottle into the crate smashing it with a look of happiness on her face. "There's something so satisfying about smashing glass."

"Tell me about it," James said, joining her.

"How'd everything go this morning?" Rose asked, " Did Zoe behave?"

"Of course not, but we didn't get caught, so that's all that matters, right?"

Rose giggled. "I'm glad."

James winked at her and then grabbed a few more bowls from the table. "I'll be outside by the burn pile."

After hours of sorting through Belladonna's strange jars, they were nearing the end of the cleaning project. James, Natts, and Rose sat around the fireplace, enjoying the rare moment of quiet.

"I can't believe I missed all these strange jars on Belladonna's shelves," Rose murmured, feeling embarrassed.

"The sorceress was crafty," Natts chimed in. "Pink lizard heads, lime green snake tongues, and lemon yellow mouse eyeballs. Who knew? Everything looked so neat in those fancy bottles."

James added, "I think the gods are smiling on us now."

"Why would the gods be happy with us?" Rose asked, curious.

Chapter Eighteen

"We got rid of the old hag," James said, his voice calm but carrying an edg. He leaned back in his chair, hands clasped behind his head, as though disposing of an ancient, malevolent being was just another item checked off his to-do list. "She'd been stealing people's life force for centuries. Ancient as sin—looked like she was six hundred years old before her own magic finally turned her to ash."

The crackling sound of paper interrupted the stillness as Natts crumpled a sheet into a tight ball. He squinted at James, then flicked his wrist, sending the makeshift missile sailing across the room. It struck James squarely in the forehead

The room settled again into a heavy silence, the weight of their recent ordeal hanging in the air. The midday sun poured through the windows, painting the worn wooden floor.

"It's over now," Rose said softly, breaking the quiet. She sat by the window, her hands folded neatly in her lap, her gaze distant.

"What's over?" Natts asked, his eyelids drooping. His voice was low, barely awake. The exhaustion of the day had finally caught up with him.

Rose sighed, her chest rising and falling slowly."My delusion of being a magical being," she said. "I need to let it go. This curse… this life. It's time for me to just… be mortal."

James nodded thoughtfully. “I agree. No more chasing sorceresses or sorcerors for their magic. They just want our gold or life force.”

“That’s right,” Natts mumbled, half asleep.

James stood, gathering more things for the burn pile. “And speaking of, is the bedroom empty? Can you check? I’m about to light this pile up once and for all.”

Rose wandered into the bedroom, where most of the furniture had been cleared. The air was cooler in the bedroom, carrying the faint scent of old wood and something else—an echo of the magic that had once lingered in the corners. Most of the furniture had been stripped away, leaving the room hollow and lifeless. Rose gathered the last few items—a single worn shoe, two tiny hats with their ribbons fraying, and a child’s torn coat. Holding them in her arms, she sank onto the edge of the stripped bed, its frame creaking under her weight. For a moment, she closed her eyes and wished it was all already out by the burn pile.

And then, something happened.

Out of nowhere, a delicate spark of light, as thin and bright as a single thread, began to twist and spiral around Rose. It shimmered like a comet's tail, moving with an almost hypnotic grace. “What...is...happening?” she gasped, unable to take her eyes off the ethereal glow wrapping around her, winding around her limbs, and tracing patterns across the air. The light seemed to pulse with life, and as it did, her hands began to glow, a soft, golden radiance that illuminated her skin from within. *Even more strangeness.* Her heart was racing. Rose felt an electric energy in the air, like the world had shifted around her.

And then, the impossible happened. The crate that had been sitting on the floor—vanished. One moment it was there, solid and real. The next, it was gone, as if it had never existed at all.

Rose stood frozen, her breath caught in her chest, eyes wide with disbelief. "Did I do that?" she whispered to herself, her mind racing to catch up with the bizarre turn of events. She could feel the hum of energy, something deep inside her awakening, but it was so surreal that she almost couldn't trust her senses.

Without a second thought, she sprinted outside. She reached the burn pile and stopped dead in her tracks. The crate was there—right in the middle of the pile, as if it had always been there. She stared at it, blinking in confusion, her mind trying to piece together what had just occurred.

"I've got magic! I got magic!" Rose cried out, her voice rising with the thrill of discovery. She jumped up and down, a wild laugh escaping her lips. The light from her hands flickered like a living thing, casting strange, beautiful shadows around her.

Natts appeared just then, looking confused. "What did I miss?" he asked, his voice curious.

"I finally did it, Natts!" Rose exclaimed.

"Finally, did what exactly?" Natts raised an eyebrow, still not fully grasping the gravity of the moment.

"Magic!" Rose practically shrieked, her face lit up with excitement. "I can do magic now!" Her hands waving wildly in the air.

Natts' eyes widened, disbelief creeping across his face. "Shut up!" He blurted, staring at her like she was some kind of impossible phenomenon.

Just then, James appeared, stepping out from the cottage. "What happened? You two are staring at me like I have three heads."

"I finally have it, James!" Rose shouted, her voice full of wonder. "It's been inside me the whole time!"

James squinted, his mind struggling to comprehend her words. "What are you talking about?" he asked, genuinely confused.

"I have the power of magic!" Rose cried out, jumping up and down.

"No way! Incredible!" A smile stretched across James's face. "Well, come on then! Let's see it!"

Rose nodded eagerly, her heart pounding in her chest. She knelt down and picked up a leaf from the ground, its green edges crinkling slightly in the breeze. Holding it gently in her palm, she focused on the transformation she wanted. "I will change this leaf into a strawberry," she muttered, the words barely leaving her lips before she began to concentrate all her attention on the leaf. She pictured it in her mind—its green edges turning red, its texture becoming plump and sweet.

A soft, white glow enveloped the leaf. It shimmered, sparkling with light, as if it were caught in a dream. Within seconds, the leaf spun and twisted. And before anyone could speak, it morphed into a perfectly ripe strawberry.

"You...you...you've got it!" James stuttered, his voice full of awe. His mouth hung open as he slowly stepped closer to her. He grasped her shoulders, pulling her into a tight hug. "Bloody hell, promise me you won't turn me into something strange if you ever get mad at me!"

Rose giggled, her eyes sparkling as she pulled back to look at him. "Maybe I will! You better not make me mad. Ha!" She gave him a playful shove, her new confidence made her feel as though she could take on the world.

With her magical powers still crackling through her fingertips, Rose spent the next few moments practicing with wild excitement. She transported bits of debris from the pile, waving her hands with a graceful, sweeping motion. The remnants of *Rose magic* danced in the air, disappearing with a simple flick of her wrist and reappearing exactly where she wanted them—in the center of the burn pile. Each success brought a louder cheer.

The three of them stood together in silence for a while, taking in the magnitude of what had just happened. The sky had shifted to a pale orange, the late afternoon sun casting a warm glow on their faces. As James worked on feeding the fire, Rose couldn't help but ask, her voice quiet but thoughtful, "So, what do you think has changed about me?"

James looked up from the flames."You believe in yourself, Rose" he said, his voice steady. "I think you just made up your mind. And now—you have *confidence*." He gave her a wink, his smile genuine.

Rose met his gaze and realized, for the first time, that he wasn't just speaking about magic. He was speaking about her, the person she was becoming. She just knew that somehow, this magic was changing more than just her abilities.

She turned her gaze to the fire as it changed color—first crimson, then violet, and finally a deep, hypnotic turquoise. The flames shifted, reflecting the transformation that was taking place within her. "You, my friend, have become more powerful than your enemies," James murmured to Rose, though she was still processing everything he had said.

"I understand now," Rose said smiling.

Natts, who had been unusually quiet, spoke up softly. "I'm sorry bad things happened to you, Miss Rose. But I'm glad you have magic now, Miss Rose," Natts continued, stepping forward and wrapping his arms around her in an unexpected embrace. "I love you and James so much."

His words caught her off guard, and for a moment, she hesitated, unsure how to respond. But the warmth in his arms felt real, and she chose to accept it without questioning it further.

As the afternoon sun began to sink lower, casting long shadows over the burn pile, the three friends stood together, mesmerized by the colorful flames. The fire had consumed nearly everything—dangerous herbs, evil-looking parchments, toxic bottles, and devious spell books—leaving only the glass remnants behind. Rose waved her hand over the remaining shards, and with a simple swish of her arm, they disappeared into thin air.

"I need a break from all this cleaning," James said, breaking the silence. "Does anyone want to go fishing?"

"I do!" Natts answered, practically bouncing with excitement.

"Count me out," Rose smiled, exhausted. "I'm going to nap on the couch, if you don't mind."

With a snap of his fingers, Natts created two fishing poles out of shimmering crystal dust and handed one to James. "Shall we?"

James took the rod, inspecting it with an appreciative grin. "Let's go!" he said, and the two of them headed off.

Rose waved goodbye. She felt sleepy after everything that had just happened. Entering the cottage, she was grateful for a moment of peace. Inside, a beam of sunlight filtered through the window, illuminating a book on the floor. It looked like it had fallen from one of the crates, its cover glowing. Rose picked it up carefully, brushing the dirt from its surface. "You look somewhat harmless," she murmured, reading the title *Tarot by Cathel Blueblossom*.

There was something magnetic about the book, a strange pull that Rose couldn't ignore. She sensed it had some deeper significance, something important. Curious, she curled up on the couch, her new book in hand, ready to explore its contents. Something told her this book was the next chapter of her journey—one that might unlock even more secrets of her power.

Chapter Nineteen

The Dagger with a W

"If I have to pull one more piece of garbage out of a pond, I swear I'll trade my soul to the devil."

Rose couldn't help but agree, but unlike her obnoxious sister, she would never say it aloud. "You know, Chloe, you better watch what you joke about. It might actually come true." The two sisters were sitting by the pond, playing cards at their well-loved table, while Zoe and Reeva shared a private conversation nearby.

Chloe flicked a card from her hand with exaggerated flair. "I have a crazy—eight! And I pick…hearts!" She placed the card on the discard pile with a satisfied grin.

"Rats!" Chloe shrieked in pretend despair, tossing her cards on the table. "Just my luck. I don't have any." She drew a card from the deck, then another… then another. "I hate you, Rosey!"

The platinum-haired nymph stuck her tongue out in playful retaliation, and they both burst into laughter.

"I don't really mean it," Chloe added with a grin.

"What do you mean?" Rose asked, confused.

"I mean," Chloe sighed dramatically, "I *love* picking garbage out of ponds! Ha!!"

Rose rolled her eyes. "Not me. I miss everything about this place. I'm glad we're home."

Now that Rose had magical powers like her sisters, she was bound by their nymph duty to travel the world, monitoring ponds. It was their responsibility until further notice.

Chloe raised a brow and gave Rose a sly look. "Are you regretting having powers?"

"Of course not!" Rose scoffed. "Are you insane? Having powers is everything I've ever dreamed of." She didn't want to admit how much she missed her friends, James and Natts, and how she couldn't wait to return home after each trip just to catch up with them. But it was becoming increasingly clear to her sisters that Rose wasn't as thrilled by their endless travels as she had once thought.

"Chloe," Zoe called out, breaking Rose's thoughts.

"What, dearest Zoe?" Chloe asked, not bothering to hide the playful sarcasm in her voice.

"What if Rose stayed in the shallows and monitored ponds on Lumiere instead of traveling with us?" Zoe's suggestion was met with a stunned silence from Rose.

Zoe added, "That way, if anything goes wrong on the Isle, she can discreetly help mortals in distress… without revealing her identity."

Chloe let out a quiet laugh. "Of course. Sounds easy enough." She winked at Rose, who looked both shocked and relieved.

Zoe nodded. "Now, if you're going to stay on top of things, you'll need to be part of society. Maybe get a job in town?"

"I think that's perfect!" Rose said with surprising enthusiasm.

"Madam Vespar's Tarot Parlor in Archmere?" Reeva suggested.

Rose's eyes lit up. "I would love that. I recently read a book on Tarot by Cathel Blueblossom, and I thought it would be so fun to try reading cards."

"If the daughter of a deity isn't a natural at foreseeing the future, I don't know who would be," Reeva remarked.

Zoe smiled. "I know Zelda. We can visit her first thing in the morning."

Rose thought to herself, "I can't believe how lucky I am. It feels like my birthday!"

After a week of apprenticing with Madame Vespar, Rose felt increasingly at home in the Tarot Parlor. The room was a world of its own. Small and quaint, it smelled of aged wood and lavender. As a golden light filtered through sheer burgundy curtains, casting intricate patterns across a polished mahogany table where readings were held. Shelves lined the walls, crammed with worn books, jars of dried herbs, and trinkets.

When a small bird popped out of a coo-coo clock signaling the arrival of five o'clock, Madame Vespar emerged. Her frail frame was draped in a flowing black dress. Her salt-and-pepper hair was neatly swept back into a loose bun, accentuating her sharp and mysterious eyes. She moved with deliberate grace, the floorboards creaking softly beneath her step.

"Thank you, my dear," she murmured, her voice warm and velvety, though tinged with the weariness of age. "You can go if you wish. I'll close up the shop tonight."

"Oh, you're so kind, Mrs. Vespar." Rose returned her smile, her movements slow as she packed her tarot cards into an ornate wooden box. She placed it on the mantle, beside an old crystal ball that caught the flickering light of a nearby candle. In just a week, Rose had improved at reading cards and weaving their stories into predictions that felt real.

"I do appreciate you working here," Madame Vespar said softly, her voice carrying an undercurrent of loneliness that she rarely let surface. "I welcome the company more than you know."

Rose paused, her expression softening. "I'll see you tomorrow, Mrs. Vespar."

"Please," Madame Vespar replied, her lips curling into a faint, genuine smile. "Call me Zelda."

Rose nodded, giving her a faint smile. "Goodnight, Zelda," she said, her voice full of warmth.

As she stepped out into the afternoon air, the transition from the parlor's mystical glow to the real world felt almost jarring. The streets of Archmere were alive with energy. But Rose was anxious to see James and Natts, her two best friends, and ran to Hillside School. Students from Hillside Academy spilled out of its grand front doors, their laughter and chatter filling the air as they celebrated the start of the weekend.

Rose made her way to a sturdy oak tree near the school gates, its branches casting long shadows over the cobblestone path. She settled beneath its branches, leaning against the trunk. With a newspaper in hand, she scanned the headlines, her thoughts drifting between the real world and the one she was leaving behind at the parlor.

She glanced up occasionally, waiting for James, the faint scent of ink and fresh evening air mingling in her senses. The distant sound of a bell tower chiming the hour reminded her that the weekend had begun.

"Valorie Snowberry of *The Fairy Tale Times* reports: A shop in Archmere, Madame Zelda Vespar's Tarot Parlor at 66 Daisy Street, has a new employee. Madame Vesper will be working with her new apprentice, Rose Grey. Mrs Vespar added," Rose Grey is a gifted young lady. I'm not sure I've ever known anyone to be so accurate with their predictions!" The store will be open from nine to five pm Monday through Friday. Please feel free to stop in and visit."

"I can't believe I'm in the paper," Rose thought, bewildered. Her eyes scanned the crowd of students pouring out of the school, searching for James. When she didn't spot him, she turned back to the article, her heart still racing.

A few minutes later, she felt a familiar presence nearby. She looked up.

"Oh … hi!" said a voice—low but with a squeaky awkwardness.

Standing in front of her was James. Over the past ten months, he'd grown taller, his voice deepening, his jawline sharper.

"I swear, you look different every time I see you," Rose said with a teasing smile as she folded the paper and tucked it into her pocket.

"Hi, Rosy Posey!" James grinned, the nickname rolling off his tongue as easily as it always had.

The two fell into step, walking down the road together. Rose adjusted the long navy dress she wore, her stylish jacket shielding her from the brisk air. Her headscarf was pulled snugly over her brow, hiding the markings beneath—a secret she guarded carefully. Though she'd lived for over two centuries, her youthful appearance made her look no older than thirteen.

She nudged James lightly on the shoulder. "How'd you do on the math test?"

James groaned, rolling his eyes dramatically. Then, sticking out his tongue, he made a deranged face and pretended to jab his fingers into his eyes. "I'd rather stick pins in my eyes than take a math test, Rose!"

Rose burst out laughing. "So…how bad was it?"

"I finished it, and I passed. But more importantly, I couldn't care less about fractions. They're just annoying!"

"Annoying, huh?" Rose said, grinning.

"More than annoying," James replied. "They're evil."

As they continued down the road, their banter filled the air, an easy rhythm between two old souls—one older than she appeared, the other growing into himself.

Rose noticed the hint of insecurity in James's tone. Rose caught the faint note of insecurity in James's tone. Not wanting to make him feel worse, she chose her words carefully. "You know," she began, "when I had the sorceress Evanora Blanco as my home-school teacher back in the shallows—what, a few hundred years ago?—I thought fractions were ridiculously hard too."

James halted, his eyes widening. "Wait. You were homeschooled?"

"Of course!" Rose said with a broad grin.

"How did I not know that about you?" James asked, the tension in his voice easing. "Enough about me, though. How was the tarot parlor?"

"It was fine," Rose replied with a shrug, her tone casual. "I liked it."

They walked on in silence for a moment, James kicking a loose stone into the shadows of the Everwood. "Are we still digging up Winifred's treasure?" he asked, breaking the quiet.

Rose rubbed her hands together like she could already feel the prize in her grasp. "Can't wait," she said, a mischievous grin lighting up her face. She kicked another stone into the brush, the sound of it vanishing into the undergrowth.

A sudden rustle from the bushes interrupted them, and without warning, a small object came hurtling out, narrowly missing James's head.

"Geez!" he yelped, ducking. He bent down to pick up the object. It was a small gold disc with a letter W carved in the middle. He and Rose both stared at it, intrigued. James finally broke the silence. "It's a deadly button!"

Rose laughed. "Right, the deadliest one around. Can I hold it for a second?"

"Sure." James dropped it into her hand.

They both stared at it, turning it over, flipping it, sniffing it—almost licking it. After much deliberation, they decided there was nothing strange about it.

James squinted at it, curiously. "Does this mean something, like, in a psychic sort of way, Miss Nymph?"

Rose hesitated. She didn't want to alarm him, but the moment she held it, she got a sharp, clear feeling of its owner. She lied, "I don't sense anything unusual about it."

"Sure… whatever. You're the psychic expert," James said with a grin, before slipping the button into his pocket. "It feels lucky to me."

"It probably is," Rose said, smiling.

As they continued walking, James babbled on about his love for baseball, as Rose smiled and nodded, playing the role of a good friend. That's when they saw a couple of James's classmates, Dylan Kruger and Wesley Goldsmith—Kruger and Smithy—riding their horses toward them. Kruger sneered. "Funny meeting you here, Le Mer."

Rose was completely ignored as James nodded back.

"I see you became a piece of art at lunch—Freak boy," Kruger snickered with Smithy.

James's shirt and pants were covered in stains from a food fight at lunch. Rose's eyes narrowed, but she resisted the urge to hex Kruger. Instead, she kept her cool.

"I think it was Kruger who threw that button at my head," James whispered.

"Probably," Rose whispered back.

Kruger and Smithy rode closer. "Did you say something, LeMer?"

"Nope." James gently pushed Rose forward. "We were just moving along. Have a great day, Kruger and Smithy!"

As the two boys rode away, Rose's lips curled into a mischievous smile. With a subtle flick of her wrist, she cast an unseen force. Kruger had no idea he was in the presence of a powerful being.

She nudged James, whispering, "Look at Kruger. He's got a bad case of poison ivy on his butt!"

James erupted into laughter. "I'm glad you're not my secret enemy!"

Rose chuckled. "Serves him right for bullying you."

James grinned so wide, it looked like his face might crack. He pulled Rose into a tight hug, something he'd never done before. Rose felt warmth spread through her chest. For the first time, she realized James was a true friend. She smiled back at him, her blue eyes sparkling as she returned the hug. James blushed, stumbling over his words, rambling about how annoying Kruger and Smithy were at school. They continued their walk home.

When they reached Cederwood Lane, where James's cottage stood, he went straight for the back door, with Rose following close behind. He slammed his books onto the kitchen table and called out, "Natts! I'm home!"

There was no reply.

"Where do you think he is?" Rose asked, looking around.

"I...actually don't know," James muttered, a hint of concern in his voice.

"When did you see him last?"

"A couple of days ago," James said, looking worried. "But that's normal. I mean. This is the longest he's been away."

"Oh," Rose followed James into the living room.

Melted candles were scattered around. A painting by Rose sat on an easel in the corner.

"I'll be back in a second." He exited into his bedroom.

She nodded with a smile and sat on a chair in the living room.

Naturally, his room was a mess. He pulled the gold button from his pocket and carefully positioned it on the corner on his dresser due to the high volume of chaos on top of it. He changed out his food-stained clothes from school and into another messy outfit. Grabbing the gold button off his dresser again, he returned to the living room.

Rose got up from her chair.

Dressed in his treasure-digging outfit of muddy boots, beyond belief dirty pants, and an icky gross dirty shirt, Rose shook her head when she saw him.

"You're a mess!"

James ignored her comment and showed her the gold button from earlier, "I want to wear this thing like a lucky charm. Can you help me make a necklace for it?"

Chapter Nineteen

Feeling guilty for not saying anything earlier, Rose divulged a secret. "I have to show you something first." She pulled out her chain necklace from underneath her dress.

"You have the same button, and it's dangling around your neck?" James said, looking stunned."What are the odds?"

Holding the two buttons next to each other, she said, "Do you think they're Captain Wilhelm's?"

"He's dead…and so was his crew. They sunk in quicksand. Remember?"

"I do," But Rose felt uneasy.

"It's a lucky gold button…that's all!" James growled.

"Okay then." She slipped the necklace back under her dress. "Are we digging up possible hidden garbage today, or not?"

"The Winifred Brown jewels, I hope," James confirmed.

Rose smiled. "You know it's probably a box filled with false teeth!"

He made a funny face, adding, "Let's wish for a pound of gold."

Carrying shovels, James and Rose pushed through the tangled brush of Everwood, the evening sun filtering through the dense canopy above. The map from Winfred Brown's letter crackled in Rose's hand, as they stopped to catch their breath. Finally, they reached the spot marked with a hand drawn "X."

"This has to be it," James said, dropping his shovel to the ground and stretching his arms.

Rose squinted at the clearing. "I don't know...looks like every other patch of dirt we passed."

"Trust me, this is the place," James replied, already driving his shovel into the earth.

They began digging, laughter breaking the tension of the quiet woods.

"Let's hope it isn't a body," Rose gripped, leaning her weight into the shovel.

James snorted. "Why would it be that? Get your mind out of the graveyard, Rose." He wiped the sweat from his brow, flashing a grin. "I'm betting on jewels. No one buries a body and leaves a map to it, right? It's gotta be treasure!"

The shovels clinked against roots and rocks as the minutes stretched on.

"This is it," Rose said breathlessly, a glint of excitement in her eyes as she struck something solid.

James crouched beside her, running his hands over the dirt. "We're inches away. Get ready—we're about to hit the jackpot."

Rose was lifting a shovel full of dirt when she accidentally flung some at James.

"Oops," she smiled a devilish grin.

James flung dirt back at her.

"Oh yeah…oops!" Suddenly, it interrupted into a dirt-slinging war. But as they were laughing at each other's clothes, there was the sound of a thud in the trees.

"Did you hear that?" James whispered.

"Sounded like something hit wood," Rose commented.

Above where they were digging, a dagger was stuck in a tree, still vibrating from the force of the throw. Rose and James both stopped digging and looked at the dagger curiously.

"It has a W on it like my button," James whispered.

"I see it," Rose gulped, scanning the area for possible intruders nervously.

There was a rustling in the trees, scaring both of them. James held his shovel, ready to swing at whatever it was.

Chapter Twenty

The Kill Shot

Emerging from the shadows of Everwood came the dreaded Captain Wilhelm, his reputation as fearsome as the stories whispered about him. The magic creature trade may have been dwindling, but the captain's lack of success didn't dampen his confidence. Rose and James stared in shock as he strode forward, puffing on a cigar like a chimney, his gold-trimmed jacket glinting in the low light. His monstrous tricorn hat, adorned with billowing plumes, added to his commanding presence. Behind him was Slade and Mongo, two of his pirate crew, both waiting for orders. And beside him was Miss Obsidian, mischief dancing in her eyes. Her silver sparkle dress and shiny black boots caught the light as she crossed her arms with an air of knowing superiority.

"Is this ghastly nymph demon the one who killed your boy?" she asked, her voice venomous.

Wolfgang growled, his lip curling in disgust. "Yes, Silvia—oh, yes, she is!"

Unbeknownst to Rose and James, Mongo and Slade had silently descended into the treasure-digging pit. With practiced precision, they slipped powerful similatra neck braces around their unsuspecting targets.

James barked, "Who? I think you've got the wrong person, old man! She's just an ordinary girl—"

Mongo, one of Wolfgang's brutes, yanked back Rose's headscarf, revealing the elegant, golden disc-like tattoos embedded in her skin. The shimmering marks betrayed her true identity.

"The phantom nymph is right beside you!" Mongo declared with a sneer.

"What?" James stepped defensively onto the half-buried treasure chest beneath his feet, oblivious that Wolfgang already knew of its existence.

"Thank you for finding my treasure!" Wolfgang laughed, his scratchy voice grating in their ears. "How thoughtful of you two!" His grin widened maliciously. "Did you know Winifred Brown was my cousin Whinny, Miss Nymph?"

Confusion flickered across James and Rose's faces. How could he possibly know about their map?

"Odd," Rose whispered to James. "Natts was the only one who knew about it. Could he have been captured and forced to tell stinky-breath here where we were?"

James nodded grimly. "That would explain why he's gone missing."

Even as Rose mulled over an escape plan, she faced Wolfgang with defiance. "I read that you were dead," she said, her voice sharp.

"Sorry to disappoint you, Miss Nymph," Wolfgang snickered, exhaling a cloud of cigar smoke. "I'm alive and well."

"Or maybe," Rose retorted, her voice laced with venom, "I just prayed to the gods that you were."

"Ha! Very funny," Wolfgang chuckled. "No, I'm alive and kicking—thanks to my little monkey friend."

From above, a vine swayed, and a small figure descended from the trees. It was Smokey, the former monkey pirate of Captain McSly and Ozzy's crew. The little devil leapt onto Wolfgang's shoulder, a tiny cigar clamped between his teeth, smiling happily.

After being abandoned by his former masters and left to survive alone in Everwood, Smokey had clawed his way back to glory. His rise began the day he saved Wolfgang and his crew from sinking in a deadly quicksand trap. Ever since, the loyal monkey had been the captain's right-hand pirate.

With a wave of his hand, Captain Wilhelm signaled Mongo to haul James and Rose from the pit. The hulking pirate flexed his considerable muscles as he effortlessly pulled James out, then Rose.

Two more figures emerged from the shadows—a pair of tall, lanky boys, their jackets marked with bold W's on the pockets.

"Sid, Dean!" Wolfgang called with delight. "You're just in time!" His tone was smug, as though the battle was already won.

Rose's heart sank as she recognized the scoundrels. They were boys she'd met long ago at the Spring Fair—though ten months had seen them grow into men. James remained under Wolfgang's control, but Rose's mind raced with plans for escape. She wasn't ready to surrender—not yet.

"If you guess how many toes I have on each foot, I won't do you in!" James remarked, boldly.

The captain didn't know what to say. "You worthless fool!" Holding his pistol like he was about to fire it at James, the Captain blew smoke out his nose like a bull, thinking. Suddenly, he pulled the cigar out of his mouth and hovered close to Sid so that no one could hear— but everyone could.

"Is there something wrong, Capt'n?" Sid asked, nervously.

"Of course, there's something wrong, you idiot! Who is this boy?" Sid and Dean didn't know the scar-faced hawk had transformed into a boy named James LeMer. So, he couldn't devise a clever answer to the dilemma.

"I'm sorry, sir. I don't know." Sid mumbled.

"You worthless idiot! Get out of my way!" the captain barked, annoyed by his lack of help.

With glassy eyes filled with hate, the captain studied James's face. Pondering the answer, the heartless captain took another puff of his cigar, then blew smoke in James's face. As he coughed from the stink, James announced,

"I'm the son of the great Rufus! God of the Pistol!"

The ridiculous response humored Captain Wilhelm. He laughed so hard, birds scattered out of trees, squirrels dove into bushes, and a gust of wind made trees sway like an evil force was present.

Wolfgang stuck his face in front of James's, so close their noses almost touched.

"There is no God of the Pistols!"

With a curled lip, James snarled, "Oh yes, there is, old fool!"

Furious at James's sassy remark, he held his pistol toward James's chest.

"I've got the son of Rufus as my prisoner! Whatever God he is!" The pirate captain shouted. His crew all laughed. "Ah! You and the nymph beast —will help me rule the world! You imbeciles made my life so much easier, son of Rufus. Ba-ha-ha-ha!"

Still held by Mongo, Rose cried out, "You better watch it, old man. I'll make you hurt yourself, you incompetent fool!"

Outraged by her insults, Wolfgang held his pistol straight at Rose, ready to shoot. His glassy eyes were riveted on the innocent nymph. “You killed my son in cold blood, and now, you dare to insult me! You wretched beast of a girl!”

Silvia Obsidian stood close to the captain, whispering, “We aren’t planning on doing her in, are we? She is more powerful than me. We must not kill her.”

Captain Wilhelm was trying to resist. “No,” he mumbled to Silvia, “But I sure *feel* like it.”

Rose, undaunted, glared at the captain with fiery eyes. “You don’t scare me, old stinky breath!” she taunted him. She leaned forward, daring him to pull the trigger. “Come on, do it. You’re too weak to face me any other way!”

Wilhelm’s finger twitched on the trigger, his resolve wavering under the storm of his emotions. Around him, his crew watched in silence, caught between fear of their captain and awe of the girl who had the courage to mock him.

Unable to contain his temper, the half-crazed pirate captain was so full of rage that he engaged his weapon, which was still pointing at the nymph. But within seconds, an unseen force lifted him into the air and threw him backward several feet.

To the pirate crew's surprise, the powerful nymph — was free.

While Wolfgang and James bickered, she had slipped her hands free and removed the similatra choker. With a graceful wave, an invisible force hurled Sid, Dean, Mongo, and Slade into the dense brush of Everwood.

Wolfgang scrambled to his feet, fumbling to find his weapon in the dirt. Before he could grasp it, James, now unbound, yanked a small charm with a bold *W* on it from his pocket. With precision born of desperation, he hurled it, striking Wolfgang square in the eye.

"Here's your button back!" James taunted.

Wolfgang howled in pain, blood streaming between his fingers. "You little rat!" he bellowed. "After them, you fools! Catch that brat and the beastly girl!"

Grabbing James's arm, Rose pulled him into the shadowy depths of Everwood as gunfire erupted behind them. Bullets whizzed past, splintering bark and striking trees in a deadly storm. Arrows zipped through the air, narrowly missing their mark. Birds scattered in a frenzy, their cries mixing with the pirates' shouts.

After a grueling mile of running, they dove into the underbrush to catch their breath. The pirates' voices grew closer, their shots echoing ominously.

Rose turned to James, her platinum hair disheveled but her eyes fierce. From beneath her jacket, she pulled out a shimmering cloak and thrust it into his hands.

"Take this," she said urgently. "It's my invisibility cloak. Wrap yourself in it and go home. Tell Natts I'm handling this."

"What about you?" James asked, panting.

"I'll be fine," she assured him with a soft smile. "Just don't take it off until you're safe."

Another arrow struck a tree mere inches from them. Rose flinched. "You need to go *now*! Let me handle this."

They locked eyes for a moment, a silent understanding passing between them. Reluctantly, James draped the cloak over himself and vanished. "Good luck," he whispered.

Rose sensed his lingering presence. "Go, James! I know you're still here. Please—just g*o*!"

"Fine, fine! I'm going," his voice grumbled. "But don't die on me, okay?"

"Deal," she said firmly. "Now *go*!"

As the rustling of his retreat faded, Rose stood taller, more determined than ever. She blinked twice, and a gleaming sword materialized in her hand. Its golden sword gleamed in the dim forest light as she tested its weight with a confident swish.

"Come out, cowards!" she shouted, her voice echoing through the trees.

Sid burst from the bushes, pistols blazing. Laughing maniacally, he unloaded a hail of bullets at her. Rose wiggled her nose, summoning a shimmering shield that deflected the shots with ease.

"You call that respect?" she snapped, kicking one pistol from his hand before slamming her shield into his stomach. Sid staggered backward, clutching his abdomen.

With a swift gesture, the earth beneath him spun like a whirlpool, forming a deep pit. She leveled her sword at him. "Get in," she ordered.

Defeated, Sid stumbled backward and fell into the dirt prison.

From the corner of her eye, Rose spotted Dean emerging from the shadows, firing his pistols wildly. Bullets ricocheted harmlessly off her shield.

"Out of ammo already?" she teased.

Dean dropped his weapons, raising his hands in surrender. Rose prodded him with the tip of her sword, forcing him to the edge of the pit. He glanced down at Sid and sighed before jumping in.

A sudden screech interrupted her. Smokey, the pirates' monkey mascot, swung toward her on a vine, brandishing a tiny dagger. With an impressive roll, he landed in front of her, striking a martial arts pose.

Rose raised an eyebrow. Her glowing eyes locked onto him, and Smokey froze. Dropping his dagger, he let out a terrified squeak and leapt into the pit with Sid and Dean.

Rose turned her attention to Mongo and Slade, who lurked in the brush. "Come on, boys," she called mockingly. "What are you waiting for?"

Mongo fired arrows rapidly, but Rose deflected them with her shield. Closing the distance, she delivered a punishing blow to his stomach, sending him flying into a tree.

But Slade, ever the opportunist, seized his chance. From his hiding spot, although several yards away, he let loose an arrow, striking Rose square in the chest.

She staggered back, stunned. The world seemed to still as she collapsed to the ground, motionless.

Slade's triumphant shout pierced the eerie silence in the distance. "I got her! The nymph is dead!" His voice echoed through the forest, sending birds scattering into the sky.

The forest grew quiet.

"The phantom nymph is dead!" Slade repeated, his voice ringing out, echoing through Everwood.

Chapter Twenty-One

The Golden Nectar

As a gentle breeze swept through Everwood, it stirred leaves into a whispering dance that gathered against the fallen nymph lying on the forest floor. Shafts of sunlight pierced through the treetops, illuminating the motionless figure. Creatures of the woodland crept from their hiding places, awe-struck by the tragic sight. To gaze upon the daughter of a deity was a rare occurrence in Everwood, but this was no ordinary meeting. The phantom nymph, her radiance dimmed, had an arrow in her chest.

Fairies fluttered above, their wings humming softly as they scribbled furiously in tiny notebooks, their faces painted with curiosity and dread. *What would the fates decree for Rose Grey?* They wondered. *Was this truly the end?*

In the distance, Slade's triumphant shrieks shattered the silence. His voice echoed, celebrating his kill shot. Yet his brow furrowed as he searched. *Where was my prize?*

Surely, if true, the death of the famed nymph would grace the front page of *The Fairy Tale Times*.

Nearby, Circe Lavenderweed, a fairy journalist, was already sketching feverishly, capturing the scene. Then, in a moment that would be retold for centuries, the impossible occurred.

The nymph's eyes fluttered open.

A gasp escaped her lips as she drew breath. Her chest was rising and falling once more. The creatures around her erupted into cheers. It was not divine intervention that saved her, but from a simple charm hanging around her neck— a lucky button. It just so happened the lucky button was positioned perfectly to intercept the arrow's fatal shot. Slade's arrow struck the luck charm—dead center!

Regaining her composure, Rose rose to her feet. After retrieving her sword and shield, her expression was unyielding and full of determination. With a leap, she soared into the treetops, seeking a better vantage point. She wasn't giving up. And she knew Slade wasn't, either.

From her perch, she spotted Slade fumbling through the underbrush, his bow slung across his back, muttering curses under his breath. Rose descended like a shadow, landing silently behind him. Her sword's tip pressed against his spine. He froze.

"Ah! I thought you were dead!" Slade groaned, his voice trembling.

Rose chuckled, sounding menacing. "Not today. Maybe in another thousand years, if you're lucky."

With a firm nudge of her blade, she directed him forward. They soon arrived at a deep pit, where Slade's accomplices—Sid, Dean, Smokey, and Mongo—already captured. The prisoners stared up, looking annoyed, as Rose gestured for Slade to jump in —the pit.

"You, like the others, belong in here," she declared, her voice commanding. "Any questions?"

Slade sighed and, with a reluctant groan, climbed in. He muttered more curses under his breath. The forest fell silent again, except for the faint rustling of leaves. Then, out of the shadows, a new figure emerged—Wolfgang.

"Well, well… who do we have here?" Captain Wilhelm growled, his cigar glowing as he exhaled a thick plume of smoke. "I've been looking for you."

Rose stepped forward, the inevitability of their confrontation washing over her. She twirled her sword with a casual elegance, the blade glinting in the light. "It's just me, your favorite nymph," she said, a mocking smile curling her lips. Her indigo dress and long jacket swayed as she squared her shoulders. "Are you ready to die, Wolfgang?"

Wilhelm smirked, unbothered by her challenge. "Die? Me? Oh no, my dear…" He chuckled, tapping ash from his cigar. "I don't plan on dying today. In fact, I have a proposal: Why not team up? Together, we could rule the world."

Rose's eyes narrowed. "Work with *you*?" Her voice sharpened like her sword, and an unnatural energy sparked in the air. Her hair lifted, glowing faintly with divine power. "You've gone mad."

Wilhelm took a slow drag of his cigar, exhaling leisurely. "Mad? Perhaps. But you'll see reason soon enough. If not, well…" He gestured lazily toward the shadows. "I'll let someone else convince you. Someone who's been dying for the chance."

From the brush emerged a figure, tall and dark, his silhouette both familiar and foreign.

"Natts?" Rose whispered, disbelief in her voice.

"No," the figure growled, his tone venomous. "The name is *Stan* now."

Standing beside him was Silvia with a wicked gleam in her eye. "We're going to get married," Stan declared proudly, a twisted grin spreading across his face. "And she wants a special gift to celebrate our union. That gift… is you."

Rose's stomach turned. "What has *happened* to you, Natts?"

Stan's dark hair glinted like the darkside of the moon, streaked with obsidian-like strands. Intricate and malevolent symbols covered his chest. He glowed faintly with an unholy energy. "Life happened," he hissed. "Silvia needs me."

"She's using you!" Rose cried. "She's a pirate—when have pirates *ever* told the truth? Silvia will toss you aside the moment you're no longer useful, and Wilhelm? He'll kill you the second you threaten to overpower him!"

"Lies!" Stan snarled, his eyes flashing dangerously. He drew a handful of crystals from his pocket, their edges crackling with energy. "Silvia *loves* me. You're just jealous—a weak little girl who always needs saving."

"You're blind, Natts!" Rose shouted, her voice trembling with sorrow.

"I said my name is *Stan!*" he roared, hurling a bolt of blue light at her. Rose darted to the side, the ground where she'd stood exploding in a shower of sparks. A whirlwind formed around him, his anger fueling. His voice shifted mockingly, mimicking her in a shrill voice: "'Please help me! I'm so pathetic!'"

Rose's jaw clenched, and she braced herself for his next attack. But before he could strike again, Silvia stepped forward, her power radiating as she raised her hands. With a flick of her wrist, she freed Wilhelm's crew from the earthen pit prison Rose had trapped them in.

"Ah, my loyal fools," Wilhelm said with amusement, watching them scramble to his side. He tipped his hat, his cigar bobbing between his teeth. "Do help Stan capture the wretched nymph, won't you? Silvia, darling, assist Stan—he needs you." His smile turned sharp. "Now *go.*"

"I can't wait to see the nymph become my prisoner! This is so exciting!" Wolfgang bellowed.

"You don't have to do this, Natts!" Rose wailed, hoping the old Natts might hear her.

"My name is Stan!"

He pulled elf dust from his pockets, barked out a command. They morphed into a ball of fire, before shooting through the air and hitting a tree near Rose. She did nothing in return. Not wanting to retaliate against her friend, Rose was sure she could persuade him to be the elf she once knew.

"Natts!" She shouted.

Annoyed by her attempt to change him, Natts shook his head "How many times do I have to tell you—My name is Stan!"

Rose could see he was not withdrawing, but he was listening.

She babbled," I… I never knew my lack of confidence stopped me from being 'the powerful and confident me' I am now."

The demonized elf called out, "Just give up. Make things easier for me. I'm going to win this battle."

The elf dust in his hand swirled into a bolt of light before he threw it at her again. She quickly reacted, dodging the bolt of energy from hitting her. With a distorted face filled with rage, he laughed. "My, how you've changed."

Wolfgang was waving his arms, cheering Stan on.

"Hurry up, fool! Capture her!"

Rose took off into Everwood as fast as light. Hiding behind trees, she escaped Natt's bolts of magic. Wolfgang shouted from below as the two friends insnared in a battle of magic,

"I think you'll look good as a pirate, Rose!"

The nymph suddenly transformed into a dragon with long fangs and breath-like fire in an attempt to trap Natts. But the elf and Silvia, together, struck the dragon in the shoulder with a lightning bolt. Screeching in pain from the jolt of black magic, the dragon fell from the sky, landing on the ground with a thud. With a horrible gash, the beast transformed back into Rose. As she lay there moaning, trying to regain her strength, her once bright platinum hair was now changing. A mysterious force was overtaking her.

"What have you done?! Fool of an elf! I hope you didn't kill her!" shrieked Wolfgang.

Straining to feel her powers, the nymph was losing her strength. But she flew up into a tree one more time, just in time to dodge another bolt. But Natts and Silvia's magic was consuming her like a poison.

Too weak to keep fighting, she collapsed again, gasping for breath.

Wolfgang and his crew scoured the forest, their foot-steps crashing through the underbrush. "Find her! Hurry!" Wolfgang barked. "Mongo, get the neck brace ready! She's weak now, but don't forget—she's still dangerous."

Chapter Twenty-One

As the hours stretched on, Rose lay motionless beneath the canopy of ancient trees, her body growing heavier with each passing moment. She struggled for breath, each inhalation a labor, the air thick and suffocating. Her gaze wandered upward, drawn to the hawk circling high above, its wings slicing through the air. The sunlight, warm and golden, streamed through the gaps in the dense forest, casting dappled patterns of light and shadow across the forest floor where she lay in her fading strength.

Suddenly, the air shifted. A soft, cool breeze whispered through the trees, rustling the leaves in a soothing symphony. But then, without warning, a violent gust of wind swept through the woods, shaking the towering trees and sending a flurry of leaves spiraling into the air. In that moment, a brilliant flash of light ignited the sky, blinding and radiant. As the wind subsided and the forest stilled, an otherworldly figure appeared.

She was a woman of extraordinary beauty, draped in an ethereal gown that shimmered like moonlight on still water, its fabric flowing with a celestial grace. Flowers, delicate and vibrant, were woven into her long, golden hair. The air around her seemed to hum with magic, her presence was calming and inspiring.

The goddess knelt beside Rose, her movements fluid and graceful. Rose, too weak to speak or move, could only gaze up at her with a sense of relief, the pain in her chest momentarily forgotten.

“Hello,” the goddess said softly, her voice like a melody carried on the wind.

Tears welled up in Rose’s eyes as she took in the sight of this radiant being. The searing pain in her shoulder had spread, now consuming her chest with an unbearable tightness. "I... I'm not going to make it," Rose whispered, her voice barely a breath, as a grimace of pain twisted her features. “I won’t... see James again...”

“All in due time,” the goddess murmured, her voice like a soft caress against Rose’s fragile soul.

Exhausted, Rose’s eyelids fluttered closed, the world fading into darkness. But then, a gentle touch brought her back. The goddess pulled a small vial from the folds of her glowing gown, the liquid inside sparkling like stardust. She poured it onto Rose’s wound, the liquid shimmering as it soaked into her skin. The air was thick with the scent of blooming flowers and fresh earth. The goddess sat back, watching in silence as the magic took root.

As the first notes of a songbird’s melody filled the air, a soft, warm glow began to radiate from Rose’s body. Her eyes fluttered open, and she was no longer lying on the forest floor, but standing beside the goddess, her body alight with new energy. The birds, chirping merrily, seemed to be gossiping among themselves, chattering excitedly about the transformation that had just unfolded.

“What just happened?” Rose asked.

"I am Cloris, the Goddess of Flora," the woman replied with a serene smile. "I was crafting some new flowers when I saw you lying here, weak and near death. You're fortunate I was close by."

"Thank you," Rose said, her voice trembling with gratitude. She looked up at the goddess, still awestruck by her beauty. "Thank you for saving me."

Cloris stood still for a moment, her head slightly tilted as though listening to something far beyond the realm of mortal hearing. "I've just received a message from Hades," she said, her voice intertwined with urgency. "I am to take you to him."

"Hades?" Rose studdered. "Have I... died?"

Cloris blinked, surprised by Rose's question. "I follow my orders, Rose. No more, no less."

The truth hung heavy in the air, and Rose's heart sank. "I'm... I'm never going to see James again, am I?" The realization struck her like a blow, and the tears welled up once more, spilling down her cheeks.

Cloris reached out, her touch gentle but steady, and took Rose's hand in her own. In that instant, the aching emptiness in Rose's heart vanished, replaced by a calm, soothing warmth. The pain was gone, and for the first time in what felt like an eternity, Rose felt peace.

"How did you...?" Rose began, astonished by the sudden change.

“As a goddess, I have the power to ease suffering,” Cloris replied with a soft smile. “You’re safe now.”

A smile stretched across Rose’s face. "Thank you, Cloris. I...I don’t know what I would’ve done without you."

Cloris’s gaze softened. "There is one more thing. The Phantom Nymph... the myth you’ve been for the last 205 years... is no more."

Rose’s breath caught in her throat.

In response, Cloris raised her hand, and the forest around them seemed to respond, swirling with life. A gust of wind swept through, and from the whirling leaves, a flowering bush emerged. Its blossoms were pure white, the same color as Rose’s hair, and they gleamed in the light like snow on a winter’s day.

Cloris waved her hand again, and suddenly, Rose’s tattered dress, jacket, and scarf were replaced with a magnificent gown of rich, shimmering fabric. It mirrored the goddess's own attire, flowing and radiant, the cloak draping elegantly around her shoulders.

“The good news is,” Cloris said, a hint of a smile on her lips. “You’ve been promoted.”

Before Rose could speak, a sudden swirl of leaves and twigs enveloped them. A gust of wind howled, and a brilliant flash of light filled the air. When it faded, they were gone, vanished from the forest in an instant.

Chapter Twenty-One

In Everwood, the forest was alive with gossip. Animals chattered excitedly, and sparkling fairies darted through the air, eager to share the miraculous tale of Rose's resurrection. Their wings glittered in the sun as they zoomed off to spread the news far and wide.

Out of the trees stepped Dean, his voice booming. "I FOUND SOMETHING!"

Wolfgang and his crew emerged behind him, drawn by his call. Captain Wilhelm raised an eyebrow as he looked at the strange scene. "What have we here? An ugly bush with strange flowers... and the nymph's things?"

"She's dead," Mongo said, rubbing his chin thoughtfully. "What do you think, Stan?"

Stan eyed the bush, his face grim. "This is what happens to a nymph's body when she dies. We're too late."

Without hesitation, Natts plucked a rose from the bush and handed it to Silvia, who blushed as she accepted the flower. "Let's go, Silvia," he said, pulling her close.

"She's dead, Captain," Stan confirmed, his voice heavy.

"Dead as dead can be," Slade smirked. The pirate gave a nod of reassurance to Wolfgang.

"She's... deader than dead," Dean added, attempting to sound cool, but only managing to look foolish.

Captain Wilhelm chuckled darkly. "Let's go celebrate, then. We'll find her sisters next!"

Chapter Twenty Two

The Promotion

After reappearing out of thin air, Cloris and Rose were at the next step of the nymph's journey— a cave.

The cavern's threshold was magnificent, far beyond anything Rose had expected. The grand archway gleamed with ethereal light, as a river flowed through the center. The water glowed faintly, as if it held secrets beneath. The only way to enter was to cross the water by boat. The walls on either side, adorned with glowing torches, casted flickers of light on intricately designed metals and crystals embedded in the rock. It was beautiful—strangely so, for caves weren't typically this enchanting. Rose whispered to Cloris, "Someone important must live here."

The goddess smiled, her voice like a gentle breeze. "Yes, indeed. Thcy do."

Rose felt a sudden calm wash over her, her worries easing in Cloris's presence. She had been assuming she was

dead, with the goddess as her guide, but she couldn't help her curiosity. "I'm not sure how death works, so it's comforting to have a goddess with me," she mumbled, hoping for more explanation.

But then, eerie, ashen faces began to rise from the surface of the river. Rose's breath caught. "This is definitely... the underworld!" she gasped.

Cloris nodded serenely. "Yes. It is."

A wave of unease swept over Rose as her mind began to race. "I get it now," she said, her voice trembling. "You're here to escort me to...the fire pit of doom, aren't you? I failed as a nymph, and now you're leading me to my punishment."

The goddess laughed softly, her eyes twinkling with amusement. "What?"

Rose blinked in confusion. "What do you mean? I saw faces in the water, and the fire pit of doom is...in there, right?" Her tone was innocent, but there was a new desperation in her voice. She felt the weight of failure pressing down on her. "Why would they waste time fixing me when I've failed? It's easier just to demote me."

Cloris chuckled, shaking her head. "They promoted you, Rose. The gods don't demote their children to the fire pit of doom." Her smile softened as she placed a hand on Rose's shoulder. In an instant, a wave of calm washed over the nymph, the anxiety melting away like ice in the sun.

"You're not being punished, Rose. You're being guided—by me."

Feeling the weight lift from her shoulders, Rose's heart stopped pounding in her chest. She was still confused, but the reassurance of the goddess left her feeling less fearful. "Where am I going, then?" she asked softly.

Cloris smiled, her eyes sparkling with wisdom. "It's time," she said, gesturing toward a boat that waited at the water's edge. Tied to a small platform, it looked like a large canoe, but elegant and refined.

Before Rose could ask any more questions, a deep voice interrupted. "Miss Grey."

Two guards, in gleaming gold armor etched with mysterious symbols, stood at attention. One of them motioned toward the boat, signaling that it was time to board.

As Rose turned to thank Cloris, the goddess had vanished. In her place hovered a glowing ethereal form—her face vast but like a ghost that scaled the cave walls.

Her voice rang out, powerful and comforting, "Do not fear, Rose. Your journey is just beginning."

With that, the goddess's face faded, and Rose, feeling lighter and more at peace, stepped into the boat, ready to face whatever awaited her on the other side.

"Don't worry. Ruta and Vax will escort you from here," the goddess's voice reassured Rose. "They will guide you to your destination."

The nymph let out a heavy muttering, "Thank you, Cloris."

"You're welcome, Rose."

With a final glance at the fading image, Rose braced herself. "Okay, here I go!"

Despite the relief of not being led into a burning pit, she couldn't shake the unease about the eerie cave ahead. After Vax and Ruta helped her into the small boat, the trio floated in silence down the river, the water dimly reflecting the faint light from the torches along the banks. The cave stretched endlessly before them, its dark walls looming like a shadow over her thoughts.

The sweet scent of jasmine lingered in the air, and Rose found herself thinking, *Nothing evil could happen with the smell of flowers around... But then again, I'm in the Underworld.*

Ghostly reflections danced on the water's surface, creating unsettling images. She swore she saw skeletons beneath the murky depths, so she quickly turned her gaze upward, trying to distract herself from the eerie sight. *I hope I'm not in trouble for dying,* she thought nervously, her mind racing.

After what felt like an eternity, the boat slowed, and they reached another entrance. Rose's gaze fixed on the massive stone pillars flanking a grand opening. Crystal-like gems glittered along the walls, their intricate patterns catching the faint torchlight. Over-sized urns, filled with unidentifiable plants, stood like guardians, adding to the grandeur of the entrance.

Ruta, the female guard, spoke, her voice calm and steady. "Please follow me, Miss Grey."

Rose stepped out of the boat, and with a final glance at Vax, she followed Ruta through the grand entrance.

Inside was a vast room, the air warmer and thicker with the scent of wood and burning embers. At the far corner, a man sat in a weathered chair, which Rose quickly realized was more of a throne.

"Welcome, Rose!" he boomed from across the room, his voice deep and commanding. "Come closer."

As she moved toward him, she couldn't help but notice his strong jaw, dark eyes, and light brown hair. For a brief moment, Rose saw her father. But it wasn't him. Although thought he resembled her father, Hades was unmistakably different.

"Thank you, Uncle Hades," Rose said softly, her voice tinged with nervousness.

Hades smiled. "Welcome… welcome," he repeated, his tone warm but distant.

Rose curtsied, bowing respectfully toward the *God of the Underworld.* She took a moment to study the room. The space was grand but sparse, with only a fire crackling in a large stone pit at one end. Ruta stood by the door, ever watchful.

"Please rise," Hades instructed, his voice gentle yet firm.

Rose straightened up and nodded. "Thank you."

With a slight tremor in her voice, she asked, "If I may… Uncle Hades, am I in trouble?"

Hades chuckled, as if he found her question amusing. "No, and there's no need to be afraid," he said, smiling. He gestured around the room. "Welcome to my home. Your father will be here shortly."

Known as *King of the Underworld*, Hades ruled the realm of the dead, while his brother Zeus governed the sky ,and their brother, Poseidon, ruled the waters.

"Please, sit," Hades said, motioning to a comfortable chair nearby.

Rose took a seat, relieved to feel more at ease in its plush embrace. She glanced up at him and, after a long pause, spoke hesitantly. "I'm sorry I died. I know I wasn't supposed to, being an immortal nymph and all. But…but I didn't want to fight back against my friend. You know what I mean? I didn't want to hurt anyone." She sighed, "I think 205 is too young for an immortal nymph to die."

Hades remained silent for a moment, scratching his head in thought. Finally, he mumbled, "You know, you chose this path for yourself when you entered earth."

Rose blinked in confusion. "I… I chose this path?"

Hades nodded slowly. "Not having magic, then setting out on a journey to find it. It was a challenge you embraced before you were born. You wanted more power, but power doesn't just fall into your lap. There are trials. You chose to test yourself. Even without magic, you sought to improve your standing in Everwood. You had the courage to venture into the unknown. That's something most immortals wouldn't dare to do."

Rose's mind reeled. "So, you mean…I passed some kind of test?"

"Yes," Hades replied. "You passed the test. The challenge you set for yourself. You wanted growth, and you've earned the responsibility that comes with it. You're ready."

Rose sat there, stunned, her mind racing to make sense of everything. She could hardly believe it. She hadn't expected any of this. There was a strange comfort in the company of the gods.

She immediately sprang to her feet and lowered her head in respect, her voice trembling with gratitude.

"Thank you, my lord," she said, her words genuine but hesitant, as if she were still trying to wrap her mind around the reality of being in Hades's presence.

Hades's laughter was deep and rich, resonating through the room like the rumble of distant thunder. "You're welcome, Rose," he replied, his voice as smooth as velvet, though there was an underlying edge to it that made her shiver.

Rose's mind was grappling with the hugeness of the situation. "So… I'm not in trouble for dying?" she asked, a part of her still afraid she might somehow be reprimanded.

Hades raised an eyebrow, amused. "No, but—"

Rose's body relaxed as if a weight had been lifted. She sank back into her seat, the worry easing from her mind. The thought of being punished for something beyond her control had been terrifying.

Hades's eyes glinted with knowledge. "You were exterminated from Earth because you told the truth. A being like Stan," he said, heavy with scorn, "couldn't bear to hear it. Don't waste your energy trying to fix everyone. They have there own path to walk."

Rose nodded in understanding, but before she could respond, a door creaked open, pulling her attention away from Hades's words. A man entered, tall and imposing, a towering figure of strength. His physique was sculpted like marble—muscles rippling under his robes—and his presence demanded attention. He was the embodiment of power, someone who could easily lift a small building with ease.

"Rose!" His voice boomed, warm and welcoming.

"Father!" Rose cried out, the shock of the moment giving way to overwhelming joy. She sprang from her seat and rushed to embrace him. She couldn't remember the last time she'd seen him—had it been years? Decades?

Poseidon's eyes met Hades's briefly, a silent exchange between brothers. And in an instant, something materialized in Hades's hands—a book. Thick, heavy, wrapped in a deep burnt sienna leather that shimmered with an ethereal light. Rose's name was embossed in gold on the cover. It was a symbol of power, and it was hers.

Poseidon, with a tender smile, handed it to her. "This is for you."

Rose's hands trembled slightly as she took the book. The sight of her name on it left her speechless. Her mouth hung open in disbelief.

"Rose Grey," she whispered to herself, staring at the title. "Goddess of Antiquities."

Her eyes teared with happiness. She couldn't quite find the words to express her gratitude. Her voice was soft. "I… I don't know what to say."

Poseidon placed a gentle hand on her shoulder. "This book will help guide you. It will answer your questions about your new role and responsibilities."

Before she could process the significance of what he had said, Hades's voice rang out, "you are a goddess now, Rose Grey. With that title comes great responsibility. So don't get too excited."

Despite his words, Rose felt an undeniable burst of excitement. To her, it felt like a lottery she had won. A fate she couldn't have imagined in her wildest dreams.

Hades gave a nod, and the small golden marks— symbols that had made her a target and a walking prize for every greedy fool on the island—vanished without a trace. Her face was now free of the marks, and she felt a deep sense of relief.

"Thank you, uncle," she whispered, a smile tugging at her lips. She turned to look at the mirror on the wall, walking towards it with curiosity. She barely recognized herself. No more golden symbols. Her hair, once platinum, was now a dark umber, and her eyes—now deep emerald. They were different now, more piercing, more profound.

"Even my eyes are different," she marveled aloud.

"You look beautiful, Rose," came a familiar voice, warm and comforting.

She turned to find Zeus standing in the corner, a proud smile lighting his features. "Thank you, Uncle Zeus."

"And," Zeus added, his tone becoming more formal, "you'll report to a council of elders now. Myself, Hades, your father, and your mother are on it. Don't worry, we're here to help guide you. Someone will reach out with your first assignment when the time comes. Good luck, Rose."

"I'm so proud of you, Rose," Poseidon added, his voice soft but filled with affection.

She had become a goddess.

"I'm so proud of you, Rose," Her father whispered. "Your mother couldn't be here, but she sends her love. She is always with you my dear. She is the one whispering in your ear when you need help. I'm around too. But she… she is your personal guide."

"I can't believe this. I don't know how to thank you.. her…I'm so happy —"

But before she could respond, the room seemed to shimmer. Light burst forth, swirling around her, and before she could even react, the world around her dissolved into thin air. And in a flash, Rose was caught up in a swirl of light and the room dissolved into thin air.

Chapter Twenty-Three

The Death of a Legend

Standing a few feet away from two magnificent gardenia bushes was Zoe. She was looking smart in a long umber dress, a tall hat with a peony flower accent, and holding packages held together with long ribbons. Unfortunately, her jacket was missing. She had just returned from shopping in Archmere and had not rematerialized all the way—successfully. Gold glistening markings were now exposed on Zoe's shoulders validated her deity status. Because of this several fairies popped out of some bushes and started scribbling what they saw.

"Rotten luck," she commented, "I must've done something wrong—as usual." She lifted her hand towards the fairy reporters sending an unseen energy to ensure they stopped writing about her in the paper. They all scurried off in a hurry. Then, with the snap of her fingers, her linen jacket suddenly rematerialized in its proper place on her body. However, unbeknownst to Zoe, Wolfgang and his crew were hiding in the brush, observing her. Stan had

been following her earlier in his dragonfly disguise. He had seen her exit the secret entrance earlier and shared the location with Wolfgang and his crew.

Wolfgang grumbled, "Now I need you all to capture this beast— don't kill her —just capture."

"Do you have the neck brace ready, Slade?"

"Yes, Cap!"

"Then GO! Capture the beast girl before I strangle you all myself!" Wolfgang's crew spread out and hid in the brush as planned.

Zoe was oblivious to the intruders. She had not heard them whispering their plans to capture her, because she was too busy repositioning her hat, which had slipped off her head ever so slightly. But as the nymph bent over to count her packages, thinking she may have dropped one by mistake, she felt something poke her in the back of her shoulder. She turned quickly.

Looming over her with a sinister smirk was Mongo. The big, burly pirate was supposed to distract her as his buddy Slade slipped the neck brace on. But no.

The eldest and most knowledgeable of what not to do immediately cast a force so that Wolfgang and his crew flew backward several feet.

"Don't ever underestimate an old lady like me," Zoe declared sharply, her scowl deepening. "I've faced down plenty of pirates—and far more dangerous—than the likes of you." Her piercing lavender eyes blazed with a chilling intensity, silencing the air around her."Don't you know it's rude to sneak up on a nymph, Wolfgang?" Zoe added, her voice steady yet laced with menace.

And with a flick of Zoe's wrist, Wolfgang, along with his crew, were now hovering mid-air, caught in Zoe's unyielding magical grasp. The pirate captain struggled against the invisible bonds, his face twisted with frustration.

"How can this be?" Wolfgang roared, thrashing uselessly. "A pirate captain of my stature, defeated by a *nymph*! Mark my words—I'll escape this treachery, and when I do —"

"Captain Delusional," Zoe interrupted with a sly smirk. "Here's some news for you. I'm smarter, stronger, and more powerful than you'll ever be. And, by the way, so are my sisters."

With a snap of her fingers, the weapons clutched by Wolfgang's crew flew from their hands, twisting in mid-air to aim directly at their startled owners.

"Let's leave! Please, Captain!" Silvia pleaded, her voice cracking with panic.

"Go now!" Zoe commanded, her voice thunderous.

"NEVER!" Wolfgang bellowed, defiant.

"Alright then," Zoe said coolly, her lavender eyes glinting with mischief. She muttered a soft incantation, and in an instant, Silvia shrank, her body morphing into a squeaking little —mouse.

Natts shrieked, "My Silvia!! What have you done? I was so in love!!"

Zoe raised an unimpressed brow. "Oh, spare me. I had no choice." However, Zoe rubbed her hands together like she had a plan for him too. "Now… you, elf."

Natts was furious, his eyes narrowed at the nymph. Revenge burned in his heart. But Zoe's lavender eyes glinted with a sudden spark of mischief, and before he could think of a plan, she flicked her wrist. With a pop, he was gone, replaced by a crocking frog."Good luck with the Goblins! I think they like frog legs for dinner from time to time!" Zoe teased.

Still suspended in the air was Captain Wilhelm. He looked like he wanted to strangle Zoe, but of course, he could not. Wolfgang growled, his fists clenching in the air. "You'll pay for this, nymph! I swear it!"

Zoe stepped closer, her lavender eyes gleaming. "Big talk for a man who's completely powerless." She leaned in, her voice low and sharp. "I think your crew needs a long vacation. Zumba Isle should do nicely."

She raised her hand, and a burst of magic engulfed the air. The pirates vanished in a flash of light, leaving Zoe standing alone, victorious!

"Pirates," she muttered, brushing off her hands. "They will never learn."

Zoe stood tall. Her fingers were still crackling with magical energy as she watched the remnants of Wolfgang and his crew vanish from sight. A brief but satisfied smile played at the corners of her lips, but there was no real joy in her eyes. It had been a long time since she'd had to deal with pirates, and the annoyance of it. The package ribbons fluttered in the breeze as she adjusted her hat again.

Her lavender eyes glinted, knowing she had done what was necessary, when she transformed Stan into a frog. *He needed to learn the hard way that one didn't provoke a nymph without consequence*s. As for Wolfgang, his delusions of grandeur would soon be crushed on Zumba Isle, where isolation was the least of his worries. "Back to business," Zoe muttered, turning her attention back to the gardenia bushes, where the fairies were still scribbling away about the chaos that had just unfolded. With a flick of her wrist, they scattered. “Ah! That's better!” Refocusing on her mission, she pressed down on a branch of the gardenia bush. An electric light swirled. Within it, leaves, flowers, and petals intertwined before morphing into the secret door to the shallows.“I have tasks to finish! There's always so much to do!” She suddenly wondered how long it would take her sisters to find out about this little skirmish. However, just as she entered the lavish gardenia door, a familiar voice rang out from the brush behind her.

“You really ought to stop attracting trouble, Zoe.”

She didn't need to turn around to recognize the tone.

“Chloe,” she said dryly, “What do you want?”

Her sister emerged from behind the flowering bush in a sharp black embroidered jacket covering a silver dress. The black peony accent on her top hat glowed in the light. Chloe had a presence that demanded attention, even if she was aggravating.

"I came to see if you needed help… or if you were planning to start another fight with pirates," She teased, crossing her arms as she stepped closer.

"I'm fine," Zoe replied with a flick of her wrist, sending the last of the fairy reporters scattering in all directions. "I've handled worse. Besides, what's a little pirate trouble? It's nothing compared to the real threats out there. Humans. They can make such messes." She looked off toward the distant horizon, her expression hardening. The unease in her eyes was enough for Chloe to understand.

"Pirates again?" Chloe guessed, her tone softening.

Zoe didn't respond at first. She simply tightened the ribbons on her packages again. Finally, she nodded. "Yes. They are stirring."

"Then we should prepare," Chloe said with finality. "We'll take care of it. Together."

Zoe looked at her sister, the faintest hint of a smile returning. "Together, then. But first, I have a few more packages to put away. You wouldn't want to get in the way, would you?"

Chloe's lips curled into a smile, but her eyes never left Zoe's face. "I would never," Chloe teased.

And with that, the two nymphs stood silently for a moment, the scent of gardenia and magic filling the air. And if a storm was approaching, but they would face it together, as always, side by side.

Wearing the invisibility cloak, James safely made it home. Bursting through the kitchen door, he expected Natts to be home by now.

"Natts?" he shouted, hoping for a response so he could choke him for making him worried. "I can't believe this is happening to me! Where are you?" James roared angrily.

He walked through the quiet house, feeling a sinking sensation in his stomach. The silence was oppressive, and it didn't help that Natts's absence seemed like a growing mystery. The house, usually full of life, felt hollow. There was an eerie emptiness in the air. Natts was supposed to be a protector and a friend, but now Natts's absence felt like a gnawing sense of failure."What is happening out in Everwood? Where is Natts?" James groaned.

Dirty plates, batter drippings, smooshed blueberries, sticky syrup, and pancake bits had been stuck to the kitchen counter since Monday night. The last meal James had eaten with Natts which looked more like a science project now.

"I'm not in the mood for this!" James lost it and shoved everything off the counter in a rage. Plates and bowls crashed to the floor.

"Rose says cleaning is therapeutic." James kicked a bowl. It ricocheted off the wall before breaking into pieces. "That felt *very* therapeutic."

After spinning in circles around the room with worry, James disappeared out the back door. There was a small barn behind the cottage. His gleaming black stallion whinnied and threw his head in the air, happy to see James—and his food.

The barn smelled of fresh hay and earth. The warm scent of oats filled the air as Ajax nuzzled against James's chest. Outside, the wind rustled through the trees, but something was unsettling about the way the birds had gone silent... as if waiting for something.

"That's weird."

After James gave Ajax his hay and oats, he raced back to the living room, grabbed the invisibility cloak, and took off into the woods. He had enough of the weirdness and wanted answers. Glancing up at the tops of several trees along the route, he noticed hundreds of birds perched in the trees. Now, they were tweeting excessively. He got a sudden chill. He wondered if they knew what happened in the battle, the nymph versus the pirates. The battle he ran away from by Rose's orders.

"Everything is going to be fine," James told himself. "I'm going to be fine. Natts is going to be fine. Rose is going to be fine. And even though I returned home by her orders, I still feel like a completely wimpy friend to her right now."

The sun was setting behind the trees on the horizon when he sensed a change in the atmosphere. Something big was stirring, something magical. After the wind subsided and the leaves stilled, he noticed a girl walking towards him. She was dressed in a flowing white gown,

"Crazy—" he thought, observing the strange girl with long raven hair. He suddenly recognized her. He flung the invisibility cloak off, shouting, "Rose? Is that you?"

"James!"

When he saw her, the world seemed to stop. The words caught in his throat as he reached for her, his hands trembling. "Rose... I don't know what I'd have done if—"

Rose's arms wrapped around him, and he let out a breath he didn't know he was holding. "You're okay," he whispered, more to himself than to her. "You're really okay."

Her once trademark platinum hair was now as dark as the night. "Your hair! It's so —beautiful!"

"Thank you, James," she laughed, then blushed. She hugged him tight, never so happy to see anyone.

"Your gold marks are gone."

"Yes," she whispered, "but its a good thing."

"You look beautiful to me…marks or no marks," James said with a smile, his cheeks turning flush.

"Thanks, James." Chloe's lips curled into a smile. Her eyes never left James's face.

They walked back to James's cottage, hand in hand. When they got there, he lit some candles and made a fire. The room seemed alive again, warm and cozy. Rose cleaned the kitchen with a snap, making everything smell better again. After Rose put things back together around the cottage, they sat down on the couch in front of the fireplace. He reached out and held Rose's hand. "I was so worried about you!"

"I'm okay… I'm better now." Rose looked like she had news for James by the way she sat quietly thinking.

"Sure…sure…you must be tired!" James babbled, not knowing what to ask first.

"Natt went to the dark side. He was dangerous. So Zoe made the decision to turn him into a frog for the time being," Rose announced, dropping a bomb of information.

"Natts? The Natts I've known? How could he...?"

Rose's face hardened. A shadow passed over her eyes. "I never wanted to believe it, either. But something twisted in him, something that Silvia... she charmed him, James. Silvia Obsidian is a fairy pirate. That's what they do. I'm afraid he's not coming back, at least not yet. Maybe being a frog will change his perspective on life."

"I see," James was surprised. "I hope *I* don't make Zoe mad."

Rose laughed. "So true… you better watch out!"

There was silence as James thought about the startling news. He'd been living with Natts as his guardian for a while. James got up, threw another piece of wood on the fire, then sat back down, quietly thinking. She could tell James was a little shocked.

"I have another announcement to make," she said, hoping to distract James with even more unusual news. "I died when I fought Natts and Silvia."

"You died?" James squeaked, shaking his head. "But...you're an immortal! I—I thought you were..."

Rose nodded slowly. "It wasn't like I died died…um I just vanished for awhile, James. I was conversing with Natts, but he and Silvia teamed up against me. I got hit with a double whammy of dark magic. But Cloris, a goddess, saved me. I went to Hades and for some odd reason— I was promoted." She smiled faintly, her voice softer now. "I saw my parents! They were there, and... well, I met Uncle Zeus and Uncle Hades too. They're not as bad as people say, you know."

"Promoted?" James wondered, "Wow…what does that mean—dying then promoted?"

Rose smiled, "I'm Goddess of Antiquities now. I got a book with instructions. Isn't it fabulous?" She showed him her new leather instructions manual with her name on the cover.

"A Goddess! Incredible! I'm speechless." James said, "I'm hoping never to make you mad again, or I'm —as good as dead."

Rose laughed.

"Geez," James remarked, dumbfounded by the news. "I can't believe Natts joined the dark side.... and ... and... you're a Goddess of Antiquities! Gabingo Bango!"

Rose laughed, "Yes...Gabingo Bango!"

James put more wood in the fire, trying to keep it going while he listened to Rose tell him about the details of everything: her experience in Hades with all the Gods, and what her parents were like.

"I will have assignments! I'm suppose to wait and I'll be contacted by someone."

"I love it. This is so fantastic!" James was feeling better already.

There was a thud on the door. James got up to see what it was. *The Fairy Tale Times* was rolled up on the doorstep.

He opened it up and started reading "A nymph...falling from the sky?" James furrowed his brow as he read. The rest of the article was a jumble of confusion, but the first sentence stopped him cold.

> "The Phantom Nymph, believed to have perished in battle, has now become a mysterious fig-

ure shrouded in myth...A shadow of what she once was? Or something greater?"

He smiled at Rose, "The phantom nymph with the platinum hair— is gone. I get it now. No one really knows who Rose Grey is—so."

Rose was happy he wasn't alarmed by all the news.

"You know what this means…Miss Goddess," James mumbled, "you can never leave me again—ever!"

He squeezed Rose tight. Their tears mingled with smiles. Exhausted but content, they cried and laughed about everything, until they fell asleep in front of the firelight.

Glossary

Nymphs: In ancient Greek mythology, nymphs are a class of minor female deities associated with nature, water, or growing things. They are often depicted as kind to men. But nymphs on Lumiere are immortal and can live forever if they choose to but not immune to death. They can be killed.

Roses: symbolize grace, gentility, sweet thoughts, femininity, elegance, and refinement.

Pixiary: A tiny magical being that lives on the Isle of Lumiere. It is always sweet, helpful, and would watch over mortals and immortals in Everwood. They look similar to a fairy but are more powerful, especially when they travel in a herd. They are also known to transform into larger-sized beings as a fairy does.

Poseidon: In ancient Greek mythology, he is the God of the Sea; presiding over the sea (and all water generally), storms, earthquakes and horses.

Amphitrite: In ancient Greek mythology, she is the Goddess of the Sea, the Queen of the Sea, and married to Poseidon.

Zeus: In ancient Greek mythology, he is the King of the Gods and the God of the Sky, thunder, lightning, rain, winds, and brother to Poseidon, Hades.

Hades: In ancient Greek mythology, he is the God of the Underworld, the dead, and riches and brother to Poseidon and Zeus.

The Underworld: In Greek mythology, the Underworld is the realm where the dead resided, and ruled by the god Hades and his wife Persephone.

Elves: In mythology, elves are believed to be the cause of illness, have strong magic, and be very beautiful. They were often considered to be a type of fairy and often seen as mischievous pranksters. On Lumiere, elves are both good and evil as far as magical creatures on Lumiere and live in the center of Everwood, called Elflin. They use elf dust to preform magical charms.

Sorcerer or Sorceress: A sorcerer or sorceress are humans who practice magic or sorcery, which is the use of supernatural or occult powers to influence the world

The Bermuda Triangle: The Bermuda Triangle is a vaguely triangular region in the North Atlantic Ocean where some claim that ships and planes have disappeared under mysterious circumstances:

Fairies (also fay, fae, fey, fair folk, or faerie): magical creatures with human appearance, magical powers, and a penchant for trickery.

Pirates: Pirates are robbers or criminals attacking ships by ship or boat-or at a coastal area, typically with the goal of stealing cargo and other valuable goods.

Gremlins: Formerly lived in England, they migrated to the Isle of Lumiere. Gremlins are smart like humans; Read human books; Are approximately 2 to 3 feet tall, are known to live underground and participate in criminal activity, til Captain Samson Shu'gar hired them to run his Krusty Puffs Empire

1 Gold Onza: In 1790's, 1 Gold Onza is equal to 387 US dollars.

8 Escudos: The spanish pirate coin 8 Escudos is equal to 1 Onza.

1 Duros: One Duro is equal to one dollar.

1 Gold Doubloon: One Gold Doubloon is equal to Four dollars in 1790's.

Cloris: In ancient Greek mythology, Cloris is the God dess of the Flora or Flowers.

Were-cat: Cats capable of shifting between human and feline forms.

Stay tuned for more books
by J.D. Milligan in this series

Rose Grey and The Crystal Disc

Go to: www.jdmilligan.com

Follow J.D. Milligan on

Instagram @j.d.milligan_books

Facebook @jdmilliganbooksandart

Acknowledgments

Without the support of many friends, I would have been zapped by a sorceress or done in by pirates as I attempted to bring this twenty year project to print. Thanks to my husband Henry for being my number one scoundrel; Linda Clark for your artistic magic; Maria and Bob for believing in fairies; John and Karen Light for being scallywags ; Christy Hannum for your artsy pizzaz; Rosamond duPont for poetry and bibliophiles; Nick Fuhrman for encouraging me to go rogue; Nick duPont for captaining a ship; Art Milward—the mythology master; Mina Austin for your artistic brain storming; Anna Biggs Seiffert for your pirate lingo; Lynda Schmid for your Arghtistic dazzle. I couldn't have done it without you!

J. D. Milligan is a story-teller artist, author, tarot card reader, pirate historian, fairy expert, a fabulous jokester, and married to the Former US Heavyweight Boxing Champion. Ms. Milligan lives with her husband and two dogs, Stella and Gigi in the United States. Rose Grey and Pirates, Nymphs, and A Smoking Monkey is her debut novel. Find out more about her at www.jdmilligan.com